KINDRED

KINDRED

TONY CHAPELLE

Kindred published by Rangitawa Publishing, Feilding, New Zealand. 2019.
©Tony Chapelle

ISBN 978-0-9951166-2-7
www.rangitawapublishing.com
rangitawa@ xtra.co.nz

Reviews and comments on other books by Tony Chapelle

Joan Curry on Flaxroots: *[On Original Sin] "What a treat! This is a fine collection [that] can hardly fail to entertain."*

Catherine Robertson in The New Zealand Listener: *[On Original Sin] "... evokes place very well, the characters and their voices are convincing..."*

Azariah Alfante on NZ Booklovers: *[On Original Sin] "To describe the whole collection with a string of adjectives won't do. Simply read the book yourself, again and again."*

Novelist Maurice Gee: *[On Merely a Girl] "It has a real Victorian voice... It's perfectly balanced, moving the characters (they're a convincing bunch) round the strong centre that Addie provides... I loved her and loved the book." [On The Youngest Son] "... a good strong novel full of entertaining things."*

Historian Andrew Sharp: *[On A Distant Belonging] "I think future historians of New Zealand literature will see it as a major contribution to the story of how tau iwi are, or become, New Zealanders."*

Harold Bernard on Flaxroots: *[On A Distant Belonging] "I enjoyed the book greatly [and] I have no hesitation in recommending [it] to others... I would like to read the other two books in the series."*

Carolyn McCurdie in Takahe: *[On Merely Girl] "[S]trong, complex characters... I thoroughly recommend Merely a Girl... It begs a sequel." [On The Youngest Son] "... skilfully captures the voices and attitudes of the time... provides a wonderful contrast between the outward orderliness of respectable society and the underlying economic and social changes."*

Novelist Sue McCauley: *[On Merely a Girl] "... presented with respect, compassion, believability and that thread of wry humour that makes [the] writing such a pleasure to read." [On The Youngest Son] "I think I like it even better than*

Also by Tony Chapelle
Original Sin (Short Stories), and the novels in the Gilbard saga:
Merely a Girl
The Youngest Son
A Distant Belonging

Dedication: For 'Senaca, with love and gratitude.

This novel can be read as a sequel to the other three novels in the Gilbard series, but it also stands on its own. All the characters are imaginary.

KINDRED

Prologue

I have decided to experiment with a Journal of my own, inspired by that of my great-great-grandmother, Adelaide Augusta Gilbard. I'll think of it as a revival of hers, as I have just turned forty-five, which means I am only a little younger than she was when she died one hundred and thirty-two years ago.

So… here goes.

Wellington, November 2017. I'm Gus (Augusta) Ashcott-Gilbard, and I'm writing this in the kitchen of my house that is perched on the hillside above the bowl of Karori village. From our lounge window we can almost see the buildings of Karori West, the school Vanu now attends. It's about the same size as her old school. She seems to have found it easy enough to fit in, and already has made some new friends. One of them lives just two doors away.

Is this Journal going to serve any particular purpose? I decided I would hand-write it, so I bought this hard covered book with unruled pages to make it a kind of match with Adelaide's. Yet reading through what I've jotted down so far (or scrawled, in comparison with her neat hand), I'm not at all sure that it will be an equal to hers. What I've written so far seems stilted and boring, boring, boring. Adelaide made hers far more interesting. Hers is much more a collection of musings about what was occupying her mind whenever she sat down to write than it is a description of what she could see, or of events in her life – though there is quite a bit of that, too. Hers, though, are leisurely thoughts generated by what she saw or what she had experienced. That was her style. But she was a woman of the mid-nineteenth century; a middle-class woman who seems to have always had at least one servant in the house and no need to worry about earning an income. She could sit down to write just about any time she felt the urge. For me, it's different. If only there were no need for me to go out five or six days a week to earn a living, or if I had help in the house so that all those necessary and time-consuming domestic tasks could be shared! Wouldn't that be nice!

I'll try again, not so boringly factual this time. Instead, I'll do a little Adelaide-like musing while I have these precious minutes to myself. In fact, it might be better if I imagine that I'm writing for her.

Hmmmm. I'm sure you'd like to know, Adelaide, if this country is now the sort of place that you hoped it might become. In some ways I think it probably is. For example, women have had the vote now for a long time, and we even (yay!) now have our third woman Prime Minister. That would please you, I think. In fact, I'm sure it would. In other ways, though, we are probably just as divided now as we were then, if not more so. Rich and poor. Workers and bosses. And there are opposing views on many issues that I'm sure you would recognise, such as justice for Māori, bi-culturalism, immigration, and on whether economic growth is more important than the protection of our natural environment (this being one I'm sure you would feel particularly strongly about). And these are just a very few examples. I think you would approve of the creation of our welfare state and especially our precious health and education systems, though I must tell you that lately these have come under attack from those who see them as an unwelcome restriction on the presumed right to create private wealth even from those activities that are designed specifically for the public good. I should also mention that there are significant problems relating to the abuse of alcohol and other drugs -- but these are probably not so very different from the ones you had in your day.

All this is a bit heavy, I suppose. I should do as you have done and write mainly about family and friends. I should start by telling about my mother, Tela (Atelaite) Gilbard, your namesake and great-grandniece, and my father James Ashcott, your great-grandson. Yet when I think about it, how much do I really know about their early lives, my parents? Yes, I lived with them for the greater part of my life – for more years, I suppose, than most children live with their parents – but that doesn't mean that I know their personal histories in any great detail, particularly how they even became attracted to each other in the first place. But then, can children ever really know or understand that? Or... do they really want to?

1

Jamie

Gus, my daughter, has just left me. As always, her leaving means that I am both bereft and enriched. Bereft, for obvious reasons. She is, and always has been, from the moment the doctor confirmed her presence in Tela's womb, a part of me. Even before then she had been like the germ of an idea or a longing in my mind. But once I had knowledge that she was corporeal, she became an integral, a physical part of me; like an arm, or lungs, or a chamber of my heart. Integral. Part of Tela, and thus also part of me.

Enriched, because when I am alone my thoughts and memories rise up to banish the momentary emptiness.

I accept my past, and I am contented and embarrassed by it in almost equal measure. It is my wife Tela and our daughter who justify it.

Tela. Practical, impish, the most complete person I have ever known. See her now as she was. She needs no one. She is complete.

It is towards the end of the sixties. She chooses me. She need not have chosen anyone. There, in that foreign yet familiar place, she chooses me. It is in Cambridge, on Clare College Bridge. The leaves on the trees that line the path across the Backs are yellowing. She leans in to me, kisses me. She smells and tastes of coffee, the colour of her skin, her warm and beautiful skin.

In that very moment, in that particular place, my life begins again. Gone are my self-doubts, my feelings of inadequacy, my hazy, lazy envy of others. I would not change places with anyone else in the entire world. Now is all the reality there is. The future is no more than a thrilling, rosy promise, and I have no thought to do anything other than simply let it happen.

What more could any man wish for? As for endings – it is as though there could never be, will never be, an ending.

Cambridge, England; a foreign yet now familiar place. Turn us inside out, and you will find it there. It is as though it was there before we ever knew it ourselves. Its presence within helps make us what we are, we two. Tela and I. New Zealanders, yes. Not tangata whenua, true, but none the less New Zealanders for that. Tau iwi.

Back in New Zealand the following year, 1968, we become engaged.

"What sort of ring do you want?" I ask.

"You choose," she says. She doesn't seem particularly interested. Certainly not excited.

"But you'll have to come with me. See if it fits."

"If it doesn't, it can be altered, can't it?"

"I suppose so." My own excitement is deflated by now; but it hasn't gone completely. Somehow, in my mind, the engagement ring has become a symbol, a soon-to-be-publicly-displayed authority that will confirm my continued and, yes, exclusive right to plunder her perfection. A shout out to the world, and to my scarce-believing self. Mine!

I go alone to the jeweller's on Lambton Quay and choose a square cut diamond in a platinum mount. It is a small diamond, but as much as I can afford. Back at her flat in Kelburn she takes the ring, slips it on her finger and smiles.

"It's nice," she says. "And it almost fits. Thank you."

She wears it for as long as we are together that day, but when I see her again on the week-end it is not on her finger.

"I put it away for safety," she says, when I ask. "I don't want to lose it when I'm doing the dishes."

But she puts it on again when we go to Fiji, to marry.

It is not a church service, of course. We neither of us give any thought to that. It is a civil service, with only her surprisingly

13

large number of near relatives and a few of her childhood friends in attendance, and only telegrams from any of mine. It is how we want it.

It is hot. I had not imagined how hot it would be here, on the western side of the island of Viti Levu. I am in shirt sleeves, but there are garlands of frangipani flowers around my neck and I am slick with sweat. Tela, on the other hand... Tela looks completely at ease, and happy, too.

There is true fondness between her and her father, I can see that, though their exchanges are only brief. I like him. He is a small, sinewy man, lighter skinned than Tela, his face creased with age. "You look after my little girl," he says. There seem to be tears in his eyes, but that, too, could just be a sign of age.

Much more demonstrative are the Fijian women who move about at the feast that follows. They look like stately galleons in their colourful sulus. Before long I am smothered in a succession of hugs, their genuine enthusiasm for the occasion overcoming whatever awe they might have felt. "You're kaivalagi," Tela whispers to me, as though that is sufficient explanation when they seem, at first, to be too shy to approach me. "I'm far more frightened of them than they are of me, I think," I tell her. "I know you are!" she laughs; and she reaches under the trestle table and secretly squeezes my thigh. "Big, brave white man, afraid of my aunties," she says.

Some of her younger female relatives mill around, looking at me with frank curiosity and giggling amongst themselves. They're a joyous, lovely and lively group, their skins ranging in colour from near-white to rich coffee. "Nice bowler!" one particularly tall, slim and astonishingly pretty young Fijian girl says to me. She's mini-skirted, all legs, and she's looking directly at me, bold-eyed yet poised to run, like a gangly fawn. I am nonplussed. 'Nice bowler' did she say? Or perhaps it was 'nice bawler'. No, it definitely sounded like bowler. I reach up and touch the heavy chaplet of frangipani flowers that someone has placed on my head. A head covering, yes... but it

14

could hardly be taken for a bowler hat. I look back at her with a questioning smile. The only response is a hand to her mouth and a fresh outburst of giggling, then she turns and skitters away.

"What was that all about?" I ask Tela. "I'm not even wearing a hat. Let alone a bowler."

"Not 'bowler'," Tela says. She, too, is grinning, though a little cynically, I think. "She said 'nice bola'."

"Oh? And what does that mean?"

"It's just sort of… slang. It doesn't really mean anything except… 'yum yum', or 'I fancy you, pretty boy.'" She glances at the girl, who has re-joined the giggling gaggle. "The cheeky thing. Her name's Virisila. Another of my cousins."

I preen a little. "Nice bola, eh?"

"Don't get any ideas. She's only about fourteen. Last time I saw her she was toddling around naked, getting under everyone's feet."

"Yeah, but still… nice bola. Good to know I've still got it."

"Ha! When I was her age we used to yell out 'car-shine', which meant much the same thing. We'd say it to any boy, just to make them embarrassed. So you can stop thinking you're God's Gift."

Both the engagement and the wedding ring are on her finger that day; platinum with its little diamond, and eighteen carat gold respectively. It is the last time I ever see her wear them both together. Every now and then she puts the wedding ring on, but mostly, from then on, she wears neither. At first I wonder why. I cannot suppress my sliver of resentment and suspicion. I ask her. She puts her hand on my cheek, fondly. "You're my life partner," she says. "That's my choice, our choice. We make it so, not the ring. I just find wearing it, wearing them, a sort of… physical irritation. Like the princess and the pea, I suppose. I don't like things, hard things, touching my skin." And it's true. She avoids all ornamentation. No rings, no earrings, no bangles, no necklaces.

No make-up, either, I remind myself. She needs none. Her skin is perfection.

She does not change her name. At her work, she is Dr Gilbard still. Between ourselves, and amongst our friends, we are simply Jamie and Tela, Tela and Jamie. Officially (when we cannot avoid officialdom), and only officially, we are Mr and Mrs Ashcott. Or, more formally still, Mr and Dr Ashcott.

When she first told me, matter-of-fact, that she would always be Tela Gilbard, I was bewildered, and offended. It seemed to be a declaration that she was not mine, and I told her so.

"Well, that's exactly right," she says. "We're together, but neither of us owns the other." She smiles; confident. "Right?"

Of course she is right. Part of me accepts that. But part of me doesn't, not for a long time. Part of me inwardly rejoices when she has to sign some document that affirms her designation as 'Mrs Ashcott'. Mrs Ashcott, my wife, and mother of my child. Our child.

And that is another thing. She makes it clear from immediately after our daughter's birth that Gus will be, formally, Augusta Ashcott-Gilbard. That is the way she is recorded on her birth certificate. Not Gilbard-Ashcott, but with Tela's own name last, most final. From that arrangement stems one of our daughter's school nicknames, 'Gag'. Fortunately, only the diminutive 'Gus' has survived into her adulthood.

Of course names do matter; yet perhaps not so much in our case. I, too, am part a Gilbard, after all. Now, I would not be at all upset if Gus decided to drop the Ashcott altogether. Besides, in these more relaxed times I have discovered it is commonplace for children to adopt the name of their mother rather than their father.

In those early days, when honesty with each other is accepted as an essential part of our togetherness, I ask her how many lovers she has had.

"I've had only one lover," she says. "You."

"No, I mean how many men have you…"

"How many have I had sex with?"

"I suppose. Yes."

"I'll tell you if you tell me how many girls you've had," she says.

"Why me first?"

"Because… I'm not sure why exactly. It just seems… Well, I need the reassurance of first having you tell me that you have… had sex with others."

"But why?"

She doesn't answer immediately. After a while I think she is not going to answer at all. Then: "When I was a kid, I used to run around with a gang of boys. I was accepted as one of them, most of the time. But they'd strip off to go swimming, and when they were older they'd sometimes even show off their erections, waving them around. Not to me especially, but they behaved as if I wasn't there. I had nothing to show them, of course. Yes, I'd go swimming with them, though I never stripped -- not even just to my knickers, not at all. I think it's a girl thing."

"Modesty?"

"If you like." Another pause. "I'll tell you. But… you tell me first."

I think over my small catalogue of successes, if that is what they can be called. It is not that I have to do any fresh calculations. They are not that numerous, and I have brought the figure to my mind often enough in the past, counting them off. A boy thing, I suppose.

"Precisely eleven," I tell her.

"Wow!" I think I see a fleeting look of resentment cross her brow; but I could be mistaken. "That's… more than the fingers of both hands. Wow! You've banged more girls than you have fingers and thumbs!"

She's not smiling. I can't read the expression on her face at all. For a moment I think that her choice of word is an indication of displeasure; but then I realise that it isn't used to shock me, but to make a distinction clear.

"Yes," I say. "If you put it like that. And you? How many men did you..."

"Just two," she says, dismissively. She lies back and sighs, and for a long, slightly uncomfortable minute we are left with our own thoughts.

She is the first to break the silence. "I'm glad that's out of the way, aren't you?"

"Yes." And I am glad. Now it is something I need never think about again.

She shifts to my side of the bed, leans over me. She has that impish smile on her face, but not quite full beam. "Remember though -- you owe me nine," she whispers. It is a joke, I hope. I try to return the smile; but she is serious again and the magnetic determination is in her eyes and I feel as though I am being tugged gently into another world. "Let's make love," she says.

2

Tela

I know it is supposed to be a girl's greatest day, her wedding day, but I don't think of mine that way. I would have been quite happy to do without it altogether, but I let myself go through with it because that is what others – Cynthia and Jamie and Fi and my sister Margie – seemed to think was essential. Maybe most of all because I know that is what my mother would have wanted, had she been alive. So there is an element of guilt, there. I know I disappointed my mother in a number of ways, especially when I decided quite early in my childhood that I could never share her unquestioning dedication to the rituals and demands of her simple and deeply-felt Christian faith, yet she rarely showed her disappointment. She let me be what I felt I had to be. So mother, I say to myself on this day… the gathering and the ceremony are for you.

I feel quite certain that in the minds of some who are there Cynthia Wallace stands in the place of my mother; but the relationship between Cynthia and me has never been of that nature. She has been my patroness, yes, but she has never even pretended to be a mother substitute. Nor would I have wanted that. Good heavens, no! We are and always have been friends, even at the time we first came into each other's company. I was only ten or eleven then and she was a woman in, I suppose, her mid- to late-thirties. But from the very start, unlikely as it may seem, we were friends: the little girl, dark-skinned for a kailoma, a Part-European, and the tall, fair and (in a slightly ravaged way) elegant New Zealand wife of the Sugar Mill's Chief Chemist. She with a Doctorate from Cambridge and me with nothing but an ambition to read everything that had ever been written. Friends.

I am a little bemused by Cynthia's enthusiasm over my wedding day when I first tell her of our decision, Jamie's and mine. She had only quite recently seen a definitive end to her own marriage, which had left her childless and with little satisfaction in any other way, excepting only what I understand to be a substantial divorce settlement. But from the very first she is excited over the prospect of a return to Fiji to see us become husband and wife. In fact, I have never seen her so excited, apart from when she announced to me, thirteen years earlier, that she had been successful in her plan to win me a Scholarship to her old school of Mapledene Hall and thus set me on the path to become what I am now – a New Zealander myself, with a Cambridge doctorate just like hers.

We fly from Auckland to Fiji together for the wedding, Jamie, Cynthia and I. We stay in the same hotel in Nadi, in adjacent rooms.

"I am very happy to see you again, Mrs Wallace," my father says to Cynthia, in his very best English, when we make our way to the village the next morning. It is my mother's old village, where he and my sister Margie and my brother, Junior, are staying. They have come over from Suva, where they all now live together with Margie's husband's family.

"And I, you, Mr Gilbard." She is full of a girlish joy and excitement.

The aunties soon warm to Cynthia, embracing her and laughing. She seems to become absorbed into the group, wanting to be one with them.

"You'd think she was the one getting married, not you," Margie whispers to me, watching her, not entirely approvingly. Margie's figure has become matronly, and not only because she is visibly pregnant again. Her second child.

"Tell me about Chrissy," I say. Even mentioning her name renews a pointless spasm of guilt. Chrissy, my other sister, my younger sister. The one who wished to be like me.

20

"She doesn't even bother to write any more," Margie says. "I hate to think what she's doing there."

"Still in Brisbane?"

"As far as I know. In her last letter she said that Frank, that's the man who took her over to Australia with him, had left her there and gone to Darwin or something. But that was months ago."

Chrissy, pretty little Chrissy. Chrissy who wanted to be like me, to leave home, to go to places like the ones she saw in the cinema and the magazines.

Quite suddenly I want it all to be over. I want us to take our vows and get out of Fiji, and so put that unwelcome feeling of guilt far behind me. My life is not going to be lived out here. I had decided that years ago. And yet…

It is not the way to overcome that feeling, I realise. In fact, I have long known that turning away is not the answer. It is at that very moment that I decide to go ahead and apply for the three year contract as a lecturer at the new University in Suva that I had seen advertised, and spend at least a few years in the country of my birth and so make an attempt to come to terms with those aspects of my past life that disturb me still.

Besides; my father is here. My father and Junior, who, along with Jamie are the men in my life; and they seem to be enjoying each other's company. Not talking much, but comfortable with each other. Yes, we will come back to Fiji; for a time, at least. Jamie will think it's a great idea. He's already said as much, in fact -- suggested I apply for that job at the University. And… and if we have a child, I would like him or her to be born here, too. Just like me.

All that, of course, was decades ago. The past. My life as lived. Now, in the fifteenth year of a new millennium, I sit here in my study remembering. Recalling. It is not difficult for me to recall some, at least, of the significant moments from my deep past, though I don't often choose to do so. As for remembering what happened yesterday, or an hour or two or even a few minutes ago... well that's another matter, and one I would rather not even think about. Mostly, my reality is either here and now, or long ago. What is in between is too often confusing, at best. An inability. A personal affront. An absence.

I can tell that Jamie believes I am in a sort of denial, that I am refusing to confront my problem; but I am not. I was aware of it long before it was diagnosed by the specialists. What's more, I have vivid childhood memories of my mother's mother, my bubu, who suffered from exactly the affliction that is now creeping up on me. I did my own investigations of the implications when the symptoms first appeared. I know what to expect – or as much as it is possible to have such foreknowledge. I now ignore those symptoms and try to employ what useful abilities and memories I still have. I don't want to think at all about how it will be next month or next year because that is something over which I will have no control, and the thought of being helpless I have always found too frightening to contemplate. I have always turned away from such thoughts, and that is what I am doing now. I do not want to imagine what it will be like – the inevitable total loss of awareness of my historical self.

But meantime the deep past, quite a bit of it, I can still remember. Meeting Jamie for the first time, for instance. I suppose I would place that incident before all others in importance. It was certainly the most diverting and emotionally disturbing moment; for what followed, much of it now beyond my recall, frequently caused me to momentarily forget all other purposes in my life. No one else has come close at all to disrupting, fulfilling, giving 'meaning' in that other sense, to this person I call me, than Jamie. Not even Gus.

Anyway, Gus is Jamie's daughter. Mine, too, of course – but almost from the moment of her birth she has been closer to Jamie than to me. I wanted to be pregnant, but that wish was in large part the result of a sense of duty. My duty to Jamie as his partner in life. The ultimate expression of the feelings I had, I have, for him. Oh yes, I had those other feelings, too – those feelings that arise from our supposedly irrepressible maternal instincts. But these were nowhere near as strong in me as that sense of duty to Jamie. Or is that love? I think I knew right from the start that Jamie and only Jamie could make me comfortable in the real world, the world outside my books. Jamie, and a child. His child. Our child.

But I need to discipline my thoughts here. I am not a selfless woman. I never have been. I am very far from being a selfless woman. Take, for example…

It is after we have returned to New Zealand from our years in Fiji, and I am well established in my new job. Funds have been awarded to allow me to attend an international conference on Victorian Literature in Japan. Yes, Japan of all places. I am in Tokyo, by myself. No, that's not quite true – a man whose office in the Humanities Building at the University is just three doors down from mine is also at the Conference, has travelled with me all the way, and he, too, will be giving a paper. His special areas of expertise are the nineteenth century essayists and political philosophers – Carlyle, Hazlitt, Lamb and Leigh Hunt especially. I once asked him why he neglected to include women such as Amy Levy and Olive Schreiner in his courses, and we have not made even a pretence of friendship ever since. He takes the lead in this, though I admit his looking askance at my suggestion certainly added to my own faint pre-existing dislike of him.

So after I have delivered my paper, a tall Scandinavian, Swedish, I think, and with astonishingly green eyes, seeks me out to ask some questions. They are not difficult questions. Indeed, I had raised and answered them in my paper, and it is immediately apparent to me that his interest is myself, not my work. His eyes are mesmerising, holding mine. I find I am not particularly attracted to him otherwise. He is earnest and lean with a floppy mop of blond hair. Hungry looking. But though that analysing part of me rejects his obvious interest, my hormones say otherwise. Something is triggered inside me, and I am certain he senses it.

I return to my room and shower in preparation for the scheduled evening activities. I am still attending to these details when there is a soft but insistent rap on my door. I open it to find him standing there.

There is no need for words. He closes the door behind him, and we are in a clawing embrace. I switch off all other thoughts and give myself up to lust. It is exhilarating. He is skilful, controlled, practised. I am wanton, wanting, more than willing to respond to his every cue.

Half an hour later he leaves me, and I go through my evening preparations once again. I see him at the dinner that evening, but we do not sit together. Indeed, not another word passes between us. I think that we both choose to have it so.

No, I am certainly not a selfless woman.

3

Jamie

When Tela returns from Tokyo, on that very first overseas trip without me, it is as though the fulcrum of my life has been restored. It is to be always like that, on all the many other occasions when her growing reputation as a doyenne of Victorian Literature takes her to conferences, or to spend time in Wellington with her friend Cynthia, or when she goes on those stints as a visiting scholar and she or circumstances dictate that she must go alone. Always. While she is away, Gus and I are like planets awaiting the return of our sun. Twin planets, to be sure, comfortable in our orbits and with each other but aware of the absence at the centre.

That night, after her return from the first of her solo journeys overseas, she unpacks her things, hangs them or otherwise stores them, I watching her, reminding myself of the economical grace of her movements. She senses my attention and gives me hers. There is the suggestion of a smile on her face but also, perhaps, a touch of uncertainty. I am immediately alert.

She sits beside me on the bed and raises a hand to my cheek. It is a very familiar gesture, intensely intimate. "You owe me eight," she says.

It is enough, as she knows it will be. In that very instant it is as though a stiletto has been plunged through my ribs.

Yet just as quickly I see and respond to her own intense scrutiny of me, her eyes searching mine. The pain vanishes, and I sink with relief into an unspoken understanding. It is nothing. Nothing has changed. Nothing at all has changed. Nothing, nothing.

The years we spend in Fiji are the very last of the sixties and up to the mid-seventies, and as an era, they are a kind of carry-over from the classic sixties. They are the years of Creedence Clearwater Revival and The Rolling Stones, Bob Dylan and Joan Baez. Woodstock, 1969. Janis Joplin singing Me and Bobby McGee. Boozy parties dancing to Proud Mary and trying to sing along to Led Zeppelin's Stairway to Heaven, Elton John's Rocket Man and George Harrison's My Sweet Lord. And there are other melodies that stick in the mind, like Blowin' in the Wind, and The Night They Drove Old Dixie Down. Acid and pot, mini-skirts or caftans, and flared trousers; gauzy tie-died shirts and men's hair as long as women's.

Not that either Tela or I indulge in acid, or even pot. The very idea that Tela might do so is absurd. Her total abstinence from such things – the thought never even enters her head – triggers a similar attitude in me. Besides, although it is apparent that plenty of pot is smoked on campus, mainly by expatriates, acid, it seems, is not readily available.

But I do continue to smoke tobacco, and she accepts that. And I do continue to drink, especially at the parties we throw or attend, and she doesn't criticise my choice to do so. Nor does she put on a martyr's face, not even on those occasions when I wake up late to find her long since arisen, and I stagger out into the kitchen with a mouth gummed up and a crying need for water and a head that seems to confirm the loss of copious numbers of brain cells, and stare blearily about me.

She and Akanisi, our house-girl, are both there, and they exchange a rueful smile at my appearance. "Coffee?" Tela says. "You look like you could do with some."

Our working life from the time of our marriage is researching and teaching and writing. She does all three. I just research and write. It is her salary rather than my intermittent payments that sustain us. She doesn't mind. "Put yours into a separate account," she suggests early on. "It can be our treasure trove." So I do. It is an account in both our names. It grows and grows over the years. It is a comfort to us both, I believe. I know it is to me.

While we are in Fiji, those momentous six years, what happens in New Zealand – indeed, in the world – absorbs us momentarily every now and then. Sometimes for even longer than a moment. At the social gatherings we attend there are discussions that end in arguments, and there are arguments that are never resolved, that strangle potential friendships and strain established ones. Tela and I don't argue about such things between ourselves, though. Tela doesn't argue about such things with anyone. She is very aware and informed, but she is not a polemicist.

Being in Fiji means that most internationally momentous events and their effects we experience only very indirectly. For much of the time that the climax of the Vietnam War dominates the headlines, dividing opinions, we are in Fiji. There is no television to give us daily visual impressions. We are aware, but removed. Most of our information comes from Time or Newsweek. The arguments there seem clinical. Unimportant, almost. The Domino effect. The attempts at justifying the use of napalm and Agent Orange. The growing opposition in the United States to the continuation of the conflict.

But we have other, more trivial problems to deal with, such as the heat of the tropics, the constant threat of dengue fever, Suva's increasing traffic, the thankfully very minor disturbances leading up to Fiji's Independence Day. We have seats close to Prince Charles on that auspicious occasion, Tela's name having been drawn in a lottery organised by the University. What we see is a final bit of pomp before another fragment of Empire is set loose to make its own mistakes.

And during this time we hear occasional reports that back in New Zealand a strange little man with a misshapen grin is emerging as one of the dominant political figures. It is only when we return home – yes, home, for Tela also thinks of

27

herself as a New Zealander, is a New Zealander – that I learn to dislike him and all that he stands for. Well... perhaps not quite all. Certainly his cocky confidence and his cynical and opportunistic populism, but maybe not his willingness to use the powers of the state to modify the swings of the market. For me, and I think for Tela too, the trouble is that he does it almost exclusively in the interests of the rich and the privileged and the bigoted, of the farmers who first put him, then kept him in power, and the white middle-class generally. At the time, though, I don't give much thought to that. I just don't like his lack of grace nor his smart-Alec put-downs of any who oppose him.

And of course throughout all those years in Fiji and after our return to New Zealand there are parts of our planet that are ravaged by wars. There are always wars. And in this age there is knowledge of every war that is taking place, in every corner of the globe -- so much information that there is an unthinking acceptance of war as natural to the human state. And perhaps it is.

I was brought up amidst the consequences of war – a brother killed piloting a Spitfire in Italy, my home fatherless, in part because of arguments resulting from my father's committed pacifism. I was too young to have any memory of my elder brother, but the household I grew up in was heavy with other people's remembrance of him, my mother's especially. What I became aware of myself as I grew up was the all-too-frequent sight of men physically or emotionally scarred by conflict, and direct knowledge of the intrusiveness of war in our lives came also when I read the headlines in the newspapers. The dominant war at that time, in my childhood, was taking place in Korea, and the papers were full of stories that used such terms as 'spearheads' and 'broad fronts'. To me, then, it was all something like a game – a serious game, where good pitted itself against evil. There was no attraction for me in my absent father's pacifism, and there was no problem sorting out where my loyalties should lie. Like just about everyone else in our domestically peaceful country, I let the natural bias of the journalists and those who governed us decide for me.

It is 1972, the year of Gus. She is to be born at Suva's Colonial War Memorial Hospital, a grim and grubby building by outside appearances but still somehow reassuring. Inside, its imposing presence suggests, is the technology to ensure safety, to save lives. Yet it has that battered look, the look of having weathered too much thunder and lightning, too many hurricanes. And there is one of those hurricanes in the offing, too, in this month of October 1972.

For weeks, ever since Tela's condition has been confirmed, I have been regularly reading books on the physiology of pregnancy that I gathered from the University Library. I have made myself aware of the various stages and religiously counted the days, making estimations as to how large our womb-bound child is, how much larger he or she will be in another week, another month. I have read up, too, on the complications that can occur, and I have shuddered at the dreadful possibilities – preeclampsia, ectopic pregnancy, oligohydramnios, placenta previa. I am both impatient and fearful.

The expected time for the infant's arrival passes without any signal that he or she is aware of the expectation. More days drag by. Meantime, the hurricane is generating to the north-west of Fiji. I become ever more nervous and anxious, but Tela is apparently philosophical about the imminent arrival—about both arrivals, but particularly the baby's. It is no more than the inevitable end of a process, she tells me, all stoical, when the contractions start at last, and within an hour become stronger and more regular. She is apparently calm. I am not.

When I ring the hospital they tell me to bring her in straight away. Even if it's a false alarm, the woman's voice on the end of the phone tells me. With a hurricane on the way it'll be better to have her here, she says.

I need no persuading. I take Tela to the car, our house-girl carrying the bag of essentials we have been told to bring. I give distracted last minute instructions to the girl regarding the house, her anxious but excited face nodding at me through the car window, then I drive out of the campus, out of Laucala Bay and over into the city. I drive carefully keeping my mind on the route I must take. Tela says nothing, but I can tell by her audible breathing and incoherent grunts and utterances that another contraction has seized her.

I park. I support her through the doors of the hospital. She is expected. She is escorted by a nurse along the corridors to a room where she is to be prepped. I am superfluous to requirements. With a nod, I am told where to wait.

And I wait, and wait. At last I am allowed in to see her, gowned and readied, matter-of-fact. I just want it to be over, she says. I sense she doesn't really need my presence. She looks small and distracted, the bulge an alien and grotesque burden. She lets me hold her hand briefly then shrugs it away.

It's liable to take some time, the Chinese doctor informs me when he comes in to make another assessment. You could go home and wait for a call, he suggests. But I don't. I want to stay. I want to be with her.

Hours and hours later, early morning of the next day in fact, I am present at the delivery. At the end it is assisted by forceps, me standing there fearing to observe yet fearing even more not to, utterly useless. I see a squirming pinkness striped with purple, and red clotted blood, and membranes shining and slippery under the harsh light of the lamps. Then I see a screwed up face and an expression of fierce aversion, tiny fists clenching. I hear stuttering yelps that become a scream of rage. The meaning of it is as clear as if it had been words:

What the hell insult is this? For the first time I see and hear my progeny, the fruit of my loins.

Earlier in her pregnancy Tela had had a visit from her sister Margie, who had just returned from a trip to the other side of the island. The aunties are all very excited, she told us both. They have it in their heads that you'll have a boy. They reckon they can tell because of the way you behaved when you were little. Tela and I both laughed at that, but I must somehow have accepted in my mind that they were right, those aunties, for as I now take in the reality of the little creature that is lifted for me to examine I see with a rush of pure horror that he has entered the world without a penis. Then: "She's a perfect little girl," the attending nurse, an Indian, assures me.

A girl! She's a girl! My heart soars with relief and unfeigned joy. It swells with love and pride. I feel as though it is about to fight its way out of my chest. I am father to a little girl!

4

Tela

Before the end of my first contract at the University in Suva I am offered a renewal for another three years, which I accept. So we spend six years in Fiji, only leaving in 1975. Fiji is where Gus is born, and it is where I get my first real boost in the world of academic literary criticism. The world of my head. More importantly, I suppose, at least for our future material welfare, it is where I come to truly enjoy teaching.

It is odd how a base in what is, after all, a place generally ignored by the rest of the world, a place that I had myself rejected when I was just a child, is what allows me to become sufficiently well-known to set us up for life. Within months of starting work I send off my first submission to a prestigious Journal. I do so rather fearfully and with little hope, but it is accepted and duly published. By my third year I am being invited to contribute papers to other Journals and I begin to receive invitations to conferences and offers of visiting fellowships. By the time we leave Fiji I have an established reputation in the world of Victorian literature and a list of publications that others envy.

It sounds easy, doesn't it. But it isn't really; and it owes at least as much to luck as to any hard work or ability. Though I suppose (no – I know) that I'm cleverer than most. Whatever that means. I don't really think about that. I simply do what I love doing.

In Fiji we live on campus, in a house with very thick concrete walls. A Ponda house, it is called. It is built to withstand hurricanes. Almost all the staff houses on the Laucala Bay Campus of the University are like that. They came as part of the parcel, for the University is on the land and in the buildings that were, during the War and after, a base for the Royal New Zealand Air Force.

And we have a 'house girl', a servant in the house to do all the picking up and washing and sweeping and window cleaning and cooking and baby-minding. I am now right up there with the kaivalagi, the Europeans who colonised these islands. I am not comfortable being an employer of a servant but there isn't much I can do about it. We do need help in the house, and within hours of our arrival in Fiji a succession of girls and older women were knocking on our door asking for work. After Gus's arrival, I'm even more willing to excuse myself the guilt I should probably be feeling.

Regardless, I don't, I can't, treat my helper as though I am the mistress and she the minion. We are friends, Akanisi and I. She keeps the household functioning, and in return she has her own small separate quarters to live in and a generous (comparatively speaking) weekly wage. And I don't join in the grousing about the faults and weaknesses of house-girls that make up much of the conversation that takes place between expatriate women on the campus.

Akanisi comes from the other big island, Vanua Levu; from the town of Labasa. It embarrasses her to even admit to it, because 'labasa', is an idiomatic term synonymous with lack of sophistication. 'Labasa!' they'll say, if a girl or woman sits down but fails to ensure that her knickers aren't on display. But in fact Akanisi is a lovely girl in her early twenties who has quickly developed a fierce loyalty to all of us. She is like one of the family, truly. Gus loves her, and has her under total control. During these days, now that Gus has begun to talk, her little voice is constantly making demands. ''Nisi, my nappy needs changing.' ''Nisi, pick me up'. 'Cook me an egg, 'Nisi.' 'Nisi this, 'Nisi that. Giving the orders that I feel too embarrassed to give. A two-year-old tyrant, but with all the charm of a curly-haired miniature Circe. I am trying to teach her to add 'please'. It is the least I can do, poor Akanisi. But she doesn't seem to mind. She is a worshipper at the little tyrant's feet.

Our house is just across a small gully from the building where I have my office and where I teach. It is one of the new buildings built with funds provided by the British Government as a parting gesture, a tangible acknowledgement that they could have and should have done better. The English language and literature section that is housed within it is a kind of afterthought, with the language element (the proper use of English being essential to entry into the modern world, or so the argument goes) given far more attention than the study of literature. What matters to the administration is what they call 'progress'. My view is that 'progress' without imagination is meaningless. My literature students, I am happy to say, are amongst the brightest and best of the lot, and I have the joy of sharing ideas and excitement with young women and men from all over the Pacific – Samoa, Tonga, Solomon Islands, New Hebrides, the Cook Islands, to name only some -- as well as from all of the many communities of Fiji itself. The only thing I first have to overcome is an initial tendency amongst almost all my students to look at me and decide that they are getting second best because my skin is not white. Within a very short time, though, they know they are wrong.

There are only a handful of courses in literature, and I teach two of them, one in each semester. I also teach an English language course throughout the year and as it is a compulsory course, the class size is always large. This means a heavy load of marking, looking for and explaining errors in sentence structure, grammar and so on, which I don't much enjoy. The students who opt for the literature courses, on the other hand, delight me. Many of them are older, and include expatriate Europeans from various countries doing the course purely out of interest. Some of them use the English language in ways I have never come across before, and this excites me. I encourage this, even when it means giving tacit approval to a bending of the rules of grammar and style.

As I am something of a curiosity, being one of the comparatively few non-white academics and a native of Fiji to boot, early in my tenure there I am invited to give a talk to the members of the oldest Club in Fiji. It is a bastion of the worst of the colonial days, and entry to it is notoriously difficult to obtain. Membership is largely confined to Europeans with the odd token right given to others who are deemed sufficiently well-drilled in acceptable behaviour -- a distinguished Indian businessman, perhaps, or a Fijian High Chief.

The audience on this evening is almost entirely white, and as I am introduced I sense an atmosphere of scepticism along with the curiosity. Most are men, but I see a fair sprinkling of well-groomed and elegantly-attired women, almost all of an older generation.

I am nervous to start with – which is unusual for me as I have come to enjoy expressing my views, my knowledge and my ideas, to groups of people. Furthermore, the topic of my talk is one that I am currently exploring with enthusiasm – how the matter of race is dealt with by novelists of the nineteenth and early twentieth centuries.

The nervousness dissipates quickly enough once I begin talking of those characters and those views that are totally familiar to me. I spend some time on Thackeray's Miss Swartz, the 'rich, woolly-haired mulatto from St Kitt's' in Vanity Fair, and on the ambiguous views of Conrad in Heart of Darkness. I cover some Americans, too; Melville's Daggoo and Pip in Moby Dick, and Harriet Beecher Stowe's Uncle Tom. I also look at the attitude towards Jews, balancing Dickens' Fagin with his much more sensitive depiction of Riah in Our Mutual Friend, and pointing out how far ahead of her time was Eliot's treatment of the whole Jewish question in Daniel Deronda. I have no particular argument to make in all this. My purpose is simply to expose the various attitudes behind the depictions of character. My presentation is factual, not emotional.

At the conclusion there is a brief and telling silence; then some stunted applause. I take my seat while the man who introduced me, grey-haired and red-faced, rumbles some rote words of gratitude then asks if there are any questions. At that, a woman in the front row of seats rises to her feet and immediately and breathlessly announces: "Yes I do, I have a question."

She pauses, defiant but visibly trembling with what I soon judge to be anger rather than lack of confidence, and she has the attention of everyone in the room. "Most people here know who I am. I am one of those who was always against a University being established here," she continues. "I was born in this country, and I am proud of that fact. It is my country. We... my family and others like us have helped make it what it is. We have... we have helped civilise it. I am of this country, I love it. But I am British, and I will always be British. I have two sons, and both have been educated in Britain. Those of us who are worthy of higher education have ready access to it in Britain, or even in Australia or New Zealand. There is no need for a University here, and, and..." Her voice breaks as she grasps for the words she wants. "What... what we have heard tonight demonstrates the dangers of having people like this, ivory tower people who don't understand us and with their foreign ideas, the University itself, in these islands. We have had all the evidence we need of that tonight. This... this criticism of the civilising influence of the British, of Europeans. Now... we can all see it, can't we... these ideas will be rife in the country. There will be... all kinds of trouble and unrest. Our whole way of life is under threat..."

The woman's words drift into incoherence, her voice breaking with the anger she clearly feels. The red-faced man rises to his feet.

"Yes, thank you Mrs Stagg. Those are interesting points. Are there any other questions?"

There is much murmuring amongst the audience, heads leaning into heads, nodding or shaking. Some of it seems to be agreement, or at least sympathy, but there is embarrassment too. I see standing at the back of the room two figures in the uniform of servants of the Club. One is Indian, in white trousers, the other Fijian, in a white sulu vaka taga. The Indian is looking straight ahead, expressionless. The Fijian seems to be looking directly at me and as I look his way his mouth twitches with a grin and he nods his head almost imperceptibly.

I grin back, though anyone seeing me do so would think that I am enjoying some private joke. And so I am, in a way. That tall, impressive, handsome man is the one and only person in the room apart from myself who seems to have understood what it is that has just happened. I take his grin to my heart. We are as one. In that moment, I, too, am Fijian, nothing more.

Gus's birth in October 1972 is an event I still think of every now and then. The beginning I remember very well. The end is hazy. The aftermath we are still living with.

She announces her determination to enter the world in exactly the way it had been explained to me, ad infinitum, by just about every woman who saw my 'condition' and felt it their obligation to offer helpful advice. My waters break, then before long there arrive the first indications of the wrenching open of the gate to freedom as it were. My gate, I remind myself, rather resentfully; but there is also relief at the thought that the seemingly interminable and uncomfortable process of reproduction will soon reach its conclusion. Then comes another welling of resentment at the fact that my own will is about to be subordinated to that of another.

Time goes on and on and nothing much seems to happen apart from what are at first irregular then more regular wrenching periodic pains. We make it to hospital and I am in the care of the supposed experts. A smiling Fijian nurse attends at first, doing the necessary preparations, then the doctor calls in to assess progress. He looks distracted and uncaring. It's his eyes, I think. It's the insincerity I imagine I see in them. For some reason – or for no reason – I dislike him. I don't want him there. He leaves after offering encouraging words and advocating patience, as though it is my choice. I don't believe him. What the hell would he know, my distracted mind asks.

The intervals of respite become shorter and shorter, the pain of the contractions greater and greater, more and more invasive. At each peak I now tell myself that I didn't ask for this. But yes, I did.

No, no I didn't, no I didn't, I tell myself as the pain gathers strength once more. I want to deny reality, I want to escape the truth.

Jamie is here smiling a weak sort of encouragement and again wanting to hold my hand. I push his hand away. I don't want Jamie. I want the process to end. I feel sweat running into my eyes. I feel the nurse's hand dabbing at my skin, and I look up. It's a different nurse. I want the first one back again. It doesn't seem right, the new face. This nurse is clumsily mopping the sweat from my forehead, my cheeks; then I feel her lifting the gown again to inspect progress. I think of Thomas Hardy, of Gabriel Oak's Dorset ewes about to lamb. 'Fecund' is the word that now lodges itself in my abandoned mind. Fecund, fecund, fecund. Right now it seems more of a curse than a gift, to be fecund.

Once again the pain announces itself then increases, dominating my mind in its arrogance, proving to me my utter helplessness. Feckfeckfeckfeckfeckund, I sputter.

And so it goes on, and on. Too long, too long. Even the periods of respite I resent. Lying there, my nether regions exposed to frequent inspection, the nurse a mechanic tinkering with a piece of machinery or a shepherd dispassionately observing yet another mundane yet necessarily grisly procedure. I am not happy. I am not at all happy. Less still, much less still, when the pain grips again. And again. And again. I want to not be here. To not be here. NOT BE HERE!

I have been told by some dewy-eyed mothers on campus that even the process itself, painful though it inevitably is, is somehow an affirmation of the supreme privilege of motherhood, but I don't sense any of that. I don't sense anything other than the pain and exhaustion and resentment, and those occasional, tragi-comical animal visions…

It comes again, the pain. It seizes me, wanting to pull me apart. It is more than I can bear. Much more. Go away, go-a-fucking-way! I screech.

I am angry, now. I shout and swear again, over and over and over, first in English. Sheeeeeeit. Sheeeeeeeit. Sheeeeeeeit. Fuckfuckfuckfuck. It doesn't help much, so I try Fijian.

Bocibocibocibocibocibocibocibociboci. Booootheeeeeeeee! There is something on the ceiling in the corner of the room that has taken my attention. It is some sort of gridded panel. It looks as though it could open. It looks big enough for me to escape through. I want to escape. I don't want any more of this. I've changed my mind. I want to go back, back to the way things were, the way they were before… Escape! I stare at the panel, imploring. Nothing seems quite real except for the pain. Not even my own thoughts, or the voices, or the light. Just the pain. The pain.

"I think a little pethidine." I hear the muffled words. They are perfectly clear to me. They have meaning, much more meaning than they should have. They echo like bells in my head. What's more, I am not so far gone in my near-delirious emotions not to register a look of self-doubt on his face. In the doctor's hitherto couldn't-care-less eyes. His pig, pig, piggy eyes. "I need to ask you," he says. "An epidural. Just to help you through it?"

"Painkiller?" I gasp. It seems like the best idea I have ever heard. Escape. The word is the key, the speaker is not a pig at all. He is my saviour. "Yesyesyesyesyes."

Hands roll me partly over and I'm given an injection. I remember little after that. I am still there, Jamie assures me later, still groaning and whispering to myself or to ghosts or other figments of my semi-absent mind. The doctor asks for forceps for the last stages, Jamie tells me later. I'm sure I don't care, one way or the other. I am torn, he tells me. He sees them use the instrument that tears me. Snip, snip. I don't care. The baby is out. Out. Out. The thing inside me is out, no longer part of me, no longer connected. Physically, at least.

She is shown to me immediately, I'm later told. I don't really remember, but Jamie tells me I smile, just like a new mother should. I look exhausted and elated, he tells me. I don't really remember.

Later, after I have been stitched up again and some feeling has returned I do have a certain amount of smug satisfaction, along with a numbed awareness of the soreness of birth passages and breasts. And dizziness, and persistent nausea and an equally persistent need to sleep. I feel, I suppose, like a new mother. It is an interesting feeling. I take the baby, our daughter, to my breast, and she suckles me. It is oddly comforting. It is actually rather wonderful. She is out of me, but still demanding. I am aware that I am smiling, now. I am happy, sore and tired; and I am also reasonably confident that I won't want to do this again.

It is October the twenty-first, 1972. Almost exactly two years after Fiji gained its independence from Britain, Gus, too, is liberated. And so am I. At some level I think I have always known that she was a girl. After, looking down at her greedily feeding, I have no fears at all for her future. She will need me, for a while. But only for a while. And that is as it should be.

5

Jamie

I bring them home to our house on campus on the very day that the threatened hurricane, which has been given the very apt name 'Bebe', begins to move south-east heading directly for Viti Levu. The house has been designed to withstand such an event – thick concrete walls and shutters that we, Akanisi and I, fasten down over the windows – but even so the feeling of insecurity is strong.

When it hits, Tela and Gus are tucked up in a bedroom on the lee side. I stay in the living room, on the side of the house that is being battered by the shrieking wind. No… it roars rather than shrieks. It roars and batters. I have a greater understanding of the meaning of relentlessness. Objects are flung .against the shutters, mostly, I assume, pieces of vegetation torn from the trees. So strong and brutal is the wind that water begins to accumulate at the base of the inside walls, somehow driven through the concrete and the shuttered windows.

I race up and down mopping up the water. I check frequently on the bedroom, on mother and baby. They are both sleeping. Sleeping, while Akanisi and I are like demented Canutes, scampering around, slipping and sliding, shouting reassuring words to each other as we try to keep the menacing waters at bay.

And such is the homecoming of Tela and Gus. My wife, and my daughter. My mind is full of them both. The hurricane makes itself felt, dramatically demonstrates its power, but there are far more important things on my mind. It seems little more than a fitting affirmation of the significance of the occasion. In a bedroom on the lee side of the building they sleep through it all.

For weeks after Gus's arrival I look upon Tela more as the ultimate earth mother than my exclusive physical companion. I know that our relationship will never be quite the same as it was, but I am unsure in exactly what ways it is likely to change. Yes, I must share her attention, but I am inured to that. Her dedication to her work means that I have always had to share her attention. I learned very early on that although when she does properly allow her mind to turn to me it is with full and total attention, those times are of her choosing. But now I wonder even if she still will want me, need me at all, in the way she has before. Will Gus now become that necessary other facet of her life, to the exclusion of me? What will the pain of birth have done to her libido? She has had stitches. She has gone through the sort of trial that I know all mothers have had to bear, but worse, perhaps, than most. I have observed it all and I will understand if it is weeks, months before she…

"I can help you," she says, when I reach out for her in bed about a week after the hurricane. All I really want to do, I think, is bring her near again. To be close. But if that is what she thinks… I let her hand search me out, comfort me.

It is a relief of sorts, but far from what I need. Yet the other, I know, is out of the question for a while yet. Anyway, I'm not at all certain that that is necessarily what I want either. I need to be close. I need her flesh close, but it doesn't, surely it doesn't mean it has to be that. I simply need her to want me.

A few nights later it is as though she has divined my feelings. "You can help me," she says; and she draws me close, against her swollen breast. "She's a greedy little thing, but even she can't handle all the milk I have."

A nipple is hard against me, leaking drops over my cheek. She strokes my hair. "Go on," she says. I hesitate, some murky part of my brain protesting at the very idea. Then that reluctance is pushed aside by a primal urge. A primal understanding. A primal wish. My nostrils are filled with the

42

scent of milk and something else, something feral. The swollen nipple is in my mouth, and from the depths of my throat comes a reflex, and milk, my Tela's milk, fills my mouth; and I swallow, and my mouth is filled again, and I swallow again, over and over; and more even than in our fondest couplings I feel that our flesh is one.

I love her. I love her, and she loves me. It is something we don't say to each other. It is something I don't believe we have ever said. It doesn't matter. It is something we know.

It is a little over three years later. We have just returned to New Zealand permanently, and I am going through the bits and pieces of my old life, my previous life, that I had left at my mother's place in the small town on the other side of the Ranges where I had lived out my younger teenage years. My old home. Now Tela and I, and Gus, will be establishing our own domestic nest, our proper and lasting home, in the compact and windy city just through the Gorge that provides the main access from one side of the island to the other. Now I must decide which of the books and other objects I had accumulated and that I had decided were not worth taking or were too precious to take to Fiji I should now make part of my life again. It is then that I rediscover the Journals of Adelaide Gilbard, or Adelaide Gerold as she should by rights have described herself according to the conventions of the time. But Gilbard or Gerold, she was my great-grandmother.

I pick up one of the old volumes and idly turn the leaves. It is labelled 'Accounts', and indeed there are neat accounting entries that take up some of the space – but turn it over and start from the back and it is a record of her thoughts and her doings. It is very old, of course, and bound partly in leather that is now cracked and worn. I reflect on how much I owe to these two Journals, and to my ancestress. Without them Tela and I may never have got together, never have discovered the bonds that now tie us. I feel the weight of the volume I'm holding, and it all comes back to me. In the overarching excitement of finding each other, the Journals that had brought us together had hardly been given another thought. But here they are, and seeing them again is a thrilling reminder of both their contents and the very special place they have in our personal histories. Of course I decide that they must be taken with me now, and looked after carefully.

But first, sitting there, for some reason I recall a passage in the one I'm holding, the earlier of the two Journals, where Adelaide wrote of discussing with her maid, her friend, matters which surprised me. Why it should be this passage that now comes to my mind I am not sure, but it is possibly because I remember it as the entry that first brought home to me that Adelaide Gilbard was not just a significant contributor to my genetic heritage, but that she was also an extraordinary, an exceptional, human being. I remember this particular entry as having to do with race and class, and with friendship, but even more vividly I remember being bemused by a colourful exchange recorded there between Adelaide and her friend, who was also her maid, regarding the sexual act.

Previous to my first reading of this entry, I had had a half-baked notion that Victorian ladies never, ever discussed the sexual act, not with anyone. Men, yes; at least between themselves. I also knew that men of the middle class in Victorian England had ready enough access to very explicit erotica, because my Christchurch friend, Anders Malmo, had shown me some of his father's collection of such material. But for women of the gentry? Never, surely! But Adelaide Gilbard had written of it, I now remember. Obliquely and humorously, yes; but she had written of it. I remember being surprised by the passages, but also delighted. They had made her seem more real still. They had made me feel the connection between us more strongly, perhaps, than anything else could have.

44

I turn the book over and seek a page that will confirm my memory; and it doesn't take me long to find the one I want. I read the whole of that entry, from a time when she had been in the colony for just two years:

15th June, 1865. I am rather wickedly amused by the attempts by some of the wives of the more 'respectable' settlers to come to terms with my skin colour. "May I enquire of your maiden name, Mrs Gerold?" they might ask – clearly expecting me to answer with 'Bellini' or 'Sanchez' or somesuch. But when I tell them it is Gilbard, and add that my father's family is from Gloucestershire, they smile and nod with vague discontent, their frustrated curiosity apparent in their expression. I can then almost see them mentally attributing my colouring to some incident that their imagination conjures as having taken place on a sugar plantation in the West Indies, perhaps, or in a leafy courtyard in Bombay.

It is not that I am at all unwilling to reveal my ancestry. Indeed, had any person persevered in their inquiries I am quite sure I would have talked of my East Indian forebear, and of my supposed African connection as well. But no one ever has. It would seem too much of a presumption, I suppose. They would think that I would be shamed to talk of it.

One other thing that seems to confuse this sort of person occasionally is my way of conversing. My choice of words and my way of pronouncing them was laid down in my childhood, mostly unthinkingly, by all that was habitual in my father's household. Although I was aware very early that my mother's English was not quite that of my father – that especially when she was angry, or otherwise excited, she lapsed into what I later discovered was the accent of the Bristol docks -- this awareness only tended to reinforce my own innate determination to imitate my father. My years at Mrs Abbott's

School certainly did not alter this. At School I was occasionally mocked for my slight tendency towards a West-Country accent, but my speech otherwise could have been, and could be now, that of any daughter of an English gentleman. I take no pride in this, it is simply part of me. I know that for the majority of the settler population here, those from the labouring classes, the way I speak puts something of a barrier between us; but if I were to make a conscious attempt to change the way I talk when I speak to them, that would be a ridiculous affectation.

So here I am – a woman whose skin has taken on an even darker hue in this climate, but who speaks and has mannerisms much like any one of those who consider themselves to be the superior class of settlers. A mystery indeed!

But I am not a mystery to Hannah. We understand each other completely. I do not hesitate to talk to her of anything at all, even the most intimate of secrets. Even... Yes, even that. Well, not in detail, of course, but in a joking kind of way. We use our own word when we refer to it, Hannah and I. The use of that particular word arose one day when we were at the kitchen sink and I was questioning her as to the Maori word for certain vegetables of a sort that were not grown in this country before the arrival of Europeans. "Mostly we just put an 'i' on the end of the English word," she told me. I lifted a carrot and silently questioned. "Karoti," she said. I picked up an onion and suggested "onioni?" This was greeted by a shriek of laughter, and her hands reaching up to cover her ears. "No! No! That is something different. We say 'aniani'," she said, emphasising the 'a'. "That is our way of saying onion." "Why did you laugh at the way I said it," I asked. Again the wicked laughter. "This is onioni;"she said; and she showed me by an unmistakeable gesture and a thrust of her hips just what it meant.

We laughed together. Since then, 'onion' has become our secret word for it -- for the veiled yet essential human activity that convention tells us should not be mentioned.

And I sit here with a smile on my face. I am a little boy who has discovered a mother's secret. A great-grandmother's secret. Once again I am delighted with myself, and with Adelaide Gilbard.

The passage read, I stow both volumes reverently in a carton along with other books and papers, and I don't look at either again for quite some time, for while we are in our rented accommodation in the city we unpack as little as possible, anticipating our permanent move to our own house.

Then I leave my mother's place, the car packed with cartons of books, papers and other remnants of my previous life. As I travel south then west again towards the city, the tall arch of clouds above the Ruahine Ranges seems to me to be a portal through which I am about to pass into the next, and perhaps the ultimately defining phase of my life.

It is an exciting yet rather daunting business, buying and setting up our first proper home -- viewing possibilities, arranging mortgages, walking or driving around to get the feel of neighbourhoods. Although we look at two possible properties across the river, up on the hill near the University, we settle at last on a house closer to the city centre on a pleasant and leafy street on the southern side of the Square. It is quite a large place, bigger than we really need, but its charm wins us over. Besides, we are flush with funds as a result of Tela's bonus for satisfactorily completing two three-year contracts in Fiji and my generous payment for a series of articles commissioned by a commercial journal. We make our decision, conclude the financial arrangements, and move in.

6

Tela

Augusta Margaret Ashcott-Gilbard. Gus. Our child. Our daughter. I realise very early on that we, Jamie and I, are very different in the way we relate to our daughter, though of course we both care for her deeply. Jamie desperately wants to share her life, to the extent that at times I think he would like to live her life for her. It seems to me that his love for her is blind, and guided only by the deep emotion he feels.

Gus, though, cheerfully goes on doing what she chooses to do, taking advantage of whatever attention she gets but not allowing it to lessen her determination to make her own way and to find things out for herself.

She is three years old when we return to New Zealand so that I can take up my position here. I am happy to have it. Now I am where I want to be, with a tenured post as a Lecturer at a University that is pleasantly sited away from the distractions and difficulties of the larger centres.

When I first applied for the job it was with a certain amount of reluctance. I had thought that my ideal would have been a post in Wellington, at Vic, with an office next to Cynthia's; but here I am only a couple of hours away from Wellington anyway, and I am much closer to Fiona. And in some ways, Fi is dearer to me even than Cynthia. For one thing, we are the same age, and our shared experiences, first at boarding school and then at University in Wellington, are of a sort that are intimate in ways that Cynthia's and mine cannot be and could not have been.

After our return to New Zealand Jamie, Gus and I live at first in a rented house near the campus, then, after negotiating its purchase, we settle easily and comfortably into our new home. I wasn't greatly interested in the actual choice of house, happily leaving most of the decisions to Jamie. As long as it was large enough to allow us both to have workrooms I would have been content to live anywhere in the town. The one he chooses serves this purpose well enough. It has two rooms suitable for our respective books and other occupational paraphernalia. One is downstairs, at the back of the house, and it has a door that opens directly on to the garden. It has plenty of space for tall bookshelves on three sides and for a big desk as well as an armchair and filing cabinets. I don't have to ask Jamie. He cedes this to me.

In contrast to my study at home, my office at the University is small; but it is adequate for its purpose, and it is in one of the older and most attractive of the buildings on campus. The University is set in extensive, treed grounds on land that once surrounded the homestead of a wealthy farmer.

I can imagine no more pleasant setting in which to follow my interests while earning a living than this campus. Over the years, I have been encouraged to locate to centres of greater population and resources and reputation both here in New Zealand and in Britain or Australia or the United States, but I have never been remotely tempted by this prospect. Why would I be? It is stimulating to occasionally visit such places, to meet and debate with other leading practitioners in my field, but I am always happy to be back here away from the tensions of the northern hemisphere and away from the constant human and vehicular traffic in the bigger cities wherever they might be. Besides, I decided long ago, when I was still a child, possibly even before I met Cynthia, that the greatest privilege the world could offer me was what it has given me – to be a New Zealander and to live in New Zealand.

And there is that other reason why I am happy to live here, in this particular city. From our house it takes only a little more than half an hour to drive to Fi and Ali's farm. Fiona is my dearest friend. It is Fiona and her family who first made me feel that I was accepted, that New Zealand was my home. She was my room-mate at Mapledene, and my flat-mate through most of my years as a student in Wellington. Through all that time we were really more like sisters than just friends.

But even though she is not far away we don't live in each other's pockets, nor would we want to. Fi and I are a constant feature of each other's lives, I know that. We don't need to be physically in each other's presence to have that reaffirmed, though it is true that our domestic and other concerns have inevitably weakened our intimacy in some ways. That is simply a consequence of circumstances.

We do telephone each other reasonably frequently, and at least every couple of months or so either she will drop in of a weekend when she happens to have come to town for some reason, or Jamie and Gus and I will drive out for a country break. Most times when we are together, at her place or mine, we are still surrounded by the evidence of our other selves, the selves that serve purposes other than our friendship. Children. Our husbands. The constant pressures of time and the ever-present evidence of the ways in which we live -- the farm outside the window in her case or the books that line the shelves in mine – are reminders that our meetings must necessarily be brief, usually little more than a cup of tea and a hurried exchange of major happenings.

The Cameron farm is beautifully sited in one of the valleys that run down to the plains. The homestead is large – which is just as well as when we first return to New Zealand from Fiji we find that Fi and Ali and their three children still share it with Ali's father and mother. He, Mr Cameron Senior, is pleasant enough in a faintly arrogant, stuffed-shirt way, but his wife is clearly an almost tragi-comic snob. This Fiona seems to have learned to live with, though she confides in me that she is looking forward to returning to teaching even though her in-laws both look askance at the very thought that she should wish to do so. Ali's objections she feels she can handle, but the seniors are far more of a hurdle. Though they often talk of retiring soon to a house in town, their plans are still vague.

Mrs Cameron Senior is evidently very keen to be closer to her bridge-playing friends, but Mr Cameron, it seems, is always finding some excuse to put the move off.

Fi's children, two boys and a girl, are all blonde-haired and blue-eyed. The youngest boy, Craig, is still little more than a baby when we return from Fiji -- a couple of years younger than Gus who is in her fourth year. The girl, Olivia, is much of an age with her, and the heir, Callum, is now almost eight. He doesn't quite know how to deal with Gus when she tries (usually successfully, as there are few, children or adults, who are able to resist her determination) to drag him into one of her complicated play sequences. Gus the Loud. Gus the Risk-taker. Gus the Irresistible Force. Fi's three are cute and quaint and chocolate-box pretty, but they are no match for Gus. I should know. I'm her mother.

Some of the most significant events in our respective lives, Fiona's and mine, we have not been able to share. Although I had attended Fi's wedding to Alistair and had, in fact, been one of her bridesmaids, she had been unable to come to Fiji for my wedding because she was heavily pregnant with her first child. We had neither of us been close at hand for the birth of our various offspring, though we had sent our best wishes on these occasions. All of which means that some of the intimacy that comes through constant sharing and that had once existed between us is now necessarily weakened a little, and in many ways I regret this. Occasionally I wish for the sort of non-judgemental, unconditional and near-at-hand support and understanding that only the three most important women in my life – my mother, Cynthia Wallace, and Fiona – have ever been able to give me.

Another woman who, I suppose, should have become important in my life after my marriage to Jamie is my mother-in-law, Win Ashcott. But she hasn't. I think I had harboured some hope that we might have become close, but it was clear from our very first meeting that there was and would remain a distance between us; though I don't think that Jamie sees it.

We are not comfortable with each other, Mrs Ashcott and I. Both of us pretend we are, but we are not. This uneasy stand-off, of which Jamie is either utterly unaware or refuses to recognise, was apparent to me right from the time I first met her just before Jamie and I went to Fiji for the wedding -- which she chose not to attend, pleading an unwillingness to fly -- and again during a brief leave we took in New Zealand when Gus was just two or three months old.

To be utterly truthful, I am happy that since our permanent return to New Zealand Jamie usually goes by himself or takes only a rather reluctant Gus with him when he travels through the Gorge to the other side of the ranges to see his mother. She has shifted now to live with her elder daughter, my sister-in-law Jenny, on a farm a few miles from Jamie's old home town.

Jamie himself doesn't seem to much enjoy the visits to see his mother either, and he makes them only very occasionally. Jenny, his elder sister, he doesn't know very well, as she left the family home to make a separate life for herself when he was just a baby, and was married and living far away while he was still a little boy. On the rare occasions that we have met I have found that I like Jenny much more than I do his mother. She is a warm-hearted and welcoming woman who has raised what she calls a 'brood' of six children, all of whom are now leading separate lives of their own but who nevertheless still dominate her thinking and her conversation.

But all told I don't feel any close affinity with Jamie's family, nor do I need to do so. I say 'Jamie's family', but I don't think Jamie himself feels that the connection is of huge significance to him any more. He maintains it only spasmodically, and chiefly then out of a sense of duty, I feel. I certainly don't begrudge his maintaining it – indeed, it is often only after my prompting him to do so that he makes one of his infrequent visits to see his mother – but I know that he is happy to put almost all of his thoughts and energies into his new, his chosen family. To give his time to me, and to Gus.

7

Jamie

On our return to New Zealand, one of the many adjustments we have to make centres on household life without a house-girl. We would have liked to have brought Akanisi with us but the difficulties this would have involved were simply too many; not the least of them being that Akanisi had found herself a young man she would not have been willing to leave behind.

Domestic adjustments, then. I suppose for most facing the same necessary compromises the result would have entailed many arguments. But Tela doesn't argue. Every time I attempt to dispute a point with her – 'why should it nearly always be me that's left to do all the outside work, and the grocery shopping, and the cooking?' – she will simply say something like 'it's easier for you to find the time' and switch off. Explanation given. Accept it. If I pursue the matter, I soon learn that she will just disappear into her study and leave me to stew in my own juice.

So the pattern is established very early in our life in New Zealand. Tela makes our bed every morning. She gets Gus ready for the day. She runs the vacuum cleaner around the carpets every week or so, quickly and efficiently. She will make a cup of tea for herself, or for both of us, when she feels the need. She will throw a load of clothes and towels and bed linen in the washing machine every now and then (though she is rarely able to wait around long enough to hang the washing on the line or put it in the drier), and she'll find time to visit the shops to buy whatever clothing she deems necessary for Gus and herself. Everything else, virtually everything else, she either leaves to me or is quite happy to leave undone.

No arguments. We had been totally spoilt in Fiji, of course, with Akanisi cheerfully doing practically everything that needed doing. So it takes me quite a while to cease my occasional mutterings to myself about perceived injustices in the distribution of domestic responsibilities, but our new habits are established soon enough. No... for me, it's more than just a matter of becoming inured to the necessary extra duties. It is an acceptance that Tela is what she is, and that it is all of her that I want, and that I will always want, even her annoying deficiencies which are not really deficiencies at all. In time I come close to actually cherishing her impatience with most of the domestic arts. That's Tela. That's part of her, and she is what I need. Simple.

In one important aspect of our lives no major change is needed. We both love books. We rarely shop together except on those occasions when we go to a good bookshop, particularly one dealing in second-hand books. We split off to examine the shelves that most attract us, and meet up again at the cashier's desk. We will each have at least one or two volumes. Hers will always be novels or LitCrit. Mine might include a novel or two, but will be mostly history, or political commentary. We have our separate work rooms at home. They are like different worlds. If I select a book from one of the shelves in her study and open it (and I do quite frequently borrow from her library), I find that the margins are densely packed with notes and comments pencilled in her compact shorthand. If she ever picked up one of mine, she'd find my mostly illegible scrawl similarly pencilled in – but she has never shown any interest in my reading matter.

Gus starts Primary school a year or so after we settle in. The school is just up the road, little more than five minutes' walk away. We go together, that first day, all three of us with Gus in the middle. We take a hand of hers each and swing her over the cracks in the pavement, until we come across other groups of children and parents behaving more decorously. Gus watches them for a few moments, then drops our hands and

56

puts hers under the straps of her little back-pack just as she sees the other children doing and trots out ahead of us.

She is a little teary when we leave her with the understanding New Entrants teacher, though I doubt she is feeling as bereft as I am about her being left there with strangers. But in truth it's not so bad, as there are two of Gus's friends from Play Centre starting on the same day, and after those few tears she settles in happily enough.

From now on, at least from nine till three during the week, my days are empty of those who are dear to me. On the other hand, I now have plenty of time to chase up more work, or to complete work in hand. Or so I tell myself.

"You should look up some old friends, or go over and see your mother," Tela tells me as she gets out of the car after I have driven her to the University one morning a few weeks after the start of the new Term. She grabs her bag and a pile of marking from the back seat, then says: "You must have some old school friends over there that you can meet up with. It's not good for you to spend all your time in the house."

I think about her words as I drive back down the hill. Friends. There probably are a few of my school-friends still living in my old town, an hour's drive away, but the idea is faintly ridiculous. The friendships I made at school were not deep. I have not had any meaningful contact with any of them for at least a decade. The whole issue of friendship is something I haven't given serious thought to for years. Tela and Gus are my world. Ever since we truly discovered each other, I have felt no compelling need of friends. I feel no urgent need to look beyond Tela, and now Gus, for companionship. I tell myself that I need nothing else.

I should go and see my mother more often, though. I admit that to myself with some guilt, as I drop my speed to conform to the speed limit across the bridge over the Manawatu. My mother has shifted out of the little old house in which I spent most of my teenage years – just the two of us, mother and son. That house is now sold, and she has gone to live with my older sister, a short distance from the town. But... for reasons I don't fully understand I have found that my visits to my mother are no longer comfortable. She is nearly eighty, and her age no doubt contributes to this. She seems to be no longer interested in sharing my news. Her responses to my reports of my family's doings, or my own, are non-committal; almost like those of a stranger who has little reason to be interested. All this means that although I think of her quite often, such thoughts are not accompanied these days by any compelling desire to go and visit her.

These rather depressing musings are diverted by what I now see around me. It is a sparkling late-October morning, and the oriental plane trees on either side of the street have come into full leaf. Ahead is a vista that always diverts my thoughts – the broad sweep of the tree-bordered roadway that ends with a glimpse of the clock-tower in the Square far ahead. I suppose it is the historian in me, but whenever I see this and similar sights in the city I think of those whose vision is here partly realised. Out of the swamp and bush that once prevailed, and not so very long ago, they planned and created a town that was intended to mimic those to be found not just in the lands of their ultimate origin – in Britain or Europe – but also those that others of their kind had created as they came, hopeful or fearful, to the Americas or to Australia or to one of the many other places on the planet that suffered the European diaspora. I suppose what I see is little more than a distorted echo of the original intentions, but a drive up the Avenue at least reminds me of what those pitifully arrogant yet, in the context of the times, worthy enough aims must have been.

I turn at the lights into the street that runs east towards the ranges. The scene is less evocative here. The old colonial houses which must once have been set back from the road and fronted by gardens, orchards and lawns, their roofs adorned with finials and their verandahs with ornate wooden lace, have now mostly been pulled down or transported elsewhere. Those that remain have had the front part of their sections sold, and sterile dwellings of stucco or stained wood and glass have arisen in front of them.

This, I suppose, is the real New Zealand, the New Zealand of today. Visions have changed. There are different priorities. Now those priorities are more likely to be the provision of shopping malls and CBD parking spaces, efficient garbage collection and traffic control. The most pressing individual concerns are probably taxes and insurance premiums and power bills rather than joining with fellow citizens in the creation of pretty townscapes. As I drive past the long line of traffic waiting at the lights, indicators blinking, I momentarily and far from seriously decide I would much prefer even the original bush and swamp. In fact, perhaps especially that.

With these and similar thoughts in my mind, by the time I have parked the car in the garage Tela's suggestions regarding a visit through the Gorge have been discarded. Neither the thought of my mother nor the dredging through of my previous life in an attempt to remember old school friends has elicited in me any sufficient reason to stir myself from the house -- from our now frequently empty house.

But once back inside I do find myself thinking about certain others from my past – about the very few people whose friendship has meant, perhaps still does mean, something of significance to me. I think of Cossy, the most unlikely of these yet the one who comes freshest and most often to my mind. Cossy, three or four years my senior, the man who for some reason known only to himself took me under his wing at the Hostel I lived in for my first two years as a student in Wellington, and then invited me to stay with him in his family house in Christchurch for the three years I was there.

These thoughts of Cossy are accompanied by a surge of nostalgia which takes me a little by surprise. It's been quite some time since he last entered my head, but now the thought of him is accompanied by an oddly urgent wish that we could meet up again. Unfortunately, though, as far as I know he is still in Christchurch. What's more, we haven't been in contact with each other for years. He wouldn't even be aware that I am married – though I'm fairly sure he won't be married himself. Cossy, I recall, has a rather jaundiced view of females; apart from a degree of grudging affection for his aunt, who brought him up and who looked after us both when we shared that house just across the road from Hagley Park. We got on well, Cossy and I. We were and surely still are very different, but we were comfortable together.

Remembering Cossy and the many hours we spent in each other's company also brings to my mind the other close friend from my Christchurch days, Anders Malmo. When he had first offered me his friendship I had been surprised and grateful. Anders was one of the brightest lights at the University – a brilliant scholar with an outgoing confidence and an obvious and infectious belief that life is given to us to enjoy. He was also, then, an extraordinarily and boyishly good-looking young man, and a hugely cheerful and successful Lothario. But the last time I saw Anders was when I stayed with him in Cambridge, in that utterly memorable year when Tela and I decided that we must share our lives. She and Anders were both doctoral candidates at the University, he at Queens' and Tela at Girton. I have remained in sporadic touch with Anders – a letter every now and then – and I know he has returned to New Zealand and taken a Lectureship at Canterbury, but we haven't met face to face since that time together in England. So that is another one I could genuinely call a friend, but he, too, is an impossible distance away. Well… impossible without tedious forward planning.

Thus even my contemplation of the wider implications of Tela's suggestion leads nowhere. Besides, after the initial rush of nostalgia has waned I'm left unsure sure that I am in need

of the sort of companionship a friend could give. Yes, I decide
– it would be good to see Cossy again, and Anders, but for the
moment that is not possible. Nevertheless her suggestion
prompts me to write Anders a letter which I then take with me
on a brief walk up the road to the nearest postal box, where I
drop it in.

Back in my rather cramped office I let my eye wander
around my bookshelves. What I see doesn't do anything to lift
the depression that now threatens more alarmingly. Rather, it
tends to intensify it by increasing my sense of guilt and
purposelessness. Downstairs in Tela's study I know she has a
shelf devoted to the anthologies and journals in which can be
found examples of her own work. She is proud of them, and
justly so. I have copies of most of my own efforts on my shelf
or in my filing cabinet, but for the most part my writing has
been for the sort of trade or commercial journals that are dated
in their contents almost before they come out. Journeyman
stuff, and about as interesting now as cold porridge. It's all
been little more than a way of contributing something to the
family pot.

For a fraction of a second I wonder at the sight of the two
large volumes squeezed into the bottom corner of one of the
shelves. Two old volumes, side by side. Scruffy looking. Then
it is with a thrill of rediscovery that I remember. Of course!
Adelaide Gilbard's journals. My ancestress. The woman
whose words spoke to me so clearly that I felt after I had read
them that she was as real, as close or closer, than any of my
living relatives. A woman for whom I felt, and feel, a deep
affection as well as a very real fascination.

I pull one of the volumes out of the shelf, and, turning it
upside down in the necessary fashion I read a passage at
random. It is one of the entries towards the end of this, the
second volume of her Journal. It concerns a letter she has
received from her brother, Oliver, who has written to her from
Fiji. It is apparently the last letter she ever received from him,

and it tells her of his desertion of the Colonial Service in which he had served as Secretary to a Stipendiary Magistrate in one of the Provinces in Fiji, and his marriage with a Fijian woman; of his children, and of his way of life in the Fijian village where he lives. And it tells in particular (and I recall the amazement at the time I first registered the connection) of George, his eldest son. George, the child who was to become Tela's grandfather. It was this very passage that first brought home to me that Tela Gilbard, the clever part-Fijian girl I knew mainly as the friend of another girl I thought I was in love with, was my distant kin.

But it is not Adelaide Gilbard's dying days that I want to remind myself of now. It is the earlier time, just a few years after she first arrived in the little settlement of New Plymouth. So I put the later volume back, and select the earlier one, and I open that, too, at random, and begin my re-reading...

September 1868. I feel I should write more of the mountain, named Mount Egmont by the British who "discovered" it. It is very much a part of life here, even though it is aloof and uncaring – or apparently so. It is a volcano, of course, but a sleeping one. Its presence gives the province its name, and it is a very special feature of the landscape to the local Maori people, who view it as an important – indeed, a defining -- symbol of their tribe. I know that it has come to be of significance to many European settlers as well. Its domination is a confirmation of all that is strong and eternal. The local people identify it as such, and show in some of their proverbs their confidence in its everlasting presence. Hannah told me of one – Kaore e pau, he ika unahi nui -- which means that the mountain, and thus also the Taranaki tribe, is like a fish with tough scales, a fish that cannot be eaten. The mountain is here now and forever, and the tribe that dwells at its feet, protected by it, cannot be defeated.

I think the mountain has extended its protection to me, also. I think the mountain has accepted me as one of its own. It is only my whimsy, of course. I know that. Nevertheless, I do have this feeling that I am no longer a girl, a woman, of the west of England; that I am, rather, a woman of Taranaki. And "Taranaki" is not simply the name of this province – it is also the true name of the mountain. And the mountain has accepted me.

This whimsy, and whimsy I suppose it must be called, is strengthened by the feelings of mutual respect and sisterly love – I do not think that it is an exaggeration for me to so call them – that have grown between Hannah and me. I know I have mentioned Hannah often in this Journal, and that is a reflection of how much she has come to mean to me. I don't think Tom has ever been able to understand my feelings for her, our feelings for each other. To him, Hannah is simply a servant. A loyal and useful servant – he acknowledges that much, as how could he not? -- but a mere servant, nonetheless, and thus one who could never be part of our intimate family as anything other than a servant. An even greater barrier, to him, is that she is Maori, and therefore not one of "us". He seems to believe that there is an inherent and insuperable difference between settler, and especially what he considers to be the superior class of settler, and Maori, and that this difference is one that cannot be, nor should be, erased.

But I am happy to say that Tom is not one of those who see Maori people as being in all ways inferior human beings with an inferior culture, and therefore unworthy of our proper concern. He has great respect for Maori men as warriors and even very real sympathy for the sufferings of the Maori people since the arrival of European settlers – but it seems he is unable to accept the truth that Maori and European are in essence exactly alike. I am even happier to say that it has never been a problem for me to acknowledge this, as, knowing my own ancestry from a very early age, I have always accepted, naturally and, I suppose, without any need to justify my belief, that, apart from the sex that defines each of us in a biological sense and determines some of our major functions in life, we are all, under the skin, one and the same even though we are, each and every one of us, our own unique selves. If that seems like a contradiction, dear reader, then you have misunderstood me completely!

And now I am wondering if there will ever be a reader of this Journal. I hope there is. I hope there is someone reading these very words. Here they are, dear reader, these, my words. My greetings to you! I hope you have not misunderstood me!

8

Tela

It is winter of 1981. Almost against my will, I have been thinking about the Springbok Tour – the tour of the South African rugby team to this country, that is. The Tour is going ahead with the backing of Muldoon and his government despite the strong protests of those who see it as giving tacit support to the apartheid regime in South Africa. It is the issue that above all others, even Prince Charles's wedding, is dominating the news here. The University is constantly buzzing with talk and action, amongst both the staff and students. Needless to say, most talk and action is directed against the Tour, though it also has a strong body of supporters here especially amongst the Agriculture students.

The atmosphere all around the campus is one of anger, determination and, yes, fear. It is simply not possible to avoid thinking about the issues involved, and really there is only one conclusion that can be reached rationally and ethically. Of course I am against the Tour. But, as usual, my reaction is that of an observer rather than a participant. I am an observer. I have been all of my life. I observe and analyse and even at times admire those who take action if they do so in what is clearly a worthy cause. Vicarious, that's me. Vicariously despising whatever my intellect leads me to believe is stupid, vicariously learning about sex when I was young, vicariously sinking into the worlds created by the Victorian novelists -- but not wanting to be more than an observer. Not able, in that latter case, to be more than an observer, of course.

Similarly, these days I quite conscientiously avoid any attempts to get me more involved in the politics of the University, just as I avoid the temptation to talk about the political direction of the country. For one thing, the topic is too depressing. It is like staring into an abyss. I prefer to keep to the boundaries of my particular discipline and interests, and to see the joy and wonderment in my students – those who allow themselves to become excited about such things – when they discover the beauty and genius behind the creations of the human mind. All of such creations. My field is literature, but I have a great sympathy for, if not a very deep understanding of, those other fields of artistic expression such as music and the visual arts.

My field. It is a rather wonderful word, 'field'. It suggests a bounded though not exclusive area in which to be joyful and safe. And that is more or less the way I see it, literature. If I even think of looking too far beyond the boundaries into that bleak world ruled by the so-called imperatives of economics, or the blind loyalties of the sports fanatics, or the pious or impious witterings of those who aspire to lead us, that is when I feel a sort of terror and despair. So I rarely look, I rarely comment. I listen to the debates then I let them pass me by. Jamie on the other hand agonises, angers, spits colourful epithets – and, of course, achieves nothing. He knows that; but it doesn't stop him from twisting himself into knots.

These days, my major passion, apart from teaching, is collaborating with Cynthia in the writing of a treatise on women novelists of the nineteenth and early twentieth centuries. This project involves my occasional travel to Wellington, usually over a weekend, to see Cynthia and talk over ideas and problems and to sort out exactly what each of us will contribute.

Cynthia's house is set well back from the harbour, snugly tucked into a fold in the Karori hills. It is not far from where Katherine Mansfield once lived. The little cottage has all the charm one would expect of the late Victorian period, and is set in a sheltered garden. Inside it is snug and modernised but it still has that nineteenth century feel.

We have arranged a weekend of earnest activity, or so we tell ourselves. Our book is in its final stages. We are both feeling the indescribable mixture of apprehension and excitement that comes when reputations are about to be put on the line.

"You've managed to read through my section on Woolf?" she asks me.

"Oh yes," I say. I can't resist a wry grin. "Anyone who knows us at all will be able to recognise it's yours, that bit."

"Too polemical, you think?"

Each time we have met over the past ten years, Cynthia has evidenced a stronger and stronger feminism. Virginia Woolf has become her latest passion, almost supplanting George Eliot in her pantheon of goddesses. "No, I won't say that. But I've been thinking more about our introduction. It's pretty clear to me that we're likely to disagree on… some things. My idea is that we each write an introductory essay, and that we include both of them in the book."

Cynthia looks at me, long and hard. It doesn't make me uncomfortable. I know that somehow her gaze is helping her to martial her thoughts. Besides, although she's well into her sixties by now, age seems to have given her added authority and even greater beauty. I am, as usual, flattered rather than discomforted by being the centre of her attention.

"Yes. A good idea," she says at last. "That'd be a good way to avoid arguments. If the publisher is willing to take the risk, that is."

"We can insist on it. I think it might even add to the value of the book as a text for students." Her notion that we might argue makes me smile again. We don't argue. We never have. If we disagree over something, we tend towards humorous banter rather than argument, yet somehow the issue at stake always comes to be resolved.

Our differences in relation to the material in our book are really little more than matters of emphases. Since she has become an ardent feminist, Cynthia is constantly looking for ways to fit both the texts and the subtexts of the books by women authors into the feminist notion of an ongoing struggle by women to find a voice in a male-dominated world. To me most surprising of all, she has even begun to question George Eliot's credentials as a feminist, adopting Woolf's view of her as one whose writing tacitly acknowledges the over-arching and largely unquestioned dominance of the patriarchy.

While those ideas interest me, and I most certainly believe that there is much of value in the feminist approach to literary criticism, I still think of the debate as being little more than a side issue. To me it is literature as art, as a way of understanding, enriching and interpreting the human condition, that is far and away the more significant and interesting question. Gender is part of this, of course, but it is just one more factor in the grand tapestry. The gender-related assumptions that are obvious in the novelists' works are, to me, of equal interest whether the books be written by men or women. The assumptions are part of the prevalent perspectives of the age in which they lived and wrote. We certainly should not judge them – condemn them or praise them – by the prevailing perspectives or the currently burgeoning fads of our own age.

But, yes, our respective introductions to the book should make the different approaches clear and make the book itself more valuable to students. They can make up their own minds. Anyway, I feel smugly certain that my approach will be the more convincing, and the more useful.

Of course I do.

"We'd better agree to let each other's intro stand without comment," I say.

Cynthia laughs, delighted. "I don't think we should even let each other see what we've written. That way we can look forward to a surprise when we get the proofs to read."

"I don't imagine I'll be surprised," I say.

"Nor I," she says.

"And we're definitely agreed on the title, then?" I ask. It seemed obvious right from the time we first discussed it, and I had no objection at all to the salute to Cynthia's current favourite essay on the subject – Woolf's Three Guineas. Uneducated Girls, our book is to be called; with the sub-title Women Novelists of the Nineteenth and Early Twentieth Centuries.

"Well, that'll have to be approved by the publisher. They commissioned it, after all."

True. They'd approached me first, and I'd suggested Cynthia as co-author. "I'll be very annoyed if they don't agree to it; though they might suggest we go with just the sub-title. How boring would that be!"

"Or something completely different. Like A Feminist Guide to Literature. Try to encourage its adoption into gender studies courses."

I grin. "You'd quite like that, wouldn't you!"

"Yes, I would."

It comes out as *Uneducated Girls,* and it is about as big a success as such a work could be. The main markets are in Britain and the United States, where it quickly becomes a prescribed text in courses at many Universities and Colleges.

It does quite well in New Zealand, too, though there are a very limited number of courses where such a book could be useful, and there is, anyway, a decreasing number of students attracted to the Arts and Humanities. This seems to be part of a general trend that creeps in to Tertiary Education from around this time. Education, even University education, can be justified only by reference to the proclaimed needs of the labour market, or so the argument goes. The very idea is enough to make any teacher of the Humanities shudder and despair. It is a major topic of conversation in the Common Room, and many seem to fear the future. I find such conversations depressing, and I try to avoid them. I can't get away from them at home, though, as the issues raised have become one of Jamie's favourite hobby-horses.

9

Jamie

It is 1983, and the routines of our lives have changed very little since the time we first moved here. Tela spends most of her time on activities connected with her work – not just teaching and writing but also attending workshops or conferences or seminars both in New Zealand and overseas. It is a busy life she leads. I wish that it allowed her more time to be here with us, and I like to believe that she wishes that too. But she doesn't complain. That is not in her nature. She just gets on with things. She has a sabbatical coming up next year and we are all going with her to Cambridge. That will be an adventure for all of us – a shared adventure.

Meantime, I have of late ever more frequently gone back again to the Journals of Adelaide Gilbard. I suppose it could be said that I am now almost obsessed by her, with a passion similar to the one I had when I was much younger. It is perhaps even stronger now, and that could be in part because Tela is so absorbed in her work that she understandably often has little time for me, or for Gus.

Gus has noticed the Journals on my desk. After I have picked her up from school, it has become something of a habit for us to spend some time together upstairs in my study, she munching on her after-school snack. She has asked me about the journals and I have read certain sections to her. She is non-committal after I have finished a reading, saying very little but nodding her head briefly by way of thanks. At least, I presume she is thanking me. I know that the words have interested her because I can see it in her expression. After I have read an entry or two to her she often leafs through the Journal wanting to read the entries for herself. I thought at first that the script would be rather too difficult for her especially as in parts the ink has faded or become discoloured, but it seems to hold her attention, her head down and with an attitude of total absorption.

I am rediscovering entries in the Journal that I paid scant attention to at the time of first reading, things that help me build a composite picture of Adelaide Gilbard in my mind. Every little detail now seems to me to be of greater significance than it had been before. For instance, I have recently re-read an entry where she reveals the sense of injustice she had felt at her brother being able to study at Cambridge while she had no option but to stay at home with nothing to look forward to other than the dubiously attractive prospect of an offer of marriage. This time when I read those words they seemed to take on an added significance. It was a little detail of perhaps virtually no consequence but it made her even more real to me. It is difficult to explain, particularly as I already knew that a young middle class woman had virtually no prospect of a career other than marriage, but to see this comment written in her own hand somehow allowed me to share her quiet frustration.

During weekdays, with Gus at school and Tela at work, I am frequently left with little but my own thoughts; and those thoughts are sometimes disturbing. There is at the back of my mind a feeling that I am in danger of becoming someone I would rather not be – a friendless recluse. Someone who doesn't want, or need (and that, it seems to me is the greater threat) human contact with any other than my wife and daughter; with my self-created and self-chosen family.

Apart from the three or four years after Tela and I were married, when I had a genuine wish to share my excitement at my good fortune with my mother and the sister who was the companion of my early childhood, I have largely neglected my birth family. From Fiji I had sent many letters and photographs to my mother and occasionally to my sister Helen as well, especially after the birth of Gus. It still seemed important to me, then, that they should be able to participate in my excitement and in my happiness and delight in my wife and my daughter. Gradually, though, and I am not quite sure why, I had written less and less often until by the time we moved back to New Zealand I no longer thought of that other family, the family of my past, as something essential to my present, or my future.

Now, with time on my hands, as Tela often reminds me, there is the opportunity for me to bring that family of the past back into my life. Yet the gulf that has opened up between the past and the present at first seems to me to be too great. Those few people who were part of my old life with whom I still have some contact – my mother, most especially – have become somehow much less relevant, my experiences with them less meaningful or rewarding. But even as I think that, I also feel some guilt. The fault is probably mine. And surely by allowing Helen, in particular, to slip out of my life, to become little more than an acquaintance to whom I send a card at Christmas, I am denying myself something of value and, more importantly, denying our daughter her birth-right – a sense of connection through me with her wider kin on my side.

With these and similar thoughts plaguing me, during the August school holidays and in response to yet another suggestion from Tela that I do so, I decide though without any great enthusiasm that I will take a few days away from home to spend some time with those two of my siblings with whom I have almost lost contact and I certainly haven't seen in person for years.

I don't phone to arrange my visits. I write. I have never quite trusted the spoken word. Growing up as a very young child, I lived with my mother and my sister in a house that did not have a telephone. Perhaps this is the origin of my distrust of disembodied voices saying things they quite likely don't mean. There is too much room for deception. Even today I use the telephone only for such business-like purposes as calling the plumber or to make a doctor's appointment. So before the holidays start I scrawl a letter to Helen, and another to Dougal, my only living brother, to ask if I would be welcome to stay with each of them for a day or two on a trip I plan; and I receive rapid replies from both, affirming that I would.

As a result of these initiatives, in the first week of August I leave Tela and Gus and drive north through Taihape and across the snow-flecked and gaunt Desert Road to Taupo. From there it is little more than another hour before I reach the town where Helen has lived ever since her marriage over twenty years ago.

What do I get from this visit with she who was virtually my only childhood companion? I hadn't any real idea what to expect before I arrived, but the greeting I receive from Helen as she opens the door to find me standing there is everything I could have expected. She seems genuinely delighted to see me, with perhaps just a hint of the same sort of uncertainty as I myself was feeling.

That vanished soon enough, the feeling of unease. We know each other too well, after all. We have had too many shared experiences to be surprised by anything we find. So there follows in the hours after our first greetings many instances of nostalgic fondness, and memories that are momentarily exciting. Yet beneath it all is a faintly regretful feeling that all of this past we are now remembering is of little importance to our futures, or even, in a strange way, to our very present. I feel a little sadness at this realisation, and I think Helen does too. But we have, in that trite phrase, 'moved on'. Our past togetherness means little enough in the light of the different lives we have by now fashioned for ourselves.

Although her husband is at his office, it being a Tuesday, Helen has three of her children at home with her. The youngest is in her last year at primary school, the other two, a boy and a girl, are both High School students. I am ashamed to

74

say that I forget the name of the youngest. I know it, but it just won't come to me.

Helen laughs forgivingly. "It's Emma," she says. I do remember the names of the other two. Carys is a delicate-looking fifteen year old who blushes when her mother praises her baking ability. The young man, I remember, is called Robert, and I calculate his age at seventeen. He is tall, gangly and awkward.

"He's off to University next year," Helen tells me. She is clearly proud of him. "He's going to Waikato to do Science."

These young people are my nieces and nephew, but I don't feel like an uncle to them. But then, I don't really know how an uncle should feel. Fondness? Familial affinity? I don't feel either of those things, not at first. Not strongly, at least. Nor do they show any great interest in me; except for the elder of the two girls who I catch looking at me shyly and calculatingly as I sit there eating the cake she has baked and drinking the coffee she has made for us.

"You also make very good coffee," I tell her; and she blushes.

"Thanks... Uncle Jamie."

And that makes me feel good. I think that makes me understand a little of what it is I should be feeling, as an uncle.

Carys is the only one of the children who stays in the house in the course of the afternoon, listening to Helen and me as we talk. She tucks her feet up under her on the large sofa opposite us, her eyes cast down.

"You don't have to stay there if you'd rather be doing something else," Helen tells her. "Your uncle and I have a lot to catch up on. Most of it you'll find very boring, probably."

She looks at me and blushes yet again. "I want to hear," she says.

"Well, okay," Helen says. "Don't say I didn't warn you."

So we talk, our auditor on the couch attentive to every word. It is not until I leave that it occurs to me that the probable reason Carys expresses a wish to stay with us as we talk is that my presence in the house provides a slight relief from the boredom of school holidays spent at home.

Our conversation is easy. It is a reconnection that we are forging – a rapid reconnection. Every now and then there will be a quiet question from the sofa. Helen and I are remembering when we made a rough and ready raft out of biscuit-tins and pieces of wood tied together with fishing line, and tried to paddle across the estuary. We had to be rescued by the owner of the camping ground who heard our shouts of distress and put-putted out to us in his little dinghy to rescue us from the disintegrating apparatus and take us to safety. When our mother was told of what happened, she was furious with us both, but especially with Helen, as the elder.

"Did you get a hiding?" Carys asks me.

"I'm the one who got the blame," Helen says, "for risking your uncle's life. But no, your Nana never hit us, though she quite often threatened to. Remember the dreaded razor strop?"

"Oh yes. The one thing our father left behind that we wished he hadn't. But she never did use it, did she?"

"No. Though she probably wanted to. On me, anyway."

"Of course everything that went wrong was always your fault," I say. "Big sister, getting me into trouble." I'm joking. As I remember it, I was just as frequently the instigator.

"I could never do anything right in her eyes," Helen sighs. Then she looks at Carys, fondly. "I was always sulking as a child. It was probably my fault your Nan picked on me. And I was quite jealous of the attention she gave to Jamie, to your Uncle. I think there were times when I wished he would get the blame. That he would feel the hurt."

Helen's casually and sadly uttered revelation stuns me for a moment. I don't believe I had ever thought that she had held any animosity towards me. Then I remembered...

"Was she really that bad, Uncle Jamie? Mum, I mean?" Carys's response was another question directed at me, in her quiet, shy voice, and it cut across my inward recollection.

I grin back at her. "No, she wasn't. A bit sulky at times, I suppose, but we had plenty of fun together. And I'm sure she wouldn't have wanted me to be hurt. Though I do remember…"

"What?" Carys asks; and this time her voice betrays a real eagerness.

"Well, once when we were visiting your Aunt Jenny, one Christmas -- I was very young, maybe only five or six -- your Mum gave me a stick and told me that I'd see something really funny if I went over and poked at one of the beehives in the paddock out the back. So I did; and naturally the bees sent out angry squadrons of defenders who stung me so badly I had to strip off and sit in a bath full of warm water and Reckitt's Blue."

"Oh, I remember that," Helen says. "I remember your terrified screams, and how frightened I was at the trouble I'd probably get into. What a horrible girl I must have been. Not worried about the pain you were feeling, just about the trouble I might get into. Thinking of myself first. Goodness, how shameful."

Carys gives her mother a look that suggests a certain amount of horror and disbelief; but she merely asks: "What's Reckitt's Blue?"

I stay overnight, and when I leave the next morning to make the brief journey across to the Thames Valley to see my brother, I reflect on the results of my visit.

I am pleased I made it. It has enabled me to look upon my childhood with refreshed eyes and with at least a temporarily rejuvenated interest. It has also told me things about that childhood I had never really known. I had not previously been aware of just how much resentment Helen had felt at what she perceived to be the favoured treatment I received from our mother. I had always been vaguely aware as a child that I was our mother's favourite out of we two younger children; but that knowledge had always been modified, made to seem of negligible importance, by the pervasive awareness that neither Helen nor I were as precious to her as the treasured memories she kept of our eldest brother, of Haddon who had been killed in the War.

Yet having talked about our family news, having regenerated much of the true fondness for each other that had its origins in our shared childhood, I drive away with the knowledge that these are nevertheless little more than side issues in my life, as they are in hers. Yes, it is also pleasant to have got to know a little at least one of my nieces and to have found her a shy yet interesting and very pleasant young woman – to get some sense of what it can mean to be an uncle – but soon after welcoming these thoughts my mind returns wholly to Tela and Gus. I feel no guilt that this should be the case as I have the reassuring certainty that my departure has meant that Helen, too, can let her present concerns envelop her once more – that she too will be experiencing an essential closing in, and a shutting out.

Besides, I need to concentrate on making the turnings that will take me to my brother. To Dougal.

Shortly after I had finished University and was resisting what seemed to be an inescapable duty to begin teaching at a secondary school and thus to honour the commitment I had made when I was awarded the bursary that had enabled my tertiary education, I had made a deliberate decision to visit Dougal and to learn the truth behind the image I had of him as an impossibly saint-like man whose life had been shattered by the death of his adored elder brother – the image that my mother had implanted in my mind and that I had been unable to either confirm or revise because I had seen so little of him.

At that time Dougal had only just established his small business, a native plant nursery on three or four acres of land on the eastern side of the Thames Valley. I had spent only one day and a night with him on that occasion, but we had got drunk together and I had learned that far from being a saint, he was a free spirit who had previous to establishing his business spent much of his time in communes where he had also enjoyed a relaxed kind of living that included smoking of weed and the company of a variety of women.

This time, I arrive to find that neither Dougal nor his establishment have changed much since the last time I was there. Well… that's not quite true of Dougal. He has grown a beard, is even more lean of body, and his face and hands are creased by, I assume, work and weather. Perhaps a little by age, too, as I calculate he is now well into his fifties. His beard is long, grey or whitish in patches, and straggly. I grin to myself at the thought that Dougal now looks very much like one of those my mother's talk of him always made me imagine he was when I was a child. A saint. Simeon Stylites, maybe, just down from his pillar and still a little stiff in the joints.

The interior of his cottage has changed little from my earlier visit. There are more bookshelves than I remember, and there is an elegant mahogany display cabinet, either an antique or a reproduction, that sits rather incongruously in a corner of the kitchen and contains a variety of fine porcelain cups and saucers, but otherwise it seems much the same.

This time we don't get drunk together. Instead, we have a meal he makes from the vegetables in his garden – a light meal, mainly salad, with hard-boiled eggs and potatoes smothered with butter. No meat. I ask him if he has gone vegetarian.

"No," he says. "Not entirely. But I mostly try to keep to what I can grow myself and what the hens produce."

He asks me if I'd like a glass of wine, but as he says he won't have one himself, I decline. I'm finding it much harder to talk with him than I had on that last occasion. Then, he had opened up to me about the effect Haddon's death had had on him. He had been astonishingly revealing about it, no doubt helped by the cheap, heavy and sweet port wine we had been drinking.

I try various topics, serious and light, but nothing much seems to interest him. When I make comments he responds only after giving what appears to me to be critical thought to what I have said, his brow wrinkled and his eyes closed. There is little warmth in him towards me, or so it seems. Indeed, I am almost persuaded that I can detect a certain amount of cynicism in him regarding the genuine nature of my interest in his answers. I am on the verge of thinking that he sees me as a burdensome stranger that he has been duped into giving a welcome.

But no... I don't want to believe that. I try raising a more personal topic.

"Have you seen Dad lately?" Our father lives on an island in the Hauraki Gulf. I haven't seen him since a brief visit after I finished University, and I never really knew him at all when I was growing up.

This time Dougal looks at me, and replies immediately. "Yes. I went across to see him just last month. He asked after you, but I couldn't tell him anything."

"No. Sorry. I haven't been a very good correspondent. Is he... okay?"

"Not really. He has... health problems. Serious, I think, though he doesn't admit it. He turned eighty-five this year, you know."

"I should go and see him."

Dougal doesn't answer immediately, but looks away with that frown of pained judgement; then he gets to his feet, wincing.

"Sore joints?" I ask.

"A touch of rheumatism, or so I'm told," he says. "Another coffee?"

"No thanks. Or I'll never get to sleep tonight."

He pours another coffee for himself, black with no sugar, then comes back and sits down again.

"Dad'd probably be quite glad to see you, though I don't think he expects it," he says.

"No. I suppose not." Is it a critical comment? If so, I certainly deserve it; but somehow I don't think it is. I think Dougal is just stating it as he sees it; though he probably knows that I won't go. "You know,' I continue, "I've never felt I'm really a part of our wider family, beyond Mum and Helen, I mean. That's just about all there was for the first dozen or so years of my life. Just Mum, Helen and me, and photographs of Haddon on the mantelpiece and on the walls. It's the inevitable result of being an afterthought, I suppose."

This time the pained look on his face is decidedly more genuine, and it is for my benefit, not his. That much I can tell.

"Yes, I can see that," he says. "And… for my part, I know I must have seemed to you to be an uncaring brother. Not simply because I wasn't there for you. It's more than that. I think… in fact I know that for a long time I was never really able to think of you as a brother, not after Haddon was killed. It seemed to me that all my fraternal instinct died with him. Haddon was my brother, the only one I really knew, and he was dead. He had been at the centre of all my adolescent plans about what my life would be like once the war ended. I didn't really think much about you at all, and with Haddon gone it was easy for me to ignore you completely, to forget about you, to think that you were not relevant to my life." He kept looking down, as though to avoid the pain of seeing me. Then: "When I was… wandering around doing a bit of this and a bit of that, trying to make sense of my life, I'd sometimes hear about you from mother, or Helen, but I wasn't as interested as

81

I should have been. What I did hear made me think of you as being – frivolous. Or at least unburdened. I think I resented that. I thought that life was too easy for you. It's still quite hard for me to admit it, but... that's the way it was."

I feel a kind of pity. For the very first time I feel that he needs something from me, and I choose my words with care. "I never thought of you as selfish. Mother made it clear to me that you were what I should aspire to be. Thoughtful, caring, tender-hearted."

He looks at me then, as though seeing me properly for the first time since I arrived. He looks at me, shakes his head, and allows himself an ironic smile. "And that, I should think, was a result of my reaction to Haddon's death. We shared an adoration of Haddon, mother and I."

"And I was led to believe that I should adore you. My saintly brother."

He shakes his head again, the pained look on his brow more evident still, but still relieved by that incongruous smile. "Saintly? Good Lord! I did go through that religious phase, though. Looking for some sort of escape from the... from what I wasn't quite ready to accept had happened."

"And these days," I say, trying to lighten the mood, "you do look the part."

His grin widens, becomes more genuine; but neither the wrinkled brow nor the pained expression disappears.

10

Tela

Gus misses large chunks of her first year at Intermediate School, as both Jamie and Gus accompany me when I take six months of sabbatical leave and return to Cambridge as a Visiting Scholar.

It is an exciting time for Gus – her first visit to the Northern Hemisphere. She is enrolled in a Primary School in the village where we stay, just a couple of miles from Cambridge itself.

Rather than hiring a car, we buy one from a local dealer with an agreement that he buy it back for an agreed price at the end of our stay. This I use to travel into town to fulfil my occasional light duties, or to visit the Library or attend lectures or other functions that interest me. And we use it for more adventurous purposes as well.

It is on this visit to the United Kingdom that we discover the tiny village where Adelaide Gilbard, Jamie's great-grandmother, and her brother Oliver Gilbard, my great-grandfather, had lived before Adelaide came to New Zealand and Oliver to Fiji.

Before I left Cambridge after finishing my thesis, not long before Jamie and I agreed to marry, one of my acquaintances at Girton, a History scholar with particular interest in seventeenth century Britain, had given me some scanty information regarding a family by the name of Gilbard which had once been prominent in the western Cotswolds and whose house there had had the name of Bowerford. The information seemed at the time to be insufficient to connect it in any way with the Adelaide Gilbard of Jamie's grandmother's Journals, particularly because the old Gilbard family influence seems to have waned quickly during the middle years of the seventeenth century, evidently after the sacking of Bowerford House by parliamentary forces in the Civil War. So I had merely recorded the information in my diary and left it at that, thinking it was highly improbable that it would be of direct significance. Later, though, I remembered the entry and mentioned it to Jamie, and he immediately showed me a part of Adelaide's Journals where Adelaide writes of the 'Gilbards of Bowerford' though it is not clear that these were actually Oliver and Adelaide's forebears.

Our planning for this six month stay at Cambridge brought all this back to mind, and before we left New Zealand we decided that we must travel to that part of Gloucestershire and see if we could make any positive connection. Soon after arriving in Cambridge, therefore, we bought an OS map and looked in detail at the countryside around Stroud, a town that I had jotted down in my diary notes as the one it had been suggested to me was possibly closest to Bowerford; and we also circled the names of villages such as Painswick and Chalford and Bisley .

Then, in tiny letters by the symbol of a church, a little removed from any of those places, we find the word 'Bowerford'. Nothing further. There are a few dots indicating cottages, and a little apart, on the crest of quite a steep hill, to judge by the contours, is the symbol for a house and the name 'Newdeane'. There seems little doubt that this is the area of the old Gilbard family's influence – but if it has any connection with Adelaide and Oliver Gilbard we have no immediate way of discovering. They could, of course, have been only distantly and laterally related to the Gilbards of Bowerford. A visit to the area may reveal nothing, but on the other hand...

One Friday in October while the days are still reasonably long we set off on our journey. We have located a Bed and Breakfast place that seems to be sited within quite easy reach of the Bowerford church, and telephoned to arrange a stay of two nights. We set off early from our little rented cottage on

Grantchester Road and travel in a leisurely fashion via minor roads across country and into Gloucestershire.

Before we left Jamie had, in his usual anxious manner, methodically studied the route we would take, which means that he finds the B and B easily enough even though it is on one of those narrow roads that make one wonder if a wrong turn has been taken. It is up a small driveway and is advertised by a quaint sign. We park in the courtyard and are charmed by the Cotswold-cottagey appearance of the buildings.

"Local stone," the proprietor tells us, when we ask about the age of the place, "but actually quite modern, for the most part. The original cottage has mostly gone, but there's a bit of it out the back. Eighteenth Century, I believe."

The proprietor and his wife, we learn, are not local but Londoners who have escaped the city and opted for a quiet life in the country. They've been in the place for less than a year.

"And you can't get much quieter than hereabouts," he says. "Not this side of the Scottish Highlands or the Welsh mountains, anyway. Rather too quiet, really. We don't get many guests. Not so far, but it's not high season of course."

He knows the Bowerford Church. "I've only bothered to go up there a couple of times," he says. "We're near the opening to the valley here, you see. You turn left up the road a bit," he points. "Straight ahead takes you back into town, but if you turn left there's this little valley with access to a house on the hill beyond it. But the church, and a few cottages, are in a kind of bowl at the head. It's a real backwater. Makes this place seem busy."

We sit at the table in the big kitchen over a cup of tea and a plate of buttered scones. The couple are in their late fifties, I should say. They talk of a son in America, and a daughter married to a violinist in the London Philharmonic. They seem eager to talk, the man especially.

He gives us directions to what he says is a good little restaurant in a pub in a village not far away, and as we decide it is too late to give sufficient time to the Bowerford Church before dark – we have the idea that the graveyard might harbour some information, though it is a long shot – we take his advice and go there for an early dinner. It has been an exhausting day, and Gus is asleep before we even get back to the B and B. We put her in the double room with me, and Jamie gets the single to himself.

After breakfast the next morning we head straight for the valley, and for the first time we all, even (or perhaps especially) Gus, begin to feel a real excitement at the possibility of learning more about Oliver Gilbard and his sister, remote though the chance might be. My interest is possibly not as strong as Jamie's – Adelaide Gilbard, the author of the Journals, being his great-grandmother, not mine – but his single-minded determination to trace her home village has certainly rubbed off onto me. Besides, although the village might also, of course, have been home to my own ancestor, Adelaide's brother Oliver, my interest in him is nowhere near as keen as Jamie's interest in Adelaide as I have practically no direct evidence of his life or his character. I have no journals or diaries or correspondence of any kind, nor any other evidence of his life apart from Adelaide's mentions of him, and one letter of his to her, part of which she copied into her Journal.

We are in the hamlet almost before we realise it, but at first there is little to see. We pass a kind of wasteland of low scrub growing amongst a jumble of concrete and other scraps of industrial detritus, then a few drab stone cottages with poorly cared-for gardens can be seen on either side of the road. Our view to the right is then blocked by a tall and overgrown hedge, but beyond this is a more substantial house set further back from the road. The garden here is better maintained, with a neat lawn and trimmed shrubs. A hedge separates it from its neighbouring building which we can now see, as Jamie edges the car further on, is the church. It is a squat structure with a square bell tower. The overall impression is one of great age.

"Bowerford Church," I hear Jamie mutter; more to himself than to me.

There is space in front of the building to park, and he stops the car and we sit there for a few moments taking the scene in.

"It'll be locked," I say. "It doesn't look as though it's in use."

It's true. There is an air of neglect or even gloom about the building itself, though the surrounds are reasonably well kept. There is no notice board giving information about services nor any other indication that it might still be in regular use.

We get out of the car and Jamie approaches the double doors to the church, a look of determination on his face. There are ironwork handles on either side and he pulls on them, but nothing gives.

"Must be locked from the inside," he says. "There'll be another door around the back." A path leads to the right and around the corner of the building. I take a few steps and see that it continues along the side of the church to another entrance and links up with a path that connects to a gateway to the larger residence next door, which clearly must be, or have been, the vicarage.

Meanwhile the ever-inquisitive Gus has disappeared through a gateway in a stone wall on the other side of the church, and she now calls back to us.

"Graves!" she says, showing her greatest degree of enthusiasm so far. Death is one of her latest passions. "Come on, Dad!"

I come back to where Jamie is still standing by the doors, clearly frustrated and dithering about what to do next.

"Yes, let's have a look around the graves, first," I tell him. "We'll see if we can find someone who'll let us into the church later."

The graveyard is quite a large one, but it is clearly no longer being used for its original purpose. Most of the gravestones are of much-weathered stone, and the inscriptions have long since disappeared. Some are leaning at odd angles, and some have toppled completely.

We wander around with a sense of disappointment – then we discover a section where some of the gravestones are of marble, with inscriptions that are still visible. Yet even here, in what seems to be the newest section, we can find no older date than 1949.

It is Gus who first picks out the name of Gilbard.

There are two gravestones close together, as though they share a single plot. Both are marble, though covered in moss. Even so, the inscription on the larger stone, whose top is a gothic arch in which there is carved a cross, is still easily enough read. 'In Sacred Memory of Lydia Gilbard. Laid to rest January 3rd 1862, aged 61 years.'

"That's their mother, Oliver and Adelaide's mother," Jamie says. He seems to be in no doubt of it. "Remember from the Journal? Adelaide wrote that her mother died when they were on their way to Australia. And that must have been in 1862. Or very close."

"Seems possible," I say; but I'm far from convinced. "It could be coincidence. They might be from another branch of the family altogether, whatever Gilbards are buried here. We need more definite evidence. Still…"

The other gravestone of the pair is closer to the hedge and more heavily moss covered, particularly in its upper portions, but we can make out the name 'Gilbard' again.

Gus needs no bidding, nor permission. She sets to work with a twig she breaks from the hedge and begins to scrape away the obscuring layers. From beneath there slowly emerges the name and detail: 'In Memory of Margaret Ellen Gilbard, dearly beloved daughter of George and Lydia Gilbard, 1846-1860.'

Jamie takes my arm, wanting me to be convinced. "'George,'" he says. "That was their father's name. Adelaide mentions that. And remember what she wrote at the very beginning of the Journal? Something like: 'Meg had already been taken from me.' Remember? These must be their graves. Oliver and Adelaide's mother, and their sister."

And my doubts vanish. "Yes," I say. "You're right. This must be the place then, this little hamlet. This must be the church she attended. It's probably where she was married. There must be a register."

We are both convinced, and that conviction leads us to look about us. For a moment or two the air seems to take on a quality it didn't have before. I take in the church, the hedge, and beyond the narrow valley to the circling hills. This is where she lived, Adelaide Gilbard. She, and her shadowy brother, my great-grandfather. This must be where she had been a girl, and he a boy. It is an instantly intriguing thought – but then it is almost as quickly gone, to be replaced by a sort of mental shrug as I discover that I don't find the realisation especially exciting.

We leave the graveyard, all three of us seemingly thinking our own thoughts about our discovery. Am I the only one left feeling a little flat, after that initial excitement? I look again at Jamie, and I detect in his expression a disappointment similar to my own. We are out on the road again, looking across what I suppose could be called the village square; but it is not a square. It is little more than a V-shaped strip of neglected grass. The lane has split in two along its borders.

"What's on your mind, Jamie?" I ask.

"It's… This is where she lived, I've no doubt about that now, but… I can't sort of picture her here. Maybe a little bit in the church. Maybe if we were able to see inside, maybe that'd help. But… Well, look over there. Those bungalows across the road. They wouldn't have been here when she was here."

I look, and I see what he means. A handful of nearly identical bungalows, like a small housing estate. They are definitely twentieth century, and probably post-War, each dwelling with its patch of lawn and its single garage, their gardens showing only perfunctory care except for one that is clearly the work of an enthusiast. "Yes. They look a bit depressing, don't they. What shall we do now?" I ask, my question directed as much at the church, the trees, the very air surrounding us, as at either Jamie or Gus.

"Let's just... walk along. See if we can find someone and just... talk to them or something," Gus says; and it seems like as good an idea as anything else. Particularly with Gus the Infallible Icebreaker in attendance.

We follow a path across the green towards the bungalows. There is a car parked outside one of them, the one with the best garden, and as we approach it a woman emerges from the house and heads for the vehicle.

With a familiar look of determination, Gus trots ahead of us intent on the mission she has allotted herself. We follow; Jamie with a look of anxiety as he always has when Gus leaves us to pursue her own agenda. He likes to keep her firmly in his sights.

"Excuse me," we hear Gus crying out, even before she reaches the gate behind which the woman is now standing, one hand on the latch.

There is a twitch of the woman's lips; not really a smile, but there are few capable of resisting Gus's enthusiasms. She is middle-aged, with greying hair swept back severely from the sort of face that must have inspired whoever first depicted Britannia.

"Yes," she says. Not unfriendly, but definitely suspicious or at least uninterested. We are close enough now to take up the conversation ourselves, and Gus looks back at us in acknowledgement of our right to do so.

"We've just been looking at the gravestones in the churchyard," Jamie says, nodding and smiling. "We're from New Zealand."

"Yes?"

"We've found two that seem to belong to our ancestors. Well… one of our ancestors, and her daughter. In fact, we're… almost certain of it."

"Yes?"

I take over, impatient. "The family name is Gilbard," I say. "We were hoping we might find someone who is able to tell us something about the village. Perhaps someone who might recognise the name."

"Oh. I'm sure I don't know. The church is no longer in use, of course. It hasn't been for as long as we've been here. The vicarage is being used as a… I think they call it a retreat, by a group of hippies or Hare Krishnas or something. They've taken over some of the old cottages on that side, too. With all their chants and bells and other noise."

She doesn't sound at all happy. I see Jamie shake his head as if in sympathy; but I'm really not interested in encouraging the woman to air whatever grievances she might have. I press on: "And… is it possible to see inside the church, do you know? Do you know who has the key?"

"I believe people from one of the churches in town come out every now and then to do a bit of tidying up. I've heard that they're planning to sell it, but it's listed, I think, and that makes it difficult. They'd have the key. It'll be the Anglican church people, of course. You could ask in town."

She passes through the gate and moves around the car, unlocking the driver's door, precluding any further questions. She is clearly in a hurry. We thank her and move on down the lane, but there is very little else to see. None of the remaining dwellings seem to be sufficiently old or sufficiently large to have been the home of a middle-class family from last century, although we do notice an area of broken land just

91

beyond the bungalows where there are some old trees and overgrown piles of stone. Further beyond this there is an area of woodland that rises up the slope of a hill on one side of the narrow valley.

We reach the far end of the triangle of grass, and wander a little further till the lane branches again, one way circling around the green on the other side and thus completing the loop, and the other seemingly going along beside the little forested area and then heading upwards. A signpost reading 'Newdeane' points in this direction.

We stand there for a while in silence, the three of us.

"Well... that's about it," Jamie says, stating the obvious. "There's not much else to see it seems."

"Unless we manage to get inside the church," I say.

"Or we could look at some more graves," Gus adds, with some eagerness.

"I say we should take a trip into the town next and see if there's anything interesting there," Jamie says. "Maybe get some lunch, and think about whether to look for someone we can ask about seeing inside the church here. Though even if we did, I doubt they'd be willing to come out here to open up just on the off-chance there might be something that would interest us."

For the lack of any better suggestion, we get back into the car and leave the little hamlet, the odd mixture of decaying old and unattractive new, to itself -- to its unexciting, unappealing self. Jamie seems resigned to a mixture of satisfaction and disappointment. On the drive back, he expresses his belief that it is enough to know that the locality is, indeed, almost certainly where Adelaide and Oliver Gilbard spent some years of their lives, but we both agree that we had not had any real sense of them there. It is as though when they chose to leave all those many years ago they left little of themselves behind -- or that whatever they did leave has dissipated, withdrawn, been shoved aside.

Nor do we make inquiries in the town about getting access to the church and asking to see the marriage register there or wherever else it might be kept. It is Jamie who makes the decision not to. We could have made the time to do so, and I remind him of that fact. He thinks for a few moments; then he says, with a most un-Jamie like firmness: "No. I don't think it'd be worth the effort even if we could arrange it. She might not have been married in the church, anyway. It just didn't feel like her place. Bowerford. It's as though it was never a very important place for her. It's almost as though she was never there at all."

11

Jamie

Not long after our return from Tela's sabbatical in Cambridge, during the Easter school break, I make another short visit by myself to see my sister Helen. This time my main reason for doing so is to report directly to her on what we have discovered regarding the village where our ancestress had lived. Earlier I had made photocopies of Adelaide's Journal and sent them to Helen, as a result of which she, too, had professed to be intrigued, and interested in sharing our discoveries.

After this visit, and an overnight stay, I drive across to the Thames Valley to call on my brother before heading back home, only to find that he is not there. The kaftan-clad woman who is looking after his business for him, and is currently keeping his bed warm I have little doubt, tells me that he will be back late the following day and I briefly consider finding a motel in Thames and staying for a couple of nights so that I can see him. The idea has little enough appeal, though, and after asking the woman to tell Dougal that I had called I drive off; but first I stop at a service station to fill up for the trip home.

I will make the journey back south a leisurely one, I decide, with an overnight stay at Taupo on the way. I had anticipated being away from home a further night or two, and Tela and Gus would surely be expecting me to do so. Little other than this vague determination not to drive straight back home is in my mind as I pay the cashier and leave to return to my car. As I walk back, however, I see standing at the pump next to the one I had used, and with a wry grin of recognition on his face, an old friend, one I hadn't seen for many years. I am both surprised and delighted.

Cossy and I spent much time in each other's company in my student days. He was three years or so ahead of me at Vic, and doing a double Law and Arts degree. We probably wouldn't ever have become acquainted if he had not also been an Assistant Warden at the men's hostel where I spent my first two years as a student. Our friendship developed there. Something attracted us to each other though I am uncertain exactly what that was. It was a friendship that lasted beyond his graduation and his move back to his home town of Christchurch, as when I myself went to Christchurch, to Teacher's College and later to the University to do my Masters, at Cossy's invitation I boarded with him in the house where he was raised as a child.

To me he is Cossy, but his real name is Cosswill. What his first name is, I don't know. It has never seemed a matter of any significance. His initials are G.J., but to me and everyone else, as far as I know, he has always been simply Cossy.

"So where are you headed?" he asks, after we've expressed out mutual pleasure at the unexpected meeting.

I tell him where I have been, and my tentative plans for my return.

"I'm based in Auckland these days," he says. "I don't like the place, but that's where the money is. Anyway, I'm just heading for my bolt-hole from the city," he says. "Up in the hills. It's not far. Why don't you follow me there? Spend the night? You say you're not in any hurry."

It is unexpected, but I certainly don't need any persuading. "Hell, yeah, Cossy. That'd be great."

I follow his car. He slows just past the Thames town boundary and turns sharp left to follow the road across the base of the Coromandel Peninsula. Some way up the valley he turns left again, and we are off the tar seal and on to gravel. We continue on this road for three or four kilometres before this changes abruptly to an even narrower gravelled lane that ends as a driveway through open gates, at the side of which is a sign reading 'Coromandel Orchids'.

Orchids? I would never have guessed a relationship between Cossy and flowers of any sort, and orchids especially – romantic, showy and delicate.

The little settlement, for that is what it looks like, is straight ahead. There is a modern bungalow and at least two other dwellings tucked away amongst the trees, and a large low building, a shed of some sort, at a little distance. The cleared area is quite extensive, but above on the hills behind there is a backdrop of heavy native bush.

"Is this a commune?" I ask, surprised, when I leave my car and walk to where he is standing, waiting for me.

"Not exactly," he says.

"Orchids?"

A faint grin. "Why not?"

He offers no further comment as we walk to the bungalow and he uses a key on his key-ring to open the front door.

Inside it is neat and new and spacious with an air of luxury despite the fact that there is a minimum of furniture and that the timber walls are unadorned. A low counter separates the living room from a well-equipped kitchen with modern appliances.

He crosses the room to one of two interior doors and opens it. "Put your things in here," he says; and I do. The bedroom is generously-sized, the bed, a double, is made up with a plain but attractive bedspread. There is a dresser, a wardrobe and a television set, and a partly opened door on the far side reveals a bathroom.

When I return to the living room I find Cossy standing in the kitchen, spooning ground coffee into a percolator.

"Pretty flash for a bach," I say. "All this."

"Serves its purpose," he says. "There's a bit more to it. I'll show you later."

There is a brief rap on the front door, and a woman enters and stands just at the entrance to the kitchen area.

"Would you rustle something up for us, Moira," Cossy says to her. "No hurry."

She nods and goes out again.

"Wife of the bloke who looks after the business for me," Cossy tells me. Nothing else. Just that.

Within a few minutes the woman returns and I hear her rattling about in the kitchen.

After we've finished our coffee Cossy goes to a cabinet and splashes tots of dark gold liquid from a decanter into two tumblers. One of these he hands to me. The glass is heavy despite its modest size. Cut crystal. I lift mine to my nose and breathe in the pungent scent of wood-smoke and history.

"Single malt," Cossy says.

"I didn't think you drank at all."

"Some things change, James. And I only have one every now and then." He, too, lifts the glass to his nose; then puts it to his lips, knocks back the contents in one gulp and reaches for the decanter that he has placed beside him. "And right now, in your honour, I'm having a second."

I take a sip of mine. It is smoky and pungent, hot on my tongue. I swallow, and its passage down my throat is traceable by a warm glow. "Well, it's bloody good whisky, Cossy. You couldn't have chosen a better way to come off the wagon. But... what made you want to?"

"Yes, good question." He eases back on his chair. "A while back I was handed a glass of the stuff by someone I didn't want to offend. So I drank it. I'm afraid I liked the taste, so I took note of the label and bought myself a bottle. I was seduced, you might say. I've been through a fair few bottles since then."

I have no doubt now that beneath the Cossy-like equanimity, almost indifference, he is indeed pleased to have me here. Excited, even. I have never seen him quite like this. It is as though my presence has given him an excuse to release some tension he must have been feeling. I take another sip and relax a bit further myself. "Don't blame you," I say. "Money well spent."

He raises his glass to the light, gently shaking it and watching the contents with a fond eye. "Besides," he says, "I find when I drink it, it's easy for me to imagine that my father was... someone of significance. Descendent of a Scottish Highland chieftain, maybe. I can see a baronial mansion and dozens of kilted minions."

His words are spoken in a totally unexpected way, softly and distractedly, as though he has repeated some sort of monologue he is hearing inside his head. But it is too good an opportunity for me to miss. Never, in all the years I've known him, lived in the same house with him, has Cossy ever allowed an opening of this sort. Even so I hesitate before I ask: "Was he Scottish, then? Your father?"

It's a risk, I know. In those days when we shared part of our lives, first at the hostel in Wellington, then in his 'aunt's' place in Kilmore Street in Christchurch, I was allowed to talk about just about anything. In fact he encouraged me in my rants and in my exposition of what were undoubtedly half-baked opinions. But it was clear to me, almost instinctively, I think, that his personal history was not a subject to be broached. Despite all that, I was interested in him. I would have dearly loved to ask questions. In fact, I think it was a combination of my natural interest in him and that instinctive awareness that I must never ask personal questions that led to him singling me out as a trustworthy companion. As a friend. And we had been friends. Our hours of sharing time together were often enough silent ones, with him offering little beyond gratuitous comments and occasional advice, but somehow it was also extraordinarily companionable.

After several months of sharing the house in Christchurch he had allowed me only the tiniest bit of information about the little old lady, his 'aunt', who kept us both well fed and the house in order. I knew that the house was hers and I suspected that she was not really his aunt, though that was the name he always used. That there was a true fondness between them was also achingly apparent. Then one night after she had popped her head into the sitting room to ask if we wanted anything before she took herself to bed, he offered: "She's not really my aunt, you know. She took me in after my mother died. She was a spinster with a house and a good income left by her father. And, it seems, a big heart." I waited, hopefully; but there was nothing more. That was all. Now, after all these years, there is at least a chance of finding out something further. Again I wait.

He seems to savour the taste of the whisky this time. It must be a fair mouthful, as his tumbler is empty. Then he swallows it and reaches again for the decanter, tips another generous measure into the tumbler, and brings it to his lips. Still no answer. I accept that he isn't going to indulge me, and I am disappointed. I can think of nothing to say and the silence becomes uncomfortable.

"Reginald Lovejoy Cosswill," he says suddenly; and I look at him, taken by surprise. "Norfolk gentleman, but something of a black sheep. Adventurer. Captain in His Majesty's Household Cavalry until invited to leave after shaming his Colonel in some obscure manner. Something to do with a woman. The details are vague. Dashing, handsome. A World War One hero. A spendthrift." He raises his glass to me. "There you go, then," he says. "Impressed?"

I am indeed rather taken by the romantic image, and not at all surprised. It seems to fit, somehow. But then…

"And a total figment of my aunt's imagination," he says.

"A figment?"

"Yes. As I found out when I was around fourteen or fifteen. I discovered my birth certificate in a shoebox at the back of the wardrobe in her bedroom. My mother's name was Cosswill. Amy Cosswill, spinster and, I have every reason to believe, a penniless and probably disease-ridden prostitute. Father... unknown."

I'm again taken by surprise. I try to take in what he has told me. I have no reason to think that he is fantasising again but it still doesn't seem quite right. "That's a bit of a jump," I say. "From 'spinster' to 'prostitute'. She might've just been a... an unfortunate girl. Might've been from a perfectly respectable family. Mightn't she?"

"I thought of that. Probably hoped for that. But I went to the library and looked through old newspapers looking for a clue. And I found it. Quite a long article in the Press dated later in the same year I was born. 1937. She'd hanged herself. Amy Cosswill, my sainted mother, hanged herself." He raises his glass again and looks intently at the remaining contents. Am I going to get any more information, I wonder. Then: "The intention of the article was clearly admonitory. The dangers of life on the street. The dangers of drink. Amy Cosswill was one that Micky Savage and his do-gooders hadn't got to, or maybe couldn't help. And her name possibly wasn't even Amy. Or Cosswill. Whoever wrote the article had talked with an acquaintance, another street girl, who said that Amy had told her that her real name was something else. She couldn't quite remember what. But she remembered Amy telling her that she'd been taken aboard a ship in Sydney by one of the crew, and the ship had sailed with her still on board. Across the Tasman to Lyttelton. And that's where she'd been left. Dumped. Discarded. Pumped out with the bilge water."

Silence again, and this time I know that it is all I'm going to get. It is enough though to summon in me some sort of utterly useless sympathy for the man. Useless, because even as

100

I feel it I know he neither wants nor needs it. I don't know how to express it anyway; which is no doubt fortunate.

"And… your aunt didn't tell you anything else? How she came to… adopt you?"

"I don't think she ever did adopt me. Not legally. I've never seen any papers that confirm it. As for telling me anything more… I didn't even let her know that I'd discovered the truth for myself, though I think she knew I had. I must have left some evidence of my visit to her bedroom because after she came home from shopping that day, the day I discovered the birth certificate, she looked at me with her knowing but forgiving expression. But neither of us said anything. We both just kept on apparently accepting what she had told me. It was a sort of polite fiction we both tacitly agreed to observe."

I am stunned. I'm not even certain I believe him. For one thing, it is not at all like Cossy to divulge a secret. Mind you, the whisky might have loosened his tongue. I don't know what further comment I can make so I just shake my head and cluck sympathetically.

He looks at me and shakes his head in turn, but clearly in his case it is to show that the topic has run its course. "We're alike in one way, you know," he says. "We both find the world a bit… curious at times. Grotesque, even. But you see many things very differently from the way I see them. Different heads."

"Well, yes. I suppose."

"No suppose about it. We do. But I think there are some things we can agree on." He holds his glass high and heaves himself to his feet. "Come with me," he says. "I want to show you something. Bring your glass."

With his tumbler and the whisky decanter still in hand he leads me through a door and into a room that is fitted out luxuriously with a deep carpet and a few items of gleaming mahogany furniture. Three walls of this sanctum are covered with an elegantly-patterned beige paper. To one side of the room is the obvious focal point, a large antique desk topped with green leather. On a table next to it is an impressive looking tape deck and turntable. In each corner of the room there are large speakers.

Then I notice that one of the walls is painted in a neutral colour and is covered with framed works of art of varying sizes. They are illuminated by soft lighting concealed in the ceiling above them. Most seem to be ink drawings, or etchings, although there is the occasional one that shows colour; pastels and water-colours, but no oils as far as I can tell.

Cossy has set his drink down on the desk and flicked some switches, and now the room is filled with gentle yet enveloping sounds. A soprano and a counter-tenor singing something baroque. I am possessed by the notion that this room is indeed a sanctuary, perhaps even an elegantly appointed tomb; or a womb. There is nothing out of place. It is discreet, intensely private.

He motions me towards the wall of art and I take the necessary steps to bring myself close enough to see the detail of the first picture. It is quite small, in a rectangular frame perhaps twelve inches by nine. It is the work of a consummate master, there is no doubt of that. A stone wall with an arched gate fills much of the foreground as it angles away from left to right. Beyond the wall there are a few trees, and at some distance further a suggestion of buildings, a town, partly in ruins. The backdrop, over half of the total area of the work, is a combination of a louring mountain and tumultuous clouds. The whole drawing, pencil or charcoal, has the sort of unmistakable immediacy that comes from a quickly observed scene recorded on paper by a true genius. It has been given a yellow wash of some sort that lends it an eeriness, as though the artist has captured the landscape during a sudden but brief appearance of late afternoon sun. It is not signed, but surely it is...

"Well, James?" Cossy says. "Surprise me."

"Turner?"

He grins. I don't think he is surprised at all. "Well done, lad. Yes. When he was on his Grand Tour. Northern Italy."

"It's a wonderful print," I say. "I don't think I've ever seen quality like it."

"It's not a print, young James. It's not a print. Take a closer look."

I don't know whether I should believe him; but I do look closely. I look closer still. I see the slight scuffing on the paper, the unmistakeable traces of surface pigment. "Shit!"

"No. Definitely not shit."

Definitely not shit. "How did you..."

"You don't want to know. Let's just say it's an indulgence. And one no one knows about except, of course, for those who find the things for me. Have a look at the rest."

I do, giving some time to each one. Some are plain drawings or etchings, not tinted. There are two or three small watercolours, exquisitely detailed. Most are unsigned or the signatures are not decipherable. They all look old, nineteenth century or earlier, including two where the scenes depicted are of New Zealand during the early settler period. One of these, a naïve yet charming portrait of a Maori girl in European dress, is signed with the initials 'PDV'.

After I have finished my perusal I turn to him again. I am still more than a little stunned by it all. He has sat himself down on the leather-upholstered armchair, his head back and his eyes closed. Without opening them he says: "Are you able to indulge your passions, young Ashcott?"

I think about that. What are my passions? Easy. Tela and Gus. And I suppose in my own way I indulge them as much as I am able. Do I have any others? I may have had others, once. Art being one of them. Art still interests me; and yes, there have been times when I have even done without other things in order to buy certain works that have attracted me and been within my reach financially. But nothing of the quality or even remotely near the value of the pieces assembled here. I suppose I have simply accepted that I could never afford such things anyway. So... no, such objects could hardly be said to be my passion, not in the sense that I lust to possess them. These days I don't really lust to possess anything at all. Once I thought that I wanted to possess Tela and even thought I had succeeded in doing so, but she set me right on that pretty quickly. I now know with certainty that one can be passionate about something, about someone, without the notion of possession coming into it at all.

I tell Cossy so.

"Things that give you pleasure, you don't necessarily want to possess, you say?" he asks.

"Not at all. No."

"How different we are, then. You appreciate these things," he gestures to the wall, "but you don't wish they were yours? You have no envy?"

Envy? I find the idea ridiculous, truly ridiculous. "No. Not at all."

He shakes his head, sorrowfully. "I think, young Ashcott, that you are a natural socialist. Irremediable. I've long suspected it. I think... from the time I first set eyes on you."

I like that idea. A natural socialist. Unselfish. The greater good. I know it's not true, but I like the idea. I would like to be. "And what are you?" I ask.

"Me?" He seems genuinely surprised that I should have asked, and he doesn't answer immediately. In fact, the question seems to have disturbed him. I had expected him to come back quickly with some cynical, Cossy-like response.

"I don't see the world as you seem to see it, James," he says finally. "To me it's always been a jungle, or... maybe more of a game. It's a place where your most necessary function is to calculate the odds and do whatever needs to be done to win. Winning is what matters. Winning... and keeping quiet about it. That's part of the game, too. No crowing. No ostentatious displays. No Paritai Drive mansion with a Porsche or a Bentley parked in the driveway. Those things are for your common or garden greedy nobody. What was it the Public School boys in dear old England used to call the townspeople, those they deemed to be lesser beings? Oiks, was it? No showing off your possessions like a greedy oik. No... not even sharing knowledge of your personal satisfaction. The knowledge that you have won is all that matters. And keeping that knowledge close, the better to enjoy it."

I can see the doubt cloud his eyes as I stand there, looking down at him. I can see it; the doubt his own words have caused him to feel. Then, just as suddenly, it is gone.

"Yet here I am, sharing my thoughts with you, Sonny Jim." He holds my gaze as he unfolds himself from the armchair and stands. He is tall, inches taller than me. Now he is looking down on me. He tilts his head, seemingly to emphasise the change in our relative positions. "So now you know what I know and a little bit about what I have and what I think. Information that we share. Just the two of us. And we'll keep it that way, won't we James. Just between the two of us."

His habitual cynicism and confidence has returned now; and there is something else in his eyes, a steely hardness such as I had not seen since those distant hostel days, and even then on only one occasion. His words almost seem like a threat... and yet, that notion is surely ridiculous. We are friends. "Just between us, Cossy," I say; and I grin, just to let him know that I know his admonition is a friendly one.

"And now you can tell yourself you're a better man than me. Right? "

"Better? I doubt it. You've done well. I can see that. How did that happen?"

He twitches a grin. "It's a bit of this and a bit of that. Anything goes, these days. James. All you have to do is keep a jump or two ahead. Be smart. Anticipate needs, then meet them. If you can do that, you can win it all."

I have no idea what he means. I don't think I want to know. "But if you get it wrong..."

"There's no 'it', my lad. That would be foolish. You spread the risk. Do you play the stock market?"

"Hell, no. Embrace filthy capitalism? Never!"

"Of course you don't. I do. But... that's only a part of it. The market's a bit boring, really. And there are too many oiks. And it's too public. It's also unreliable. Let's just say I've found a surer way."

"Oh?"

"I'm not going to tell you, James. You wouldn't want to know, anyway."

"But it's working?"

"Oh yes. It's working."

"And you're putting your success to what I'd agree is good use," I say, nodding towards the wall of art. "Though... it's a pity more don't get to see them."

He casts me a look that tells clearly what he thinks of my comment; then: "The great unwashed wouldn't appreciate them even if they had the chance." He crosses the room to the wall and stands there, feet apart, surveying the exquisite collection. When he resumes talking, it is as though he is addressing the wall, the art, not me.

"They're little flakes of gold I've rescued from the great garbage dump of human activity." He turns back to face me. "You still have some sort of faith, don't you James? In humanity, I mean, not the other stuff. Not the fairy tales. But I don't. I've never been able to find anything other than these beautiful things to put my trust in. Nor anyone."

"Harsh, Cossy. Too harsh."

"I don't agree. Most people are essentially greedy and stupid. Even most of the ones who pretend to an interest in... higher things, things greater by far than themselves. Things like fine art or opera or literature. Most of the rich who pretend to an interest in such things only do so because they think that by doing so they will be identified as one of an elite that they envy but they don't understand. But they would like to be one of them. So they pretend to an interest even though they couldn't care less about those reputedly higher things. Money is the only thing that really interests them. As for the rest, the ones they now disassociate themselves from and despise even more because they are in essence exactly the same as them... well, at least they're honest. They drink their beer and lose what money they make at the TAB, they watch the soaps while they eat their KFC and cuff their kids' ears or wipe their snotty noses, and if they have a dream, it's to buy a time-share on the Gold Coast or spend a weekend in Las Vegas. Bread and circuses, some clever Roman called it back then, and things haven't changed. They haven't changed at all. I'm not a great one for romantic poetry, James, but do you know your Wordsworth? 'Intimations of Immortality?' Life corrupts people, James, and most of the fools welcome it. They leap at any chance to corrupt themselves."

"You are a true cynic."

"And you are a true innocent if you believe that the common herd are ever going to choose the greater good over the satisfaction of their immediate and unthinking hungers and lusts."

"And I say it again – you're too harsh, Cossy. We all have to satisfy our basic needs first. Ensuring that everyone's able to do so should be the first business of any government. Otherwise... well, yes indeed, life will inevitably corrupt us. Turn us against each other. Make us selfish."

He shakes his head at me and gives an exaggerated sigh. "And you, a historian," he says. "You really believe there's any evidence in our history as a species that we value compassion or altruism over greed and selfishness? And, yes, life experience has corrupted me, too. Or it could be that I was corrupt from the start, that I was never a dewy-eyed innocent trailing clouds of glory. And that has been to my advantage because that's the true nature of this world."

I don't like the image of himself that his words are painting, even less the image of humanity. I don't want to believe him yet somehow I fear that he might be right, especially with regard to humanity. But I recall something that Graham Greene once wrote, something about one being unable to love humanity, but only people. And I like Cossy. I always have. I like the man, and he likes me. "I don't see you as corrupted, Cossy," I say.

"No, James?" He shakes his head. "Well you wouldn't, would you."

As I'm about to get into my car the next morning, he hands me a business card. It reads 'G.J. Cosswill & Associates, Property and Financial Consultants'. The Phone and Post Box numbers are both Auckland. There is no physical address.

"In case you're in Auckland and at a loose end. No guarantee I'll be there, but leave a message. Let me know where you are and I'll sort something out." He pauses for an instant, then adds: "You, James, are something of an exception."

I am not at all sure what he means by that. An exception to what? It could be a compliment but I'm even less sure that I want to know, so I let it pass without comment. I get in and wind the window down. "It's been great to see you again, Cossy. I'm glad we bumped into each other."

He doesn't say anything else; he just raises a hand and taps a goodbye on the roof of the car, then turns away.

Yeah, goodbye Cossy, I say to myself as I drive off. I look in the rear vision mirror as I head out the gates, but there is no sign of him.

12

Jamie

Gus is eleven, not far off twelve, when my mother dies. She and I are alone together, as Tela is at the University in Auckland for a week-long seminar. My elder sister Jenny phones.

"She just... died in her sleep. It was a blessing, really, the way she's been."

"I should have come to see her more often."

"Poor Jamie. She wouldn't have even noticed, I think. This last year or so she hasn't really been aware of much, as you know. Senility. Sad, really."

"You've been wonderful."

"Well, she hasn't been any trouble, pottering around in the sleep-out. I've just been sort of... keeping an eye on her. Making sure she eats properly. She refused to let me do much more than that. Mostly she just sat and watched her telly. Or pretended to."

It doesn't do much to ease my sense of guilt, this picture she is painting of mother spending her last days in a semi-vegetable state. Mother, who is lodged in my memory as a tough, stubborn woman, dead-set on ensuring that Helen and I are brought up healthy in body and mind despite our father's absence and a perpetual shortage of money. A mother I owed far more regular visits in her old age than I did make.

I am not good with sickness or old age, or death. A feeble excuse if ever there was one; but sickness, even my own, I resent. In others (always excepting Gus, but even then I would rather overlook it than deal with it) I tend to ignore it or run from it or simply despair, putting my trust in the experts. Tela... well, Tela is rarely ill anyway, and when she is she resents it, gets professional help to deal with it, and carries on. Mostly, though, the only indication I get that Tela is not feeling as well as she would wish is a certain degree of grumpiness. As for old age, I have not been much around it – and death is something I have had absolutely no close dealings with at all. I hadn't even gone to my father's funeral. No, I had not been close to death. Until now.

When my mother's mind first began to deteriorate it was simply an inevitable part of aging, or so I was told. So I thought at first that nothing would really change. She was mother, after all. She would still be, essentially, what she had always been to me; full of bustle, getting on with things. Cheerful enough on the surface but with that blunt cynicism that was the result of too many disappointments in her life. Supportive and sympathetic but never quite satisfied with things the way they were. I thought her problem would be simply a degree of forgetfulness, and I had detected those symptoms long ago. I hadn't worried much about it. I had thought it would be nothing too hard for her to bear.

But I soon realised that the mother of my mind was really no longer there, that the mother who cared about everything I did, that fiercely interested and judgemental mother, was inexorably changing into something else – an old woman of still stubborn but now also apparently entirely selfish habits who barely acknowledged my ever less frequent visits beyond an apparently grudging nod of her head.

Now, my sister tells me, she is dead.

It is still the school holidays so Gus can come with me on a quick trip just to be with Jenny for an hour or two to share our grief. I see no need to let Tela know immediately what has happened even if I could have located her. I'll let her know later when she phones home in the evening as she usually does when she is away. I'll let her know then that Gus and I will also be going over later in the week to the funeral, which is to be held back in my old home town nearby.

Our initial visit is brief. Gus and I are the first of the family to call in but Jenny tells me that both Helen and Dougal have said they will come down together the following day and stay at the farm until after the funeral. We sit for a while. Gus is on her best behaviour, solemn and silent. She seems a little overawed at being this close in time and (I can see her speculative look) possibly space as well, to death; to its reality. I can see her visibly relax a little when Jenny tells me that our mother's body has been taken away by the undertaker. I ask if there is anything I can do, but Jenny shakes her head. I don't pursue the point. I do what I have always done in my dealings with Jenny – I defer. I feel like the very much younger brother I have always been.

On the day of the funeral we leave early, Gus and I. Mother's body is at the Funeral Parlour, laid out in her coffin. I leave Gus with Jenny and others of the family and go to the Parlour to sit for a while. It is not something I truly want to do. It is, though, something I feel that I should do. In my mind I see it as making one more visit as an attempt to make up in part for the many more I should have made but did not.

I force myself to look at her lying there. They have prepared her well it seems to me, but I am still shocked by what I see. Her face is thin, her jaw locked forward in a parody of her habitual stubbornness. For some reason I think of the rows of hydrangeas that she planted along both sides of the plot of land at the back of which sat the cottage I had spent my early teenage years. In summer the blooms made rich borders, mainly of blue but with random touches of white or pink, then as autumn progressed they would elegantly fade until at last all colour had left them and they waited, dry and brittle, to be snipped off and composted.

No, she is not there at all, the woman who was for many years the most significant human being in my life. She has gone. But then for me she had gone long before this day. But was that because I chose to treat her as gone? Did I try hard

112

enough to find her, the mother I knew as a child and as an adolescent? That is the thought that plagues me now.

The answer is obvious. No I did not. I am and I probably have always been a most unsatisfactory son. Is it, then, that I had meant far more to her than she had meant to me? I know she loved me. I know she worried for me. I know she forgave me when I disappointed her.

Or did she? Had the evidence of my being not at all what she must have hoped I would be in the end overwhelmed her? But then, I was never quite sure what it was she wished me to become. What is certain is that in those last years she had never seemed very interested in my visits. Possibly that was because she had not been fully aware of my presence. Or could that apparent disinterest have been something she deliberately chose to show? I remember that it had occurred to me at times – a thought that I had quickly tried to dismiss from my mind -- that she might have been making her own choice to be out of my life and beyond recall.

But now I realise that my judgement then might well have been accurate; and that thought triggers a bellowing groan that rises up from somewhere deep and escapes through my throat, at first shocking and then embarrassing me. I wait, half expecting someone to rush in to see what has caused the sound; but after a minute or two have passed without that happening I get up and without looking again at the coffin or its contents I walk uncertainly out of the room.

Several weeks later Jenny phones to ask me if I could come over to help her sort through some of the papers and other items that mother had packed away in boxes and stowed in her granny-flat at the farm.

I knew that she had greatly reduced the amount of her life's accumulations when she first moved out of the old cottage in town to go out to the farm and live with Jenny. The cottage itself had been sold, the money going to Jenny's husband as it was he who had bought it so that we, mother and I, could make our move south from the isolated community where I had spent my younger childhood. I knew, also, that by the time she died she had in her possession very little of anything other than family or sentimental value, and that what she had left was now Jenny's. I am not surprised, therefore, when I arrive at the farmhouse to find that the boxes that Jenny has asked my help to go through and sort out are few in number.

"It's mostly letters and photos, and a few books and china ornaments," she tells me. "I've been through them in a haphazard sort of way, and taken out some things that should be kept safe. Haddon's medals, for instance. Let me know if you find anything you'd like to have."

I sit out in the sleep-out and go through the boxes. I set aside a couple of items, one a porcelain miniature of a dog asleep in a basket that I had vague memories of examining with fascination when I was very young, and another a cup, saucer and plate, ornately decorated with pink roses, that had once belonged to her Aunt Inez -- my Great Aunt Inez Gerold, the elder daughter of Adelaide Gilbard. The set is not to my taste at all but the notion that it could even have belonged to Adelaide, the only one of my ancestors for whom I have huge and unconditional admiration, determines me to ask Jenny if I can take it back with me.

One box seems to contain nothing but letters and photographs. This interests me, as I have already looked through the photograph albums that mother has always been meticulous in keeping up-to-date – or at least until she began becoming inward and uncommunicative. Strangely, I thought, I hadn't found in them anything relating to myself after about my mid-twenties, and nothing at all of Tela and practically nothing of Gus despite the fact that I had sent her, from Fiji, a constant stream of letters and photos to demonstrate my excitement and happiness during the early years of my marriage and especially at the birth of our daughter. In one of the albums, the most recently assembled I presumed, I had found a formal photograph of myself at my graduation, and next to it the very earliest of the photographs of Gus, taken when she was a sweet new-born tucked up and asleep under a pink blanket. It was the very last photograph in the album. It had a page to itself. Under it, in her own hand-writing, very shaky by then, mother had written 'Jamie's daughter.' Nothing else. Not even Gus's name.

I hadn't given it much thought at the time, but now, sitting amongst the scattered photos and letters I have removed from one of the boxes I begin to suffer from an aching sense of loss. It creeps up on me only gradually but as it does so a numbness envelops me, a cold and pitiless revelation. It is as though much of my past life has been revealed as being little more than a personal myth, as being unacceptable, ignored, by the one person whose interest in it I had always assumed to be insatiable.

None of the letters surrounding me are mine to her even though I had written scores of them during those years I was in Fiji. She had been, then, still very much the reference point of all – yes, all – my previous life, my life before Tela and Gus. Up until the time Gus and I had become a couple my mother had been the one and only person whose approval I had consistently sought and on whose approval I had depended. She had been, I unthinkingly believed, an avidly interested observer of my life.

But she had kept none of my letters. Nor are there any of the photographs I had sent her from Fiji. None, apart from that one in the album and…

I pick up the one lone loose photograph from Fiji that I had found. I remember exactly when it was taken. I remember handing my camera to our house-girl, Akanisi, and asking her to take it. It was Gus's second birthday and we had had a few of her little friends around for the occasion. This was taken just after the last of them had left. The three of us are there – or should have been. I am crouching, and Gus is holding on to my knee. Behind us is the view of Laucala Bay from our house. Tela had been sitting right beside us on the pandanus mat. Me in white shorts and a bula shirt, Tela in a colourful sulu.

Except Tela isn't there. She has been cut out; carelessly cut out, the scissors also having excised one of Gus's hands. This, it seems, is the only one of the dozens of photographs of our little family I had sent her from Fiji that my mother had chosen to keep.

I am bewildered. I cannot quite believe the only conclusion it seems possible to draw. Dazed, I pick up the items I have selected and go back into the house, and to Jenny.

"Did you make any progress?" she asks.

"There are a couple of things here I'd like. If it's okay with you," I say. I try to keep the hollow bitterness I am feeling out of my voice. Besides, I don't really care if Jenny agrees or not. Except for the tea-cup and saucer. Yes, I would definitely like that, overly ornate though it is. Adelaide Gilbard might well have held it in her hands. My Adelaide. At least she can never be disappointed in me.

Jenny doesn't do more than glance at the items. "Oh, that hideous cup and saucer," she says. "Are you sure you want that? You're very welcome to it."

"Yes, I would. Not that I like it much. It's just the fact that it's old family stuff. I remember when Mum brought it home after her Aunt Inez died."

"Did she? That must have been long after I left. But that little dog. I remember her telling me that you'd always liked that. Good choice."

"Yes. Thanks."

She sees I have the photograph in my hand still. "Nothing amongst the letters, no other photographs?"

"No. Nothing." Should I say more? I'm not sure what I should ask, and even less sure that I want the possible answer. "Did… Mum ever say much about… Tela? About Gus?"

Jenny seems a little flustered. "She… well you know how she was. She would even get us -- her children, I mean -- all confused. Mixing our names up."

"Yes. I know that." It was very true. Even when I was a kid and she wanted me to come in from outside she'd start off calling for Haddon, then Dougal. She'd get it right on the third try, maybe. But that's not what I mean. I persevere, putting it differently. "When she was here with you did she ever talk about us? About Tela and me? And Gus? After the times when we visited her?"

Jenny looks at me then. It is a pleading look. She is not at all comfortable. "No. She wouldn't say much. After you'd gone."

"Not even about Gus? No comments about her?"

"No. Not really."

"Never? Nothing at all? Not about… any of us?"

Jenny is struggling with something in her mind. I can see it clearly. I can see her kindness struggling with her honesty. She doesn't want to lie. I don't know Jenny very well at all. I never knew her properly as a child. Now she is a woman of over sixty. My sister, old enough to be my mother. A kindly, generous-hearted woman who would shrink from hurting anyone; least of all, perhaps, the younger brother she hardly knows.

"She was… always rather proud of you. What you've done. You must know that. But over the last few years… well, she wasn't her old self, really. It was as though something had already died inside her. As though she'd had one disappointment too many or something."

I take pity on her now. The answer is there, anyway, in what she has said. I don't question her further. I feel the full weight of my mother's judgement. Being conscious of it

117

makes me flinch. I feel the cutting of a last, stubborn tie. But what does it mean, after all? Surely it means no more than that I didn't know my mother half as well as I thought I did. It doesn't alter anything. She was my mother. She loved me once.

Yet I feel a welling of sadness, too; a great yawning emptiness at the thought that she could not love my wife, or my daughter. And thinking back on it now, remembering Gus's scarcely veiled discomfort in her grandmother's presence, of the arguments we would have on our return journeys about her stand-offish behaviour and her eagerness always to disappear outside to avoid being in her company; remembering, too, how Tela and my mother would greet each other with smiles that I can see now were as artificial as the polite greetings they enunciated to each other, I can only wonder at my own blindness. Tela and Gus could sense what I could not. It had never, till now, even occurred to me as a possibility.

I crumple the mutilated photograph and shove it into a pocket, then I pick up the other items, say a brief goodbye, and trek outside to the car. I drive home not in the best of moods. I shove a cassette of Bach cantatas into the car's player and turn up the volume. It helps, but the depressing thoughts keep intruding. When I reach home I leave the car parked out the front knowing that Tela will soon be phoning me to get me to pick her up from work, and walk up the path to the front door. I feel leaden; both my feet and my spirits.

Inside, I am tempted by the sight of the bottles in the wine rack. But of course I can't. Gus will shortly be arriving home from school and I have Tela to pick up and the dinner to prepare.

I look at the time. It's not quite two-thirty.

I head up the stairs to my study and there I go straight to the shelf where Addie's Journals stand. I pick one up and open it at random. I know her words will divert my thoughts. They always do.

March 1877. It is possible that I am imagining it, yet I feel that Harriet Harborough has been less friendly towards me of late. She and her husband and children have recently returned from a three month stay in Wellington, during which time their house here in town, next door to our own, has been vacant, as Clement (my Clement!), very much against his true wishes, has spent the period of their absence in their place near Stratford, looking after the management of the Harborough lands .

As soon as possible after the return of his brother's family from Wellington, Clement returned to the house next door, as did Harriet and her younger son, Ralph, who, as he is not yet ten years old, is still receiving his schooling here. The elder son is at school in England.

Harriet was present when Clement and I greeted each other warmly on his return from Stratford; but our pleasure at seeing each other again was not, I believe, expressed in a manner that could possibly have led to any suspicion. Yet Harriet has a guarded, more abrupt manner towards me now whenever we meet. Or do I imagine it? We have never been very close as friends. It may be that I am merely being reminded of that.

Anyway, what is there for her to be concerned about in the friendship that her brother-in-law has for me? We are not physically lovers. Alas, I know that we can never be. He is too concerned for my reputation to ever allow it, and my awareness of my vows to Tom and my duties to him as a wife are sufficiently strong for me to resist the exquisite temptation.

119

I have thought and thought about this. I am nearly thirty-seven years old. I have a husband and three children. The very idea that I could have found love outside this family of mine still seems absurd, and unfair. Yet I have, and so has Clement, but the hardest guilt I have to bear springs not from my love for Clement, but because he, who has no ties to bind him elsewhere, feels bound to me. I have told him of my guilty feelings. He knows that I wish him to feel that he is free. But he loves me. It is the most wonderful and the very saddest thing imaginable.

Today I have taken my mind off such matters by throwing myself into the hot and messy but very satisfying business of fruit-bottling and jam-making. Some of the bottles of delicious produce that Hannah and I have made will be taken down next Sunday to a picnic and games organised by the Church. There will be contests and prizes, and a cricket match at which Tom will do quite well I have no doubt, as well as a shooting match at which he will do very poorly, I have equal lack of doubt. Because it is a church-organised occasion, and a Sunday, he will probably not drink overly much, which will be a blessing. I will be able to spend some time myself at the picnic, with my joyful little Ellen at my feet when she is not tripping around hand in hand with her little friend Arnold Harborough, trying to make everyone happy. I will encourage George to join in the foot races and Inez to soften her prickly defences and laugh with other girls her age, though I probably won't succeed in either of these aims. My poor, meticulous, serious, George and my poor, afflicted and sharp-tongued Inez – they are both of them happiest when they are alone.

13

Jamie

June 14th 1984, and the National Government crashes to defeat in the snap election called by Muldoon. It's a year with an ominous ring, 1984, though the poll result promises that it will, at least for New Zealand, usher in a new socialism very different from George Orwell's dystopian vision.

Among those to find themselves no longer on the Treasury Benches is a big, bluff, apparently genial and wealthy car dealer by the name of Geordie Hicks. While not numbered among the inner circle of the governing party – now the ex-governing party – he nevertheless is reported to have a degree of popularity amongst the rank and file, and he also has one of the safest National seats in the country.

"Pity some of them like Hicks have managed to keep their place," I say. "Mind you, the Nats could've put up a donkey in his seat. Might've even got more votes if they had."

"You say you don't like Geordie Hicks?" Tela says, after listening to my rant against him and his kind and my belief that they are in politics only for what advantage it might give them in accumulating more wealth for themselves. "I'll have you know that we went on a date once. It was in my first year at Vic. I take it you didn't come across him there?"

"You went out with Geordie Hicks?" I ask, incredulous. "He was a student?" I'm not sure which piece of information is the more startling.

"Yes, but not a good one. He didn't even last that first year."

"Well that doesn't surprise me. Thick as two short planks I imagine. Except for the cunning of a greedy man."

"Anyway, yes, I went out with him. He was in the same footy team as Ali Cameron. And he and Ali had known each other from High School rugby matches, when Collegiate used to play King's. It was Fi who arranged for the four of us to go out that night."

"Hah! Hicks went to King's? Now that doesn't that surprise me. Good Lord! I can't imagine the two of you together. Did you… enjoy yourselves?"

"He, um… tried to enjoy himself. But I… let's just say I caused him very considerable pain, and he gave up his attempt."

Do I want to know? Yes! "What did you do?"

"I… scrunched his stones together. Very hard."

My momentary confusion becomes a broad, broad grin. That's my Tela! "Whoa! Ouch. Did he scream?"

"Oh yes. And he called me a fucking black bitch, among other things. He was very angry, and with good reason I must admit. I bolted out of his flashy flat leaving my shoes behind. Fi rescued me from the garden later."

I love it, I love it. I heave myself to my feet and cross to her chair and give her a hug. "The woman who brought Geordie Hicks to his knees. I wish I'd known at the time."

"It's a wonder you didn't." she says. "It was all around campus. He tried to claim that I was a nymphomaniac, but Ali let everyone know what really happened. Geordie wasn't seen around for long after that. Ali said he went home to New Plymouth and sold cars for his Daddy. Now look at him."

"Geordie Hicks, eh. What a prick. Typical." Yes, typical of the whole Right Wing establishment. Ex-establishment, I remind myself. Dog eat dog, and the devil take the hindmost. Let's hope the new Labour government adheres to the socialist principles of old.

But of course, they don't. They betray just about everything they have ever stood for.

By the following year the whole country, it seems, is talking about the policies of the new Labour Government, particularly the removal of controls over the New Zealand dollar and the

122

wholesale scrapping of trade protections. Alarm bells ring in my head; but my unease is diverted when, early in the new year, the government takes a firm anti-nuclear stance over a proposed visit by the United States warship the Buchanan. At least they're getting something right.

But as the months go by I am increasingly disappointed and despairing at the direction the government is taking the country. Tela, on the other hand, is unconcerned. Indifferent. I know she has processed what is happening, and is aware of the possible implications, but she has dismissed it all from her mind as something she is essentially powerless to influence in any way. "The great majority of people don't want to bother with thinking", she explains to me. "That's just the way things are. Why argue?"

That is the practical way to look at it, I admit. Yet it seems to me that it is also annoyingly arrogant. If Tela has a fault, it is intellectual snobbery. I don't mean that she flaunts her knowledge. In fact she is remarkably modest, or at least reticent, about her many achievements. But she is quick to dismiss from her mind as unworthy those who appear to take refuge in ignorance, especially those who have no interest in reading. To Tela an interest in reading equates with at least a minimal intelligence. A lack of such interest, to her, equates with... well, unworthiness; or worse.

On the day of one of our aborted conversation on the implications of Roger Douglas's economic policies an urgent problem relating to our kitchen taps requires a solution so I ring the plumber to get his advice.

The plumber we have always called on is one of the most intelligent people I know. He can sum up a problem in a second and suggest solutions in another second. Most significantly of all he can implement the solutions quickly, skilfully and (as far as I am able to tell) perfectly. Tela is polite to him. She even jokes with him in what sounds to me to be a somewhat condescending way. She obviously has him listed as a non-reader, or worse. He doesn't appear to mind. He gives back as good as he gets. He is, as I said, a highly intelligent man.

This day he has completed the fitting of the new set of taps in his normal efficient manner and I tell him that the way he goes about his work puts me in mind of Adam Bede and his wood-working perfectionism. It's a book that's in my mind because I've only just got around to reading it, to my shame and to Tela's horror. But almost before the words are out of my mouth I regret them, thinking that he'd wonder what I'm talking about and maybe be embarrassed. But he's not put out at all. He laughs, and replies: "Adam Bede, eh? Well, I can tell you that my wife's name's not Dinah, and the only preaching she does is when I spend too long at the pub." And that's me taught.

I later relate the story to Tela, but she gives me an oh yeah look of disbelief. "He's probably been watching it on video," she says.

Rather than any of these issues, Tela is much more interested in dealing with the question of where Gus should go for her secondary schooling. For myself, it is not a matter that I consider to be urgent at all. Gus is just about to start her last year at Intermediate but my mind doesn't yet want to think of her as a High School girl.

"I'd like her to go to Mapledene," Tela announces. It takes me by surprise at first, her preference. But then I think it's not really so surprising. She herself did well there. She must have a fondness for the place. Even so, I'm not ready to take her suggestion seriously.

"No need to send her to boarding school," I say, trying to shrug the suggestion off. "The schools here are good." The very thought of sending her away gives me a sinking feeling. Or is that feeling a foreknowledge that this is yet another argument I'm not going to win?

124

"We should decide now, if we're going to send her. Book her in. There's still time. There's probably not even a waiting list these days, the way things are."

"But… There are good secondary schools here. And there's Girls' High if you don't want her to go to a co-ed. In fact, yes… I'd agree to that, if that's what's worrying you. Single sex school. Yes. Good idea. No need to send her away, though."

The thought of Gus not being with us wrenches again at my gut.

"It'll be good for her, to be a boarder," she says. "And we can afford it. Even if it were difficult for us financially I'd still want her to go."

"But… What can she get there that she can't get here? What'd be the advantage to her?"

"You're thinking of advantage in material terms. And that's just the point. Here, at home, she's getting all she needs and more as far as material things go. She's being pampered, you must admit. A typical only child. There, at Mapledene, she'll have to make do with what every other girl has. It'll be good for her."

"We haven't spoiled her. We've just… looked after her."

"She's got just about everything she's ever asked for."

"Yes, but she's not been greedy. She's always had a good reason to ask for the things she's asked for."

"She's persuaded you that she has, you mean."

She looks at me as she says it, with half a grin. She's not accusing, merely pointing out what is undoubtedly a fact. I'm always open to persuasion when it comes to Gus.

"Besides, it's a private school," I try. "You know what I think about private schools."

"It's not really private any more. Not like when I was there. It's integrated into the state system. As far as what they teach, it's the same as anywhere else. But they probably do it better."

She's got the answers, but there's still some fight left in me. "It's a bit of a snobby school, though, you must admit. I mean, okay, you won a scholarship, but most of the girls there are from rich families, aren't they? They're the daughters of those who feel their money means they're specially entitled." I feel left-wing righteousness armour me. "Probably all their Dads are Nats, or worse. Mums too, for that matter. They'll probably look down on her because we don't drive a BMW or a Range Rover."

"There are some like that, but plenty of down-to-earth farmers send their daughters there, too. Yes, there's quite a bit of pretentiousness amongst some of the parents, but you shouldn't condemn a person just because they drive a flashy car, or even because they vote National." That half grin again. "They're just misguided. Anyway, living with the offspring of the privileged for a few years didn't do me any harm. Everyone there's treated exactly the same. How much money their parents might have or how high they might stick their noses in the air doesn't make any difference. Besides, she'd probably convert any girl who wanted to argue political points with her. You know Gus."

She's right there. No one can beat Gus in an argument. And Gus is already showing clear signs that she is a humanitarian and a natural socialist who hates seeing the exploitation of people or the environment. She's a twelve-year-old mixture of Jacques Cousteau, Sonja Davies and Dame Whina Cooper. I'm far from convinced yet, though. "Why don't we ask her what she'd rather do?"

"Well of course she'll say she'd rather go to a school here. With her friends. All nice and easy."

"What's wrong with that?"

"Too easy," she says.

She can see that particular logic doesn't sway me, and tries another tack. "Besides, it's nice to think she'd be carrying on a tradition, from mother to daughter. I'd like her to." It's a sneaky move. She knows I won't want to disappoint either of the two most important people in my life.

"But…" I can think of no immediate counter.

"And she'll get a wider range of opportunities there. After school activities. No other distractions. No boys hanging around at the gates, like the one you saw yesterday."

Another sneaky one. I'd told her that the previous day I'd noticed a boy in uniform hanging around just outside our gate, waiting for something; and sure enough, a girl from the Girls' High had appeared and the pair had provided a spectacle for anyone passing, kissing with considerable apparent passion and urgency until they staggered off together, presumably to find somewhere a little more private.

"Gus would never do that."

Again that half smile, and a toss of the head. No need for comment. I know what she is thinking. Girls aren't angels. Not even Gus. Then the final two nails: "It's probably the best school for girls in the country, and you want her to have the best, don't you? Anyway, it'll give us some time together. We haven't really had time together, just the two of us, have we? Not for years."

"I suppose…"

"I'll phone and ask what the registration procedure is. We could get her registered, at least. Then we could take her up to see the place when it gets closer to the end of the year. They have Open Days. She'll love it. And there shouldn't be any trouble getting her in even if there's a waiting list. Daughters of Old Girls get preference, I know that much."

"Well… it won't hurt to register her, I suppose. But we need to talk to her about it."

"Of course. Get her used to the idea. You can do that. She'll take it better coming from you."

Yet another sneaky one; but I know she's right. I even feel a little smug at the thought. Leave it to Dad and his special bond. But I privately decide that I won't be sounding very enthusiastic.

When I first broach the idea of boarding school with Gus, I am dumbfounded by her reaction.

"Yes, I want to go to boarding school," she says. "But not there. I want to go to Turakina. That's where Nora's going to go. She told me. It's where her grandma went."

"Turakina?" It's a Maori Girls College. I know Nora Watene is one of Gus's closest friends at school, but it doesn't seem a good enough reason for her to choose a secondary school, not on the basis of a single friendship. On the other hand, I can understand the attraction of going with someone she knows and likes. "But your own Mum went to Mapledene. And you'd have a friend there. Livvie Cameron will be going there, same time as you."

She pulls a face. "All she ever talks about is horses."

"But you like her, don't you?"

"She's alright. She thinks I'm boring because I don't ride."

"Surely not. Anyway, you've ridden her pony. You did pretty well, as I remember."

"But I didn't like it. Well... the riding bit was quite fun, but the horse hair made my eyes sting."

"She's quite a sweet girl, really."

"If you say so."

"Well... think about it. Mapledene. You don't need to decide now. We can go up when they have their Open Day. See what you think."

She shrugs. "Okay."

Such enthusiasm; but at least she doesn't reject the idea outright. I feel quite relieved, for the moment; in the period between talking it over with Tela and broaching the subject with Gus I'd given it some thought and become much more accepting of the plan. But I know that this is just a preliminary skirmish. We'll have to just wait and see if the year she still has to go at Intermediate School will make her more or less keen on it.

Later that term, Tela is at work and I am home alone when I hear the front door slam shut and I know that Gus has arrived home from school. I wait in anticipation of her coming upstairs to my study as she almost always does, to let me know she is back. Then, if she maintains her usual routine, she will go back down to the kitchen and organise a substantial snack from whatever she can find in the fridge.

But this day I wait in vain. Instead, I hear another door slam, then silence. Curious, and a little perturbed by the thought that it is someone else who has come through the front door, I leave my desk and go cautiously down the stairs.

"Gus?" I call.

There is no answer. I call again. Then I hear, faintly, a muttered reply from behind the door to her bedroom.

I go to it and cautiously knock, then turn the handle.

"Gus?"

She is standing in a corner of the room, her back to me.

"Go away," she says, her voice still scarcely audible.

I take a step or two towards her but she turns and shrieks at me. "I said go away!"

I hesitate. I want to go to her. I want to know what it is that is causing this mood, but I also know my Gus. We respect each other's wants, Gus and I. She will tell me what it is that's worrying her but only when she is good and ready.

"I'll be in the sitting room," I say, with a calmness I certainly don't feel, and I pass out through her door again.

I wait. All sorts of dire possibilities pass through my mind. Has someone at school been nasty to her? Maybe even physically attacked her? Or was she frightened by someone while she was walking home? Or was it something a teacher has said to her? I know there is one male teacher at the school she doesn't get along with, one she says is always trying to make her look stupid, or so she claims. Good luck with that, I mutter to myself. An impossible task he's set himself if that's his aim.

Then I am aware of her standing a little away from me, her head hanging, her jaw set hard.

She mutters a few words that end with something that sounds like 'period', but it doesn't register properly with me. I can see that she is angry, bewildered and upset, and there is no one but me for her to talk to. I ask her to repeat what she said but she simply stands there, silent. But I can hear her breathing, much more rapid than it should be.

Clearly she doesn't want to tell me what is wrong, but I cannot let it go. I can't leave her the way she is. "Tell me sweetheart. You're breaking my heart. Tell me, please."

She looks up at me. I see a look of decision, then her head drops again. He words are addressed to the floor, muffled, yet clear enough.

"I... bled. Down there. I didn't know what it was."

Period! My mind scurries to make sense of it. Surely not! She is too young. But she has said it, told me. I must accept it. She needs me to accept it, to reassure her.

"It's alright, Gussie. It's alright. There's nothing wrong."

"I know that, Dad," she says. Quite sharp. "I know now. But... I didn't know what it was when it happened."

"Is that why you're upset? Because you didn't know?"

"Yes. It was... I felt scared. And stupid. Afterwards, Lisa told me that although she hasn't started yet her Mum's talked with her about it already. Sophie, too. And Nora. Their Mums told them. Why didn't Mum tell me?"

"I don't know, Gus. She probably didn't even think of it. You're... quite young to have it happen."

"She should have told me. I was scared. I felt really silly when Mrs Boag took me to sick bay and told me. She gave me stuff to put on. A pad thing... I felt like a freak."

130

"That's silly, Gussie. It's quite natural, you know. It happens to all girls."

"Mum should've told me."

"Well… you're not much past twelve years old yet. She wouldn't have thought…"

"You're just making excuses for her. I hate her."

"Of course you don't."

"She should have told me. She's always thinking of herself, the things she's doing for herself. She doesn't care about me. Other mothers would've told their daughters. It's… embarrassing. She doesn't care."

"Of course she cares."

But Gus stomps off to her room just about as unhappy as I've ever seen her. My heart aches. I only ever want happiness for Gus.

Later I tap tentatively on her door and go in. She is on her bed, reading a Maurice Gee fantasy. She doesn't look up.

"Gus?"

"What?"

"It was going to happen sometime, Gus. We should have let you know what to expect. Our fault. Forgive us?"

She turns a page, angrily, slapping it down. She pretends to continue reading, but I know she is not. Then, quite suddenly, there are tears in her eyes. She doesn't cry, though. She makes no noise at all. As I watch her lithe little body, rigid with whatever emotion is torturing it, suddenly relaxes.

She puts her book down and gets up, comes to me. I fold my arms around her and hers are around my waist. She is still small for her age. I kiss the top of her head, pressed against my chest. I don't want her to be hurting. I don't want her ever to be hurt. My Gus, our Gus.

"Mum should have told me," she says, her voice muffled, her breath warm and moist against my shirt..

131

"We should have, yes. Sorry. I'm really sorry. Is there anything you want to know about it now? Do we need to get anything urgently?"

"Mrs Boag explained it to me. She gave me another... pad thingy. And it's not your fault, Dad."

But it feels like my fault, the unhappiness she is feeling. I give her another hug, and then, in typical abrupt Gus fashion she breaks away and stretches out on her bed again, picks up the book. Episode over. Back to *The Half Men of O*. She looks up, annoyed that I am still standing there. In her space.

"It's alright, Dad. I'm alright. Really."

I'm dismissed, but still uneasy.

I remember very clearly looking at Gus's fingers when she was a tiny baby just back from the hospital. Translucent, the flesh seemed. I fancy I remember seeing the tiny bones, as though I was looking at an x-ray photo. Translucent flesh? Clearly it can't have been, and yet... Then later, when she was a toddler, watching her pick up minuscule, scarcely visible items from the floor or the path, thumb and forefinger coming together a little uncertainly, like delicate pincers. Things as small as an ant held there as she peered at them, her face close, concentrating. Gus, wondering at the world. Gus, together with her mother, the joys of my life.

14

Jamie

I have at times thought of Gus and wondered if I could claim to have played a part in the creation of the perfect human being. Then I have envisaged Gus's reaction if I ever made such a claim to her. She would explode in derisive laughter, I know. Yet... I think in some private corner of her mind there would be a little preening at the thought. She has her mother's self-belief, at least … and, I think as great or (dare I think it?) even greater reason for it.

Between Gus and me there is a bond of mateship -- in the Australasian sense, of course. She is my best mate, and as is the case with true mates, we are honest with each other. She will tell me when she thinks I am being foolish, and I will tell her when I think she is. Mind you, the occasions when Gus behaves in what I deem to be a foolish manner are far less frequent than the occasions when she feels the need to pull me up.

When she starts at Mapledene, I write to her every day. Yes, every day. Mostly I don't have very much to tell her, but I have a vision of her waiting for mail call and not having anything and her feeling miserable and homesick. So I write to her every day. At first.

We are told it is better for the settling in process for us not to visit her for the first three weeks or so. Three weeks without Gus! It seems like half a lifetime. But I have to content myself with writing those letters. In that first three weeks, we get one brief reply. 'Dear Ma and Pa, I don't like it here much, not yet. The food is terrible. They have Vegemite, not Marmite. There's a girl here in the Fifth Form who has been sent to three different boarding schools already. She says there are just two types of boarding school, Marmite Schools and Vegemite Schools, and this is a Vegemite one. She's happy about it because she doesn't like Marmite. But I don't like Vegemite. It might get better though. I've joined some special activities, especially learning to Scuba Dive and Drama and Debating. You'll have to pay extra for the Scuba stuff. You won't mind, eh? Thanks for the letters, Dad. Love, Gus.'

So she sounds reasonably happy, and I am relieved. I write to tell her so. That's two letters I write this day.

The weekend of her first day leave, our first chance to visit, I am excited and anxious. I go up by myself, because Tela has a conference call she has to be at work to take. She asks me to give Gus a special hug.

Gus is in full uniform. I'm a bit surprised, as I had imagined that in the weekends they could wear what they liked. I notice many of the girls that I see are in mufti, but some are not.

I ask Gus what it's all about. "If we leave the school grounds, we have to be in uniform, even the seniors," she says. "The girls that aren't in uniform aren't going out. We're only allowed out if we're in prison dress. It makes it easier for them to find us and take us back to our cells if we break the rules."

She is joking, I know; or I certainly hope. "It's not all that bad, is it?"

"No, it's okay."

"You don't miss us too much?" (What answer am I hoping for?)

"Well… yeah. I did cry a bit the first night. But it's okay. I'm pretty busy."

"It's good that they keep you busy."

"Where are we going?"

"I thought we could go down to the waterfront. Maybe get an ice-cream."

"Could we get some chicken and chips?"

"Of course. If that's what you want."

"Oh, and Dad?"

"Yup?"

134

"You don't need to write to me every day, okay? It was nice for a start, when I was feeling… you know. But it's okay now. The others are beginning to think I must be a dork. Getting letters every day."

"Heaven forbid! We don't want that. How about… twice a week?"

"Once'd be alright."

"Oh. Okay. And… do you think we could get one a week from you?"

"Well… I mightn't always find time. I'll try. I might miss sometimes. Would that be alright?"

"I guess so."

"It's… you know. You'll be coming up to take me on day leave every three weeks or so. So I won't need to write much."

Put in my place, yet again. I try for a little comfort. "Are you looking forward to half term? I know we are."

"Yeah. It's a long way off. Oh God! Don't stop here, Dad. There's Harriet and her parents. I don't want her around. Let's go somewhere where there's just us."

Just us. Yes. I like that idea. I like that idea very much. Me and Gus. Just us. I drive on.

After I bring her back, parking in the courtyard in front of the half-timbered, mock-Tudor administration block, we get out to say our farewells.

"Next time you come, Dad, would it be alright if we take Livvie with us? She's asked her Mum to put your name on her approved list."

"Livvie Cameron? Yes, of course. If she wants to," I say, a little surprised. "I thought you didn't like her much."

"No, she's okay. She talks with a bit of a plum, but she's okay. She can't help that. Her Gran has paid for her to get elocution lessons."

"Elocution? That figures."

"I know. She comes up to me and says, 'How now brown cow?' All posh."

"That's not very nice."

"It's just a joke. I don't mind. She wouldn't say it if she thought I'd mind. I like her."

"Well that's good. I'm glad you like her."

We stand there for a moment longer. There are two girls, also in uniform, a short distance away. They seem to be eyeing us. Gus leans across and kisses me on the cheek. "Thanks Dad," she whispers, husky voiced.

I'm surprised, but hugely chuffed. Surprised, because of late she has developed a reluctance to indulge in what she calls PDA – though I'd had to ask her what that means.

Then, after she gives me my peck, she grins at me. "Those two over there," she whispers in my ear, still husky-voiced, and with a slight inclination of her head, "they probably think now that you're my Sugar Daddy. This'll keep them guessing."

"'Sugar Daddy'," I say. "How come?"

"Well you're white. Their tiny brains won't be able to process that. Clearly you can't be my father if you're white!"

"Whoa, Gussie! They can't be that silly. Anyway, how come you even know what a Sugar Daddy is?"

She grins, then just before she turns to leave me, she says: "You'd be surprised what I know. 'Bye Dad."

As I drive off, I think to myself: yes, I probably would. Or… come to think of it, maybe not, maybe not.

15

Tela

At the beginning of 1987, just as Gus is about to begin her second year at Mapledene, we collectively decide that it is high time she visited her Fiji relatives, as she hasn't seen them at all since we left Fiji when she was three years old. The prospect appears to bring a sparkle of excitement to her eyes, though it is rather hard, with Gus, to differentiate excitement from a myriad of other controlled emotions. We decide that she and I should go together after the end of the first School Term.

So it is in the first week of the May holidays that we fly to Fiji, just the two of us. Gus and me together, without Jamie. It feels a little strange. It feels, in fact, like a major adventure, and not simply because of the passports and the flights and the arrival at Nadi and Gus's first steps in over eleven years onto the soil (well… the concrete) of our other island in the Pacific.

The worst of the flights is the one from Nadi to Nausori, a bumpy scamper over the central highlands, but the airport welcome is more than sufficient compensation for the minutes of anxiety. Margie is there, and Dad is there. So is one of Margie's boys, Roland, a handsome lad of nineteen who gives Gus one look and moves in for a hug with a distinct look of delight. Gus is smiling, but otherwise is as inscrutable as ever.

Margie drives us all back to Suva, to the large house in Toorak where the whole family now live. There, all is babble and bedlam, and at the centre of it all is Gus, fussed over as though she is royalty. And she does look spectacular, I must admit. Her cousins (Margie has five children), are an attractive looking group themselves, but there is no doubt they are outshone by this exotic cousin from New Zealand.

"She's lovely, Tel," Margie whispers to me. "Those beautiful curls!"

"Little madam. Soaking it all up."

"Do you think so? She looks a bit overwhelmed to me. I'd better rescue her." She leaves my side to offer some instructions to the noisy mob, and I sit down next to my father. He looks tired, but his grin is broad.

"Tela, Tela," he says, taking one of my hands in both of his, kissing it. "My little girl, still. Now you bring my special granddaughter to see me again."

He doesn't let my hand go. He rubs it against his cheek, his wrinkled and stubbled cheek, then looks up at me. Quite suddenly I feel and see that that cheek is wet with tears.

The lurch of emotion I feel then is so strong that it almost makes me faint. Stupid, I know; but I now can feel my own tears, hot and stinging. He is looking old and frail yet his grip of my hand is strong. This man, who would boast drunkenly to his friends of his clever daughter who had won a scholarship to New Zealand, who seemed to see in me the qualities and the determination that he himself had never quite had and who had encouraged me to be what I dreamed of becoming. Unconditionally supportive.

I don't welcome the emotions that seize me. I don't trust emotions. I try to dismiss them from my mind, but they won't go. Regret. Guilt. A yearning I don't understand. This old man. My father. Forgiving me. Understanding me as perhaps no one else ever has.

And that first get-together sets the tone for the rest of our stay. I can leave Gus with her cousins. They are delighted to take her around Suva, giving her no chance to be alone even if she had wanted to be. In fact at first Gus and I have little chance to exchange any words ourselves. She does, though, deliberately seek out my father, her grandfather, on more than one occasion, and they sit and talk together. They seem happy with each other's company. I wish I could hear what they are saying to each other but I don't try to join in. I just keep glancing at them as Margie and I talk. They deserve to know

138

each other a little. It warms my heart to see them. More than that – it soothes my guilt and remorse. What else could I have done but leave him? Now my little recompense, my gift in return for his unstinting and uncomplaining belief in me -- the chance to know again my beautiful daughter.

That night, in our shared bedroom, Gus and I do have a chance to talk a little about the family, my family.

"Do you remember any of them from before we left Fiji?" I ask.

"I'm not sure. A bit, maybe, but not very clearly," she says. "I think I remember granddad. Maybe Aunt Margie."

"And… what do you think of Roland?" He has been especially attentive to Gus, Margie's eldest, hardly able to take his eyes off her.

"Yeah, he's… quite nice. He's been asking me about New Zealand. I think he wants to go there when he's finished his degree."

"He seems to like you."

"Yeah. Talei reckons he told her he wished I wasn't his cousin. Which is a bit creepy, especially as he's almost twenty. But he's okay."

"You're getting on with Talei, then?" She is just a year or so older than Gus, freckled like her father, and from my observations, perhaps a little jealous of all the attention her cousin has been receiving.

"Yeah, she's cool. She's boy crazy, though. She wants to leave school, but Uncle Ant won't let her. She asked me to ask her Mum if we could go to the pictures – except she calls it the cinema. She said her boyfriend would come with us and bring a friend for me."

"You didn't ask, I hope."

"No. I told her I didn't want to go to the pictures with some boy I didn't even know tagging along. I wouldn't have minded just going to the pictures with Talei though, but she dropped the idea. You know she wears make-up? She tries to cover her freckles."

"How silly. I'm surprised Margie lets her."

"I know."

"Well, I'm glad you're enjoying being with your cousins. You seem to be getting along with the oldies, too."

"Yes, especially Granddad."

We're about to get into bed, but she steps across and gives me a hug. It doesn't happen often. "What's that for?"

"Just... thanks for bringing me, Mum."

Then, on our third day, a Thursday, as Margie is showing us around some of her favourite Suva shops, we see armed soldiers in the streets. They wave us away when we keep moving towards them, in the direction we were intending to go. They look nervous, dazed even, their rifles slung menacingly at their sides. Go back home, they shout at us. Stay inside.

We are bewildered, but not yet frightened. This is Fiji. Peaceful Fiji. Fiji has no enemies.

When we get back up the hill to Toorak, Ant, Margie's husband, is there, having left work to see to his family.

"There's been some sort of an army coup," he tells us. He looks as though he can scarcely believe it himself. A coup? The government overthrown? This is Fiji, peaceful Fiji. True, there have been some rumblings of discontent between Fijians and Indians, and also between the western and eastern division and between the chiefs and the ordinary people, and there always have been those who would rather voice loud complaints than get down to the business of surviving together. But it has never been much more than that. Rumblings; then everyone has got back to sorting out whatever differences there might be. That is the Fijian way. The way the world should be.

But Ant tells us of marches that had taken place earlier in the week to protest the new Coalition Government, which is dominated by the Labour Party. There is support from both the Indians and Fijians for the Labour Party, which I would have thought was a good sign. But: "There's been trouble brewing, for sure, but this…" Ant says. He tells us of the arrest of certain firebrand politicians, of threats and counter threats, of shop windows broken.

The uncertainty as to what exactly has happened continues all day, but there is no sound of shots being fired, no indication that law and order has broken down completely. I am worried for us, for Gus and me – but not terribly worried. This is Fiji, I keep telling myself. This is the land of my birth. Nothing bad can happen to us here.

Ant takes the car out to see what he can see, but some of the roads have hastily erected barriers that are guarded by armed soldiers. The radio station is broadcasting what information it can verify, but the reports it has to make are often conflicting, and the most important questions, such as what has happened to the Parliament and its members, and who is in charge, remains unclear until late in the day. Then it is revealed that the leader of the coup is a moderately high-ranking army officer who has taken over control of the major organs of government purportedly to prevent violence being committed by what he terms 'Fijian terrorists.'

Gus, I notice, turns to my father for reassurance; sitting with him and listening to his commentary on events. "Don't you worry, girl," I hear him say at one point. "It's Fijians in control. They won't hurt you." Gus leans in to him; a thankful little girl snuggling up to the one who tells her what she wants to hear.

What I feel is anger, but not with anyone specific and certainly not with my father. I am angry with Fiji. I feel betrayed. This is the country where I was born. It is not supposed to be like this.

The phones are out for a time but eventually I am able to get through to Jamie to tell him we are fine. He wants us to try to return immediately but I tell him that as we are booked for the day after tomorrow there seems little point in trying to get earlier flights. Everyone seems to think it will sort itself out peacefully, I tell him. This is Fiji, after all; not Latin America. Not Africa. And indeed, we awake after a restless night to a new day that shows little sign of being different from any other.

Despite a general wariness, curiosity triumphs over caution, and Ant, who has rung his office and been told that he need not come in, takes us out in the car again, cautiously nosing around the streets. Schools are closed, but the banks appear to be functioning normally and there are plenty of ordinary people apparently going about their business. I begin to relax a little and I see that Gus, with me in the back seat, is also once again taking in the sights, like a tourist.

Then, in an instant, the terror of it strikes again. Ant stops the car when he sees some sort of melee in front of him. Apparently out of nowhere armed troops appear. The car in front stops and is surrounded by the military, then, with gestures made menacing by guns, Ant is directed to make a U turn. Now it is our car that is surrounded. Gus suddenly lets out a whimper and leans into me, clutching at my arm, and I look to the window on her side and see an automatic rifle pointed directly at her head and the face of the Fijian soldier who is holding it. His eyes are blank, his face expressionless. An automaton. Then just as quickly he and the weapon vanish from the window and Ant is turning the car around, driving away.

And still, although my heart is thumping it is anger that is my main emotion. A seething anger. This is Fiji. It is wrong, wrong, all wrong.

We spend the rest of our stay indoors listening to radio reports and reading the papers. Junior calls in from his work at

142

the Port Authority and tells us of rumours, many of them terrifying: Fiji Nationalists are planning to massacre Indians, the Members of Parliament are being shot one by one unless they swear allegiance to the Council of Chiefs. Ridiculous rumours, almost certainly untrue, Ant says. The radio is much more reassuring, and the editorials in the papers thunder against the coup. They seem to echo my own self-righteous anger. What is behind it all? Who is to blame? How did it happen?

But really all I want to do now is go home. Get away. Leave the country that has betrayed me far behind.

And we do fly out on the day we had booked, each of the flights we take leaving at the scheduled time. It is almost as if nothing untoward has happened, is happening. Superficially, at least. Yet underneath it all is a deep unease. Already there are signs of people wanting to leave the country permanently, Indians in particular. There is an atmosphere of nervous tension at the airports in both Nausori and Nadi, and there are armed soldiers looking rather purposeless, their guns hanging loosely at their sides. There is palpable fear and panic in the air even though it is lurking under the façade of near-normalcy.

Lifting off from Nadi, rising higher and higher until the anonymous offshore islands are left behind like abandoned orphans in the sea beneath us, I feel huge relief. Gus is beside me, in the window seat, her expression as inscrutable as ever.

"Not quite the holiday we were hoping for," I say. She is looking out, still, at the clouds and the sea. Is she, like me, grateful to have escaped? To be heading south to where we belong? I want her to be sharing my relief. "I don't care if I never see the place again."

She looks at me then, a faint frown on her face. "Really?"

"Oh yes, really."

"I do," she says. "I want to go back. I want to see them all again."

143

And I sit back in my seat and think about her words, her reactions to the events of the past few days, and mine – about why I should feel so betrayed and alienated by what we have experienced while she appears to be simply bemused. It is partly her youth, of course. Inexperience. Naivety. Her lack of awareness of the sort of deep-seated hatreds and resentment that the relatively small pieces of ugliness we did experience only hinted at. But it is more than just that. Fiji is where I spent all of my childhood. It is not simply the place where I was born. I chose to leave it, but until now I have always felt that it was part of me and I have always carried a feeling of guilt at the thought that I am a deserter. While I think of myself as a New Zealander now, and have for a long time, until the events of the last few days I have looked on Fiji with a degree of fondness – perhaps as I might look on a near relation that I no longer live with but that I trust will always welcome me. But that is shattered, now, that feeling. I truly never wish to set foot in the land of my birth again. My own feelings that I might have betrayed Fiji have been exorcised by the much stronger feeling that Fiji has betrayed me.

I am overseas again, this time in Perth, in Western Australia, when I learn of my father's death. The AVSA Conference I am attending is a five-day one, and I am scheduled to be on the panel in a Workshop on the penultimate day as well as giving a paper at the start of the proceedings. It is on that first day that I receive the message, passed through Jamie almost half a world away in New Zealand.

Quandary. The news comes as a blow, of course. The funeral, it seems, is to be on the same day as the last day of the Conference.

Dad. The parent who always encouraged me in my ridiculous dreams – the dreams that turned out to be not so ridiculous after all. The parent who took obvious pride in the snotty-nosed ease with which I came top of every class and who arranged that first, prodigiously incisive meeting with Cynthia Wallace, the meeting that set me on the path that was to lead to… well, right here.

And oddly, I suppose, it is that thought that leads me to decide that there is little point in excusing myself from my Conference responsibilities and trying to get to Fiji in time for the funeral. Would Dad have understood my decision? Of course he would, I tell myself. My grief at his departure from my life is not lessened by the physical distance between us when he died, nor would my presence at his funeral be any comfort to him. Too late for that. Too late.

I arrange a long distance phone call. I talk to Junior. I promise funds for our father's memorial and promise to try to get there for that occasion; although even as I say it I know I will find some excuse not to go. I never want to be in Fiji again. Junior says he understands. Oliver Junior, but the junior Oliver Gilbard no longer. He must be in the second half of his thirties now, I realise. Yet he hadn't seemed anywhere near that age the little we had seen of him when we spent those few days in Fiji earlier in the year. We had hoped to see more of him but the Coup had put an end to that plan. Now he is the senior male of our family, yet I still tend to think of him as a child. That is, after all, the only way I truly knew him. He was always closer to mother than to father; yet it is Junior who was dutiful to him in his last years in those ways that I could not be. He and Margie. The two who stayed behind.

We share our grief. We return to being matter-of-fact, talking of the details. He wasn't unhappy to go, Junior tells me. He will be buried in Suva. Dad. My father.

And when our conversation is over I cannot rid myself of the unbidden pangs of remorse. Of guilt. But, decision made and delivered, made ineluctable, now I must turn my mind to other things.

145

And when I return from that Conference, I learn that another towering figure from my Fiji childhood, my dear friend Cynthia Wallace, has been diagnosed with cancer. As soon as I am able I drive down to Wellington to see her.

She is at her home, having accepted retirement from the University soon after the diagnosis was given.

"It wasn't a hard decision to make," she tells me. "And it's not as though I need the money, and I'm into my seventies now. Though they give me a reasonably generous pension, anyway. Then there's the royalty cheques that keep arriving."

We have kept in reasonably regular contact over the years. Our collaboration on that textbook on Victorian Women Writers was one result of this. A new edition is still prescribed for use in courses all around the English-speaking world. I look at her, thinking of how much I owe her.

"And this..." She knows what I'm referring to. "How serious..."

"It has spread. From my breast. To other places. Even to my brain, it seems."

"Oh God! I mean... Is there..."

"It all depends on the chemo. It's not terribly, terribly advanced, I'm told. There is a chance."

"Oh God, I hope so."

She smiles. "So do I. But let's talk of other things. Tell me about the Conference. I had considered offering a paper myself when I first got wind of it. Just as well I didn't."

So we talk. As we have always done, we share our mutual love for the women, and men, whose works we have studied all our lives. Her special, life-long dedication has been to George Eliot, though that weakened a bit after she so wholeheartedly embraced modern feminism. My early passion was for Geraldine Jewsbury, though even back then I knew that Jewsbury's genius bore no comparison to Eliot's. My mind is not entirely on the topic of our conversation, though. I

146

keep looking at her face, being diverted by what I imagine I see there.

She has been a woman of striking beauty. I recognised that even as a child, when I first met her. It was there, behind the superficial gauntness of one who drank too much gin in an effort to see herself through the boredom of life as the wife of the Chief Chemist in the Sugar Mill, there on the western side of Viti Levu in the middle of the Pacific Ocean. Through boredom, and, as I learned much later, regret for a marriage that was not working.

Now that gauntness has returned, but it is the ravages of age and illness this time and not of drink.

Then I notice that her scrutiny of me is probably more intense than my scrutiny of her.

"You've come such a long way from that scrawny little ragamuffin who astonished me by telling me that The Mill on the Floss was the best book she had ever read. How old were you then? Ten? Eleven?"

"I'd just turned eleven, I think. And full of myself. I was overawed by you, though. Especially when you told me you had studied at Cambridge. And seeing all those books on your bookshelves. You instantly became a sort of priestess in my mind. A keeper of the flame."

"And you saved me. Rejuvenated me."

She couldn't have said anything to upset me more. I don't cry much usually. I don't cry much at all. Yet tears are welling in my eyes now. Uncontrollably. And I am sobbing, not wanting to. "I'm so very sorry," I say, trying to control it, dabbing at my eyes. Feeling as though I am betraying her.

"I don't mind if you cry for me, Tela," she says. "I don't mind at all."

147

16

Tela

It is mid-winter in 1987. The telly and the papers are full of the sinking of the Rainbow Warrior, flagship for the protests against nuclear bomb tests in French Polynesia, while tied up at a wharf in Auckland. It was a sneak attack by agents of the French Government. But for me there is more immediately distressing news. Fi phones to tell me that her father has been killed after rolling his quad bike on one of the many tracks on the Finlay farm near Weber, the place where I had spent many enjoyable stays during the school holidays when I was at Mapledene.

The hoarseness of Fi's voice tells me that she is far more upset by the news than her words imply.

"Silly old fool," she says. "Ever since he got the bloody thing Mum tells me he's been roaring around the place like a teenage hoon. He's over seventy. Silly old fool."

She is talking of him as though he is still alive. I am momentarily confused, but then I realise that it can't have been processed properly yet, in her mind. "How is your Mum?" I ask. "She must be devastated."

"Yes, I think she is. She must be. Though you wouldn't think so to hear her. She sounded much the same as ever. I'm going over today. Ali and the kids'll come over for the funeral."

"I want to come with you. Can I come with you?" Fi's Mum was my Mum in those days. I feel a surge of fondness and genuine concern for her. Her Dad… well, I never felt quite as close to him, but we'd got on well enough. It is hard to imagine the Finlay household without him moodily stomping around the place.

"Would you? Mum'd love that. I'd love that."

"Yes, of course. I've got a tutorial tomorrow that I can cancel, then nothing timetabled for the rest of the week."

"Give me say… an hour and a half and I'll pick you up. Thanks, Tel. Thanks, really," I imagine she is about to hang up, but then: "Oh shit. I'll have to pick up Craig from school and take him to his Gran in town. Ali's taken the ute and trailer up to Taihape. He's picking up a couple of rams. Oh shit. That'll take up time."

"No matter Fi. Just whenever. I'll be here."

We aren't the only visitors at the farm. The word has quickly got around, and people have dropped in to offer support. It is like that in the country, and Goldie Finlay had been well enough liked; by most, anyway.

His body has been taken into town. There's to be an inquest but Mrs Finlay has been assured that it will be little more than a formality. She is her usual matter-of-fact self. There is nothing of the recently-widowed about her demeanour and she clearly does not want to be seen as a weeper, in need of support. It is, in other words, exactly as I would expect.

She does greet Fi with a long hug, though. Then me, and I get a hug just as long.

We take our places in the house just as if the visit is the result of nothing special at all. After she has given the essential facts of the accident, Mrs Finlay doesn't talk further about it. Though occasionally I can see that her mind returns to the event, to the inescapable consequences, I can also see that she immediately shuts the thoughts out and forces her conversation back to other matters. To her own grandchildren or to my Gus, to anything other than the death of her husband.

The next day there is an even more constant stream of visitors, a few of whom I remember seeing from the times I spent at the farm but most I don't. Then, just on lunchtime, Murray

149

arrives, having left Auckland in the early hours of the morning to drive down.

Murray. Fi's older brother. The man who had relieved me of my virginity.

"Good to see you, Tel," he says; and he advances and gives me an uninhibited hug. I pat his shoulders tentatively, a little awkwardly. He is tall. The top of my head doesn't even reach his chin.

It's around seventeen years since I last saw him. Not since just before we left for Fiji to get married, Jamie and I. He had come down to Wellington, driving Fi who was heavily pregnant and all weepy that she couldn't come to Fiji to see us married. That same year, I know, he had himself married, and was now the father of two boys. He must be close to fifty but his hair is still blonde without a touch of grey, and his body is as lean and fit-looking as I remember. It is only his face, creased now by crows' feet around his eyes, that shows he has aged. I can't help it. I wonder how he thinks I look. Then I remember why we are here.

"Are Carol and the boys coming down?" Fi asks.

"Yeah. She kicked up a bit of a fuss because she had something planned with her girlfriends." I see a knowing look exchanged between Fi and her brother. "But yeah, they'll be flying down. I'll be going over to Palmy tomorrow morning to pick them up."

He looks at me again then. It is a more considered look than the one he had given me in the first confusion of his arrival. I can see he is surprised by what he sees; surprised and appreciative.

"Jeez, Tel," he says. "You're looking good."

I try not to simper, but I probably don't succeed.

Murray arrives back at the farm with his wife and his children in time for lunch the next day, the day before the funeral. It is strange, but when we are introduced, the immediate suspicion

150

in his wife's eyes is palpable. Yet how could she know? Surely Murray has never talked of it with her. Never talked of me at all.

She is tall and thin, like a catwalk model gone to seed. Her hair is that silvery blonde you know must come from a bottle and her smile is as false as her hair. I don't like her; and she doesn't like me. That much is instantly apparent. After we are introduced, she turns to her mother-in-law and says something to her. She offers me nothing beyond that temporarily fixed smile that slides over me like a smudge of grease. Certainly not her hand, or even a nod. Mind you, my own reaction, a twitch of my lips and a slight upward movement of my chin, wouldn't have been any sort of encouragement.

Her two boys, Murray's sons, are both teenagers, one about two years older than the other. The contrast between them is astonishing. The older boy has spiky blonde hair and he looks at the world with the same suspicious caution as his mother, while the younger is much shorter, dark-haired and with a tanned skin that hints at his grandmother's ancestry. This one – his name's Ricky -- also has his father's lop-sided grin and his father's sociable nature to go with it.

On the morning of the funeral, Fi's Alistair arrives in their double-cab ute with all three of their children in tow. He'd picked up the elder son from Collegiate the day before, then he'd left their farm early with the two boys and travelled up to Havelock North to pick up Livvie from Mapledene then back down straight to the church where the funeral is to be held.

The little church is in a settlement a few miles from the farm, on the way to town. It is a typical New Zealand backblocks village. Apart from the church and its graveyard and a scattering of mostly dilapidated houses, there is a school, a hall, a war memorial and, of course, the ubiquitous old weatherboard hotel, kept afloat by a bar that when there was six o'clock closing was open far beyond the legal hours.

There are also notional streets laid out when the hope must have been that it would become a market town for the district. Those streets are now no more than tracks leading at right-angles from the main road. Half a mile past the village there is a rugby field set in the middle of a broad paddock that becomes a showground during the gymkhana season.

There is a good turnout for the service with people who have travelled from miles around. Most are pakeha, but some of them are Maori, from Mrs Finlay's whanau I assume. The people all seem to mix easily, gathering in clusters. There is much hand-shaking and observations on the weather, interspersed with phrases that include the words 'poor old Goldie' or 'good old Goldie'.

'Goldie' Finlay. Mr Finlay's nickname was a salute to his corn-gold hair. Even though he was my best friend's father I would never have called him by that name as he was also, of course, the head of the household in which I spent nearly every holiday for the three years I was at school, at Mapledene. Well... that's how he might have described himself, head of the household, though it was apparent to me that Mrs Finlay rather than her husband was the one who kept things together in that house. It was easy for me to think of her as my surrogate mother but Fi's father never came close to being a father to me. Nevertheless, I do have a certain reasoned fondness for him. Or for his memory. It is a jolt to think of him as being no more in the world.

Ali takes Livvie back to Mapledene straight after the funeral, bundling the two boys into the car as well so that he can then return straight to the other side, while Fi and I wait till after lunch.

On the drive back in the Cameron ute we have a proper chance to talk. It is a chance, too, to forget death and the funeral, though we do find ourselves talking of Murray and his family.

152

"He should come back and take on the farm, but he'll never persuade Carol to leave Auckland," Fi says. "Stuck up cow. It looks like Mum'll have to get a Manager in to run it."

"That's a real pity."

"It is. Though I think Mum is looking forward to setting herself up in Havelock North. She knows quite a few people there. Not just farmers' widows or exes – she's become interested in her Maori side. She's taken to calling them her whanau."

"I noticed quite a few Maori at the funeral. That's good, isn't it?"

"Yes. I'm pleased for her." She purses her lips, concentrating on the twists and turns of the road through the Gorge. Then: "Hey! What was it like for you, meeting up with Murray again?"

"It was good to see him, of course. Why do you ask?" There is something in the sly glance she sends my way that alerts me.

"Well, you know. His wife being there, and you two having…"

The implicit suggestion hangs there for several seconds, until I simply have to ask. "Having what?"

"Come on now, you think I don't know?"

I am honestly shocked. I had no idea that Fi had ever had any suspicion of the encounter we had had, those many years ago. We had agreed to keep it to ourselves, Murray and I. Or is she just fishing? "What do you mean?"

"Come on Tel! When I came back after that weekend you told me that Murray had slept overnight at the flat with just the two of you there. I know he'd always had the hots for you, and that you quite fancied him. Overnight together? Just the two of you? You can't tell me he slept in my bed that night."

Of course she is right. It is pretty pointless to deny it, I suppose. I decide I just won't answer.

"Tel? I won't mind, you know. Why would I mind?"

"You've… you've known all this time?"

"You needn't feel bad about it. Anyway, you didn't get to see anything I hadn't seen."

"What?" Surely she can't mean what she seems to mean. She and Murray? Her brother?

"Don't worry. It's not as bad as it sounds. And it was when I was about eleven and Murray'd just come home from his first term at Collegiate."

"Oh?"

"The boys in his dorm had probably been boasting about how much they knew about girls. Something like that, I reckon. Anyway, he must've thought he'd take advantage of having the real thing on tap, as it were. We were mucking around in the woolshed, and he came out with it. He asked if he could have a look. He was quite embarrassed about it, I think."

"Have a look?"

"Yes. If I'd take my pants down. Of course, I thought, ick, no! But then I remembered what I'd seen just the day before."

"Oh?"

"I'd gone around to the Crosswell's, and it was the day they'd arranged for some flash stallion to come and serve Fliss's little Arab mare. God, I used to be jealous of her, having that pony. Beautiful thing, it was. Anyway, we went out to have a look at them both, Fliss and I, and God! What a sight! Have you ever seen a stallion excited?"

"Well, I've read about it."

"I was really impressed. You couldn't help but be. The wonders of nature! His donger was so long it was almost dragging on the ground."

"What's this got to do with…"

"With Murray's idea? Well, I remembered what I'd seen, you know, with the stallion, and I wondered if boys were the same. I didn't think they would be, but although of course as a farm girl I knew all about animals – well… except for excited

154

stallions. I can't have seen any of those before. But I really didn't know anything about boys. I just wanted to be sure, you know. I thought maybe they stuffed it down their trouser legs."

I am laughing by now. Giggling like a schoolgirl. "And?"

"So when Murray asked, I said the classic thing... you show me yours first. I had no intention of honouring my promise, of course."

"And he did?"

"Yup. Down with his jeans. Rather sweet and trembly he was. He must have been so keen to see what I had -- you know, get a gawk at the real thing and be able to boast about his anatomical familiarity or whatever -- that he was willing to subject himself to my inspection even though he clearly didn't want to. So I had a good look, but it wasn't at all like the stallion's. He obviously wasn't lusting after me, I'm happy to say. In fact I could hardly see it. Like a little blue flower bud, it was. Peeping out. Does that description ring any bells?"

"Fi!" But I'm laughing so much I can hardly speak. "No, it doesn't."

"Well I'm relieved to hear it. For Murray's sake. As it was, I think I must have sniggered at it because he pulled up his jeans and raced out of the woolshed without even asking me to keep to my part of the bargain. I've occasionally wondered since if my reaction blighted him for life."

"We shouldn't be making fun of him," I say; but I'm still giggling at the picture she has drawn. I know her so well. I can see it all so clearly.

"So... he's well enough equipped then?" she persists.

"Ummm, I didn't really pay very close attention. He... felt well enough equipped, as I recall. Why am I telling you this? It's embarrassing."

"You didn't pay much attention? You mean you didn't... Oh, of course. You were probably still a virgin then, weren't

155

you! You probably just lay there and let it happen. Was he your first?"

"Well..."

"Oh God! He was!" she shrieks. "Lucky old Murray!"

Somehow, after these revelations, I feel as close to Fi as I had in our schooldays. Even closer. Truly like sisters again.

After she drops me at home, I think about our conversation, and I remember how Jamie had spent years thinking he was in love with Fi. Fi was aware of it, too, of course. We used to laugh together at his infatuation, though for me it was actually painful to think of it. Only a bit painful, because I felt in my heart even then that nothing would ever come of it.

I remember my frustration and, yes, my jealousy. I remember the Swinburne-inspired poetry he wrote to her and showed to me but never to Fi herself. I remember the years, yes, years, of watching him build a picture of her in his mind that bore no, absolutely no, resemblance to the Fiona I knew and loved. It was nothing at all like the warm-hearted, good-humoured, staunch and rather prosaic-minded Fiona of reality.

Jamie's Fiona was neither of the flesh, nor of the intellect. Jamie's Fiona was his own construct. It seemed to be in part an awe-struck and fanciful apprehension of her status as the daughter of a landed family. Another part of it was probably her curvy figure and her honey-blonde hair that added (purely in his mind) a hint of Marilyn Monroe's impossible sexuality – a sexuality that really has nothing to do with flesh and everything to do with fantasy. I know all this not simply because I had eyes to observe but also because in those student days we used to spend time talking together as friends over coffees in the Vic Caf, Jamie and I. He bared his foolish soul to me. Over and over.

I know I am not, have never been, and could never have been a rival in Jamie's mind for that Fiona. I knew I simply had to wait for the real Fiona to be revealed to him before there was any chance of him shifting his focus from me as a friend and for him to see me instead as a potential partner, in all the meanings of that word. And when he did see it, when his hitherto distracted mind suddenly began to consider me as his sexual partner, he saw the whole of me and he wanted me. Sudden want. Revelatory want. I saw it. I kissed him. I helped him to destroy the Fiona delusion. He had always admired my intellect but when he stopped seeing me as a casual friend, as merely the brainy brown-skinned swot who hung around with Fiona, and saw me as an attractive girl who was willing, who wanted, to partner with him, his reaction was total and immediate.

But my feelings for him then, as now, are only partly akin to his for me. Yes, I wanted him physically; but what had attracted me to him and kept his image like a precious secret in my head was something in his nature. Even now I'm not sure what it is exactly, but it was there then and it has been there ever since. It is still there. It is a steadiness, a sharp but accommodating wit, a self-effacing willingness to deal with whatever comes along not only with a kind of naïve curiosity but also with patience -- with apparently infinite patience -- and loyalty to us as life partners. Being who I am, I needed that. I knew that instinctively right from the beginning. And I need it still.

17

Jamie

In May of 1988, during the school and university holidays, we decide to spend a few days in New Plymouth. It is my idea, though I have no difficulty in persuading Tela that it is a good one. There is rather more of a problem persuading Gus, though, as she has a half-formed notion about spending a week with Nora on a marae near Feilding. A good idea it would have been, too, and one I certainly would have encouraged – except that when she first mentions it to me it is still little more than a notion in her head whereas the journey to New Plymouth is a plan put in place by the time I collect her from Mapledene on the last day of school and bring her back home.

"Sorry, we didn't have a chance to discuss it with you first," I tell her on the way back.

"And you're not discussing it now. You're just telling me."

"Well… you didn't tell us you were thinking of going to the marae."

"I didn't have a chance!" Exasperated.

"Ditto."

"I could still go with Nora. You don't need me there."

"I need you to come with us. It's a family thing. Without you, there's no family."

There follows a long pause. She appears to be considering her options. Then she utters a kind of harrumph, which I take to signify a reluctant acceptance, and she assumes a frosty silence most of the rest of the way. And when we reach home she drops everything in the hallway and stomps off, I presume to phone Nora.

So the next day when we set off together I am in rather optimistic spirits and Tela seems happy enough to be getting out of town for a while. Gus, though is still sullen and clearly believing that she is being bulldozed into doing one thing when she is much more interested in doing another. For most of the journey west and then north she is a little cocoon of grumpy ill-temper in the back seat.

The idea for the trip had come to me while I was reading from Adelaide Gilbard's Journal once again. It was her descriptions and her feelings regarding New Plymouth and Taranaki that made me realise how little I knew about the province other than what was written there. I did visit New Plymouth once shortly after I left University but that was at a time before I had read the Journal, and I really had felt no association with the place at all apart from the knowledge that my mother had spent her childhood years there. The mountain had impressed me then, true, but only because it is hard not to be impressed by such a constant backdrop, such a dominating presence.

So on the journey up through Wanganui and then north into southern Taranaki there is only desultory conversation, and that almost entirely limited to the passing between Tela and myself of odd comments about the scenery. After we reach far enough north to be able to see the mountain we are disappointed to find that it is obscured by cloud.

"You can sort of sense it's there, though, can't you?" I say.

Tela doesn't reply, but there is a disdainful snort from the back seat.

Gus's mood doesn't improve after we arrive at the New Plymouth motel we have booked into and begin our settling in. She has her own bedroom, and she disappears into this, shutting the door firmly behind her.

"Shall we get a takeaway? Or something simple we can heat up here? Or would you rather we went to a restaurant?" I ask Tela.

"A restaurant? With the mood that one's in?" she says, with a nod towards the decisively shut door.

"Shall I ask her?"

"You know what her answer will be. We could just go by ourselves, I suppose."

"Well… I'd be a bit uneasy about leaving her here alone."

"Good Lord, Jamie. She's not a baby. It'll be good for her. Little madam. Yes, let's go and have a decent meal out. Leave her to think about the consequences of her moodiness."

I might have anticipated the reaction. Tela has been smouldering away at Gus's behaviour ever since we left home. The only words they have exchanged have been like sniper's bullets.

I stand outside Gus's door. "We're thinking of going out, looking for a good restaurant. What do you say?"

There is an indistinct mumble in reply. I tap lightly on the door and open it, stick my head in. The light is on and Gus is lying on the bed, her head turned away from me.

"What did you say?" I ask.

"Not hungry," she says into the pillow.

"Are you… okay?"

She swings her jeans-clad legs over the edge of the bed and sits up. Her curls are in disarray. Her eyes are glistening as though she might have been shedding tears but the look on her face is one of stubborn sullenness. A fifteen-year-old powder keg. "I'm just not hungry, Dad," she says. "And I need to be… on my own for a bit."

"Your Mum wants to have a proper meal, so…"

"Go, then."

"You'll be alright? We won't be long. Not much more than an hour, I hope. We'll lock the door, of course." It is already quite dark outside. I am struck with a renewed spasm of anxiety. "I'd be happier if you came with us, though. You don't have to eat anything."

She is silent, but she gets up from the bed and crosses to the window, pulling the curtain aside and looking out. Then she turns back into the room and approaches the mirror above the dressing table and runs fingers through her curls.

160

Miraculously, they are restored to some sort of order. Wayward, but just right. My stunning daughter. She looks at me, purses her lips, and shrugs.

"Let's go, then," she says.

The rest of our stay in Taranaki turns out rather well. As we take in the sights Gus's mood becomes more positive and she and Tela reach a tentative but touching détente.

There are two secondary-school age young fellows staying with what I presume are their parents in a unit a couple of doors down from ours. I see the first exchange of looks between them both and Gus -- just glances, but full of mutual somethingness. The checking out and the studiously indifferent looking away that follows.

By our third day there Gus can offer a report on both of them.

"They're actually cousins, not brothers. They're almost the same age."

"Oh."

"One of them's quite sweet, but the other's a bit of a boof-head."

"And that's not good?"

"Myeh. I've got nothing major against boof-heads. They can actually be highly decorative in their natural environment."

"Which is?"

She gives me an inter-generational look of wonder at my ignorance. "On the rugby field."

I've still got a lot to learn, but I'm getting there.

On the face of it, it seems faintly ridiculous – but I come to the conclusion that it is the mountain that is having the most effect on Gus's mood. I know it is affecting my mood. To feel its presence is one thing, but to see it from various perspectives all around the city is the real stimulant. It is not at all a threatening presence, as one might expect a volcano, even a dormant one, to be. At least I don't find it to be, although Tela expresses a minor degree of nervousness and asks for my reassurance that it is dormant.

"But note, I said it's dormant, not extinct," I tease. "You never know. We live in a geologically active landscape."

"Gee, thanks," she says.

But Gus doesn't need that sort of reassurance. She seems to be feeling the same sort of exhilaration as I.

We are taking a leisurely walk around one of the many fine gardens that the city has to offer, and we come to a little artificial lake that some English settler had long ago created to grace the grounds of his substantial house, now part of New Plymouth's publicly-owned heritage. It is a fine, crisp autumn day, and the foliage on the exotic trees that stud the park is gloriously multi-coloured, reflected in the lake's placid waters. But more jewel-like still is the image of the mountain, snow-capped and with its flanks painted in shades of blue, from indigo to brushstrokes of cerulean through to lightest turquoise.

We stand side by side, Gus and I. We exchange a quick glance then Gus turns her attention away from the lake to take in the sight of the actual mountain, aloof yet somehow with us, like a fourth person viewing its own jewel like image limned on the lake's surface. The real mountain is a tangible presence, both felt and seen. It is also a strangely familiar presence. It is almost déjà vu, what I feel. Does Gus feel the same? The look on her face is reflective, slightly puzzled.

"I like the real mountain more than the reflection," she says. "It's free, not framed."

"Yes," I say. I know precisely what she means.

Tela is standing a little way from us. She, too, is clearly taken by the beauty of the park with its magnificent back-drop.

"I'm getting some sense of my mother, here," I say to her. "She used to talk of the mountain a lot, as though it was one of the most significant elements in her childhood. I think I can understand that now. And Adelaide, you know, in her Journal, she said much the same. I can sense her, too. Very strongly, in fact."

"Yes," Tela says. "I'm glad we came. It's been good for you. And for Gus."

From the Journal of Adelaide Gilbard

September 1879. The sudden departure of Hannah's husband – his desertion of her, some years ago now – left her a little tearful, but has since also made her more willing, indeed eager, to talk to me of her earlier life, before she became my maid-of-all-work, my companion and my friend.

It is not that her husband's departure was unexpected. Hannah had long known that he was unhappy with his situation here, far from his own people whose lands are the other side of the dividing mountains. Furthermore, he had grown increasingly morose and critical of Hannah for her apparent inability to provide him with children.

In talking with me of these things after his desertion, Hannah also told me more than she ever had previously about her life before she came to live here with us; and what she told me has made me appreciate even more what an exceptional woman she is, and how fortunate I am to have her as a friend.

She was an only child. The year she was born was the same year that numbers of her Taranaki people as well as Te Atiawa and others whose ancestral lands were situated around the mountain returned after having spent many years in what she calls Whanganui a Tara, or Wellington. They had gone there (to that part of the North Island the Maori people

163

call the Head of Maui's Fish) to escape from marauding northern tribes.

Her mother died when she was about six years old. She had told me before that her mother had been a taurekareka – a slave woman – and thus of the lowest status. Though her father was a ware, a free man, he, too, was of low status, and when her mother died, Hannah's upbringing was largely given over to one of her father's aunts, an old woman who had herself been childless all her life. Hannah has none but fond memories of her, but she was aware also that she was frail and ill. It seems that Hannah was therefore increasingly little more than a nurse to the old lady. So it was that when the old lady died, and shortly after the opportunity was offered to Hannah to go away to a mission school to be trained fully in the ways of the pakeha, she left the village in a mood of both apprehension and excitement. She was fourteen years old, then, and as she had attended the village's own school whenever she had had the chance to do so, she had already learned to read and write in Maori. She had also become quite fluent in the use of English, as the wife of the local white minister had befriended her and ensured she had a good knowledge of the language as well as many of the European domestic arts. It was this woman and her husband who arranged a place for her at the mission school.

So she travelled to Auckland, where she joined twenty or so other girls at St Stephen's School for Native Girls. There, she had come to be known as Hannah, rather than her given Maori name of Hahana. She stayed at the school for four years, and towards the end of that time she was taken aside by one of the English women associated with the school, a Mrs Kissling, who asked if she would be willing to become the wife of a certain young man who was at St Stephen's training for the ministry. There was, it seems, nothing unusual in this, as

164

other girls at the school had been taken as wives by young Maori men who had trained at St Stephen's.

This particular young man Hannah had already noticed watching her whenever he had had an opportunity to do so, but while she had taken his eye, he had certainly not taken hers. He was a thin fellow, she told me, always neatly dressed, and carrying himself with an air of exaggerated piety and humility. She had secretly given him the name of 'St. Paul of Parnell', a soubriquet that had then been picked up and used by some of the other girls as well. He had, indeed, been looked upon by them all as something of a joke. And so, as firmly as she had felt herself able to do, she had declined the suggestion.

Mrs Kissling had been understanding, and the matter was not pursued further – at least, not officially. The young man, however, had not taken kindly to her rejection of his hopes, and she found that within a short time rumours of her supposed flirtatious behaviour and easy morals reached her own ears. Convinced that these rumours were the work of the rejected one, she held her head high and tried to ignore them, but once again she was called to the presence of Mrs Kissling who questioned her as to their truth. At this, Hannah told me, she had lost her normally equable temper and told the lady how disappointed she was that she should even ask her such things. "She went red in the face," Hannah said. "She was really a nice lady, and I shouldn't have shouted at her. But I did. I was ashamed of myself, afterwards."

Once again, the matter had been dropped; but Hannah had taken the first opportunity offered after that to leave the school. She agreed to a suggestion by the family of a military man visiting from Napier to accompany them back to Hawkes Bay as their maid. She had spent the next four years with them, and it was while she was in their service that she met her husband, Amako. "I was never very happy there, though," she told me. "I was treated well enough, but I had no friends." No friends. How sad it seems that the sunny-natured Hannah found no friends in that family she was with for four years!

After leaving service in Hawkes Bay, Hannah and Amako had an uncomfortable journey to Wellington on a small and ill-fitted ship. There they stayed for a number of months, with Hannah eking out a living for them both by long hours of work in a laundry. During this time, she told me, she and Amako were happy enough together, although Hannah constantly dreamed of a return to te maunga, to Taranaki, even though news of the fighting between Maori and European settlers there was the talk of the town. A little later, there was also much talk and rumours of even bigger troubles afoot further north, where the King Movement was strengthening and seen by the government to be an increasing threat to British rule. This was around the same time when Tom and I were making our own plans to cross the sea from Australia.

In Wellington with them at the time were several young men from Amako's tribe who saw in the rumoured conflict in the North an opportunity for adventure or to gain revenge on other tribes for past indignities, and who were therefore eager to join the ranks of the Queenites who were prepared to fight on the side of the government. Amako, too, was attracted by this possibility, and readily agreed when Hannah suggested they make their way north to Taranaki by whatever means possible, and there to see what chances lay even further north – though Hannah's reasons for wishing to make this journey this were very different from Amako's.

When they finally reached Taranaki a tentative peace had been established here. Hannah was thus readily able to re-

establish contact with her people, though she found that although those in her village accepted her, many did not do so at first with any great warmth or enthusiasm, especially when they grew suspicious of her husband's Queenite sympathies. Amako, though, had sufficient sense, she told me, to keep quiet about his intentions, and eventually to drop them altogether.

Things had changed greatly in her village in the ten years or so since she had first left for Auckland . More of their lands had been lost by confiscation or purchase, and fevers had taken the lives of many, adults and children both, her father being one of them. And as she herself seemed to be looked on by some with a degree of suspicion because of her long contact with Europeans, when she heard that there was the possibility of service in the houses of some of the new English settlers in New Plymouth she immediately decided that she would make enquiries. Although she did not truly wish to go back into service with a European family, she thought there was little else for her to do.

As a result of those enquiries, she came here, to me. Sometimes fortune smiles -- on me, at least, especially as we had only just arrived in the town ourselves.

After some years, she renewed regular contact with her local whanau, her ancestral family, on a warmer basis in most cases. But not entirely with all, she tells me. She is still looked on with some suspicion and even disdain by a few, so she says. It saddens me to hear her say so.

18

Tela

It is late in 1988, and I am only two years away from turning the much dreaded fifty; except these days, it doesn't seem like such a turning point after all. I have taken time off to go and see Fiona, and it is she who has brought the prospect to our notice, spurred on by a description of the difficult menopause she is experiencing.

"God! Not just all this, but the prospect of soon reaching half a bloody century. Ali too, of course, but it's not so bad for a man, eh? But for me... Not far off fifty years old and looking like it. Dyeing my hair and desperately trying anything that claims to banish wrinkles. And my belly still marked with horrible pink stretch marks I've never been able to get rid of. Carrying too much weight. Whereas Ali... It's so bloody unfair. Age seems to make men more interesting – to some women, at least."

There's something in her tone of voice that alerts me. "Do I detect a smidgeon of bitterness?" I ask.

Ali's out on the farm somewhere, and I haven't seen him since I arrived for the short visit with Fi – a visit I've made in response to the evidence of low spirits I'd detected when we had earlier talked on the phone – but I think of the last time I saw him just a few weeks earlier. He has that slim, stockman's look, with rather glamorous touches of silver streaking his dark sideburns. So he is still long and lean with a touch of manly elegance. Yes, an attractive man. More attractive now, it seems to me, than he was when he was younger.

"He probably looks at me and sees just another well-worn piece of furniture. Something he thinks he must get around to chucking out one day. An old sofa with broken springs and its innards leaking out."

"That's rubbish," I say. "You're a lovely mature woman. I'm sure Ali would agree. Wouldn't he?"

She shakes her head. "Oh God, Tel, I don't know. He doesn't tell me. He's a man. And there's another woman…"

She's looking down as she says this; but then she looks directly at me. "It might be nothing, but… They've only recently moved to the village. I think her… her man is a contractor of some sort. Builds dams and stockyards and that sort of thing. And she's… she's quite young. Late twenties, I'd say."

"And?"

"I've overheard Ali and one of his friends talking about her, saying that she's probably a goer, always looking for a bit of excitement. She has no children, and her partner's away a lot. I don't even think it's a proper relationship."

"And?"

"I know she's at the village pub most nights, and Ali's taken to calling in there much more than he used to. Then a couple of weeks ago when we were on our way back from the Feilding Stock Sale we stopped because he wanted a beer and a yarn, and she was there. As soon as we got through the door she was joking with him, coming on to him. She virtually threw herself at him. It was as though I was invisible for all the attention he was giving me."

"What was her partner doing?"

"He wasn't there. Like I said, he's away a lot."

"Well… how did Ali respond?"

"He looked distinctly uncomfortable once or twice with some of the things she was saying to him, actually. And of course that made me more suspicious than ever."

I take a good look at her then. I've never known her to be like this before. She looks defeated, hollow-eyed. "And that's it?" I say. "It doesn't sound like anything serious to me."

"It's not just that. It's other things, too. The way he looks at me then looks away. Like he pities me, almost. I hate it."

"Have you said anything to him?"

"I tried. After we left the pub that night, I said he seemed pretty friendly with the woman. He just laughed. Told me not to be ridiculous."

"There you go, then. Any reason you shouldn't believe him? Any other evidence?"

She shrugs, then looks up at me and smiles. "No. Not really. Am I being a stupid cow?"

"I would say so. Yes. Think about it, Fi. He needs you. Probably now more than ever. You've never had any doubts about him before, and that evidence you talk about is pretty slim. He might have been a bit flattered, that's all. Like you would be if some young Brad Pitt type started flirting with you."

She snorts. "Fat chance. Anyway, she's not all that pretty. Quite hard-faced, in fact. Brad Pitt, on the other hand…"

"That's what I mean, you see. We can all have fleeting fantasies. Even staid old Ali. It doesn't mean anything."

I can see the light coming back in her eyes, the burden of her fears lifting. "Yeah, you're right, aren't you. I'm just being a silly cow."

I nod. "Yes. I'm pretty sure you are. Put it down to your crazy hormones."

The smile on her face becomes broader, even more sincere. "Thanks, Tel."

On the drive back home, I wonder if Fi's suspicions were justified. I don't know, of course, despite my assurances. I don't know Ali sufficiently well to judge whether or not he would have succumbed to temptation; but I do know Fi. I could see by her look of relief that she wanted to believe me when I suggested she was mistaken. And whether or not my reassurance was appropriate it seems to me that Ali would have been given a sufficient shock by her questioning of him to shrink away from any further involvement with the woman – if there had been anything at all.

Anyway, I can't see the question of whether or not Ali has had a meaningless fling with the woman as being of any real significance. But that's just me, I suppose.

I think of my own experiences in infidelity. No, it's the wrong word, infidelity -- the wrong word for what I have done on those rare occasions when I suppose some might think the word is the appropriate one. I have never felt truly disloyal; or, perhaps just a little bit and only momentarily, for the occasions have always been quite separate from my domestic milieu both in terms of distance and nature.

I am a passionate woman. No – again, that is not quite true. Mostly, I suppose the precise opposite is true. I am, in most of my dealings with the world, a dispassionate woman. Passionate about the world of my head, yes, but mostly dispassionate in my encounters with the physical world. Except…

I enjoy sex. On my terms, that is. I am very firmly of the belief that Tiresias, the old Greek who spent time as both a man and a woman, had it right when he said that women have the capacity to enjoy the act far more deeply than men. I think to women it is something beyond what it is to men. Or it can be. I know for me an orgasm is a little like a reaffirmation of life. Like giving birth, I suppose, but with the pain replaced by an intense pleasure. Men, it seems (or so we are told) die a little after they have had their orgasm. The little death I have heard it called. Whereas with me, although a good orgasm might leave me momentarily tired, within minutes I feel rejuvenation rise like a tide through every fibre of my being. But, like most pleasures, the wise will only take it in moderation. And I have to believe that I am wise.

Nearly all my physical satisfaction, and certainly the most emotionally meaningful of it, I have gained within the warmly comfortable bounds of my marriage to Jamie; but there have been other episodes. These have nearly always been almost totally meaningless. Something done in passing. Enjoyable, yes, but not anything that lasted very far beyond the moment. That's how it has seemed to me; and for them, the men, too I suppose. Except for one man, just one, who wanted more.

It had started, as usual, when a passing spark ignited in me an interest quite different from any of the intellectual issues that were the topic of most conversations around us. It was at another Conference, this time in Boston, in the aftermath of one of the papers delivered. We had both been standing in a group that was discussing Continental and British influences in the novels of Henry James and Edith Wharton, though we later admitted to each other that neither of us was especially interested in the topic. We exchanged a glance that clearly meant: let's drift away and have our own chat.

He was black; tall and youthful-looking with the sort of wry arrogance in his expression that for some reason has always triggered a rush of adrenalin in me -- the sort of look that signals both an exciting promise and an irresistible challenge.

He told me within the first few minutes of our private conversation that he was from the island of St Lucia, that he taught comparative literature at Boston University, and that he was himself a writer. I think I was attracted by both his manifest intelligence and his beautiful body. No doubt I was also flattered by the excitement in his eyes as he looked at me; slowly, deliberately, very appreciatively.

Later, in bed in my hotel room, I learn that he is not as young as he looks – that he is, in fact in his late forties, recently divorced and desperately unhappy. The last piece of information disturbs me. It isn't that I don't feel pity for him – it's rather that I do not need the complications that any sympathetic response I might make to his unhappiness might bring. So I make inconsequential noises but I plead weariness and he eventually and reluctantly leaves, with my promise that we will meet up again the following day.

We do, but I have had time to get my thoughts in order and I keep him at arm's length. There is no repeat assignation. Despite his efforts at persuasion, his protestations that he would agree to anything I stipulate if only we could let a relationship develop between us, I remain adamant that it has been only a passing encounter. At the end of the Conference we part, I believe, as acquaintances, nothing more. I really do not want to have any further contact with him.

But in the weeks that follow, after I have returned to New Zealand, he tries twice to contact me at work by long-distance phone calls. I take those calls but I make it clear that they must stop, that there is absolutely no point to his efforts; and for several months thereafter he leaves me in peace. I relax, and his protestations pass from my mind.

Then the very next year he appears unexpectedly at a Seminar I attend in Auckland. I look up from my opening address as Chair of one of the sessions to find him there at the back of the room – a startling and highly visible presence. There he is, all the way from Boston, attending a seminar on the indigenous literature of the South Pacific.

I don't quite know what is the best way to respond to his presence. Later I do talk with him privately, of course, but I deflect his attempts to tell me how much he needs me. There is no room in my life for another man who needs me. I think that this time I must have been sufficiently brutal as he accepted what I had to say in the end and returned to America before the Seminar had concluded. I have not heard from him again.

These and other similar thoughts and memories are still in my mind as I approach the outskirts of the city. Why is it that I and many others, too, I presume, are tempted into throwing all restraint aside and indulging such sudden passions? What is it that causes them? Well, yes, we know. The eruption of hormones at the behest of signals from the brain, those activated in turn by images that the eye imprints on the cells of the cerebral cortex. All of these things and more trigger rushes of blood that take glandular secretions to various parts of the body. The symptoms are manifested in the thrumming passage of blood, in breathing that becomes panting. And arching above it all is the sheer, primal thrill of it, the consequence of the rush of adrenalin. It really is the possession of one's self by another, usually dormant, self -- the self that subjects all else to the imperative of self-satisfaction, that most basic manifestation of survival. Excitement in the purest, most primitive sense.

It is all just something that we must accept and adjust our lives to. Everyone has their own methods of doing so, or so I presume. I know that many simply shut their minds to temptation until they possibly even imagine that they are no longer tempted at all. This technique becomes, I suppose, something like aversion therapy. It was (and is) supported by the precepts of most religions and also, more subtly, by the orthodox customs of most societies.

Others, of course, make only limited or no attempt to suppress these urges. Perhaps the young woman who flirted with Fi's Alistair is one of those. But I believe, and hope very much for Fi's sake, that whatever did or did not happen between them, it is now all over.

19

Jamie

These are strange times. We are instructed that our new heroes are those who go out and tirelessly strive to make deals involving the buying of companies or government-owned enterprises that they decide are underperforming and then stripping them of any easily-realisable assets and selling the rump off to the highest bidders. Or those who buy gold and store it to sell when the price reaches its peak. Or those who produce any one of the new rash of magazines presuming to tell us how to become one of the new wealthy. But I am not a believer. To me it seems that these new 'heroes' have the sole aim of making themselves rich at the expense of the gullible who are led to believe that they, too, can become instant millionaires.

Even super-rational Tela is afflicted by the madness. She has on occasions come home from work to tell me of breathless common-room conversations where otherwise cautious academics have talked of the paper profits they have made from putting their spare cash, or money that they've borrowed from the banks that seem to be falling over themselves to provide it, into property investment companies or gold stocks or any one of the myriad of new ways to turn dreary old salaries into sparkling personal unearned wealth.

"Should we be doing the same?" she asks me.

"No," I tell her. I shudder at the very thought. My determination seems to convince her, at least temporarily.

But it is not just the common-room that is feeding her with these ideas. The television, the radio, the newspapers, the very air around us seems to be full of glittering temptations. Telly advertisements purport to show gallant agents of investment companies wearily travelling back to little old New Zealand (business class, of course) presumably after having successfully negotiated yet another financial triumph; then, martyr-like, rising to their feet to walk down the aisle and open up negotiations with fellow passengers for more deals yet. What heroes they are! They are giving their all to give us all the opportunity to make unearned millions! Quick! Be in to win! Surely no one wants to be a loser!

I prefer to put our savings into the state-owned bank and thus ensure that whatever profit that is gained from making use of it will be returned to the people; to all of us, collectively. When the state-owned bank is privatised I transfer our savings to a community bank. I am sticking to my principles. Our principles, I remind Tela when she once again comes back from work anxious that we might be missing out on untold riches.

"Why do you want riches anyway?" I ask. "We have all we need."

"Well, you know. Just in case."

Another journey. Gus is near the end of her second-to-last year at Mapledene when we return, all three of us, to the United Kingdom for a holiday. We make our plans when she is at home for the August holidays, and although, in what is presently her customary manner, she displays little overt excitement at the prospect I pick up clear evidence that her mind is already partly on things connected with our proposed holiday when I find her curled up on the armchair in my study, reading. She is there for hours, occasionally reaching out for a handful of the mixed nuts that she has placed in a bowl on my desk, turning the pages of Adelaide Gilbard's Journal with the utmost concentration. I wonder why, because this time we do not plan to go again into Gloucestershire, to the village where Adelaide spent her days before coming to New Zealand, but rather to spend most of our time in Cambridge and in Wales. But at least it is an indication of her interest in the proposed trip and it's true that there are many references in Adelaide's

Journals to her husband – to Tomas Gerold, the Welshman. To Gus's great-great-grandfather.

It is November when we catch the plane to Auckland on the first stage of the journey. We have had to get special permission from the school to remove Gus for the last two weeks of class so that we can all go together.

This time, although we first stay a couple of days in Cambridge where Tela calls in to Girton College to spend time with an old friend from her student days who is now a Senior Research Fellow there, our major aim is to explore North Wales. To this end, on the Wednesday of our first week we hire a car and head west.

We establish ourselves in a comfortable holiday cottage near a lake in a valley that runs down to the sea. It is the part of Wales that impressed me most during my first and only previous visit, in the late sixties. Then, I had driven down the valley from its head, and been awed by its grandeur, by the evidence of the massive power of the glaciers that had carved out the landscape. It is for that reason that we decided to make the valley our base for a few days of exploration of North Wales, including at least another sighting of my great-grandfather's ancestral home high on the hills overlooking Tremadog Bay.

And we do all we intended to do; but for both Gus and I the most affecting parts of our stay are our visits to a site within easy walking distance of our base in the Dysynni Valley. These are the ruins of a thirteenth century castle built on a rocky outcrop around which those ancient glaciers must have slowly ground their way leaving behind this perfectly protective site. The place is called Castell-y-Bere, and the castle was built, we learn, by a Prince of Gwynedd as he tried to protect his people and his lands from the incursions of the Norman King of England, Edward I.

I had not even realised that such a ruin existed when I first drove down the valley on my youthful journey all those years

177

ago. Now, from the very first time that the three of us visit the site Gus and I are both struck by a feeling of mystical awe. This is the Wales that something in us both responds to in ways that we cannot even begin to understand. Side by side, we look down the valley from the highest point of the complex fortification. To the north is the dominating bulk of Cader Idris. The Valley itself runs south-west towards the sea and we can visually follow its course for a long distance.

"I can't imagine how the Norman English could possibly have captured this place," I say.

Gus is silent, but I can see by her expression that she is absorbing the same sort of energies that are flowing through me. It is an elusive feeling though. Indescribable.

"I don't think they did," Gus says. "Not at first. And not at last. Maybe in between, but not at last. I think this place must have just become irrelevant to whatever purpose it was supposed to serve. In the end. "

"The English did capture it, but only much later in the century. That's in the notes."

"Yes, but it must have been taken by the Welsh again."

"How do you know?"

"Well... I don't. But can't you feel it? The... defiance. The sadness? It's a... native sadness. It hasn't been... wiped out."

I know what she means, and I couldn't have put my knowledge into more understandable words. There is something intensely native about these ruins. There just is. Their Welshness has not been relinquished.

While Gus and I are exchanging our words, Tela stands beside us but is not really with us. She doesn't offer any comment.

"The feeling I get here is sort of like the feeling I had when we had that school tramping trip and camp at Waikaremoana last year," Gus continues. "Everywhere there, wherever you looked -- the lake, the bush, the mists -- it was Maori. The very essence of Maori. It was so intense, that feeling, that all the girls seemed to feel it. This is like that. But…"

"But?"

"But even more so, for me. When I had those feelings at Waikaremoana I felt like an outsider. We all did, I think. Not… unwelcome, but not really able to participate or share. Here… there is a part of me that is… sharing." She gasps, and shivers. "God, it's strong. I think I'd like to stay here forever. To die here. That maybe I already have."

And I know exactly what she means. I don't even have to reply. We just stand side by side, Gus and I, seeing and feeling, sharing that temporary resurrection of a long-gone once-belonging. And next to us yet quite, quite outside, Tela remains silent.

Later that week we travel north to Harlech and into the hills beyond. We go to see Tan-y-Bwlch, the ancestral home of Tomas Gerold, Adelaide Gilbard's husband.

It has changed a little since my earlier visit twenty years or more ago. There is a new building to one side of the house. An effort has been made to ensure it is of the same materials and style as the old structure, but it still looks alien. There is no trace in me of the excitement I felt on my first visit. Of that recognition of affinity. It is gone.

We don't stay long, and when I move the car on I take the same route as I had twenty years earlier; up the hill to the little church then turning to loop back past the house again on the way to the main road. All three of us are silent. It seems that even Gus has nothing to say. I am a little disappointed, yet I also feel some satisfaction that leaving Tan-y-Bwlch behind again, almost certainly for the very last time, is in no way difficult for me.

In the village below, I slow down as I pass the tea-rooms I remember from that earlier visit. I remember, too, the woman who had served me my coffee and cake. Nel was her name.

Very Welsh, and proud of it, she was. Thinking of her invokes the only real sense of nostalgia I feel this day.

It is New Year's Eve, the final night of our stay in Britain, and we spend it in the hotel we had booked into quite close to Heathrow.

There is a festive air about the place, with guests and staff exchanging New Year's wishes in a distinctly un-British fashion. One of the staff looking after the guests in the waiting area outside the restaurant downstairs is a fresh-faced and good-looking lad who gives Gus an admiring look as he approaches to ask if he can bring us a drink. By some process entirely beyond my comprehension she correctly judges his nationality and asks him, in her impeccable French, if she can have a bottle of Evian water.

His face lights up with pleasure and he eagerly assents.

She absents herself from our company several times in the course of the evening and we suspect she is taking the opportunity to track him down again. There is quite a crowd in the hotel's reception rooms, all seemingly intent on celebration.

"His name is Christophe," Gus tells me when she returns from one of these excursions. "He's from the Moselle. His parents manage a pension in Pont-a-Mousson. He's here for a few weeks to learn more about the English way of doing things."

By the time midnight comes around I am heavy with fatigue, but we have decided to stay up to see the New Year in though we stay seated in our chairs. Gus has left us yet again as she joins in the continuing revelry.

By half after the midnight hour, I am too tired to stay awake any longer.

"We should find Gus. I'm going to be asleep here soon."

"Just leave her," Tela says. "You should trust her more. She's old enough to look after herself."

"No. I'm not happy with that." I begin to wander groggily around the room, looking for her. The couple of glasses of champagne I'd had pressed on me mean that I can hardly keep my eyes open. I go to the side of the room from where the lifts operate, and despite my doubts I am tempted to press the button and gain the blessed relief of my bed. Then, just as I'm about to turn away from the lifts, my fatherly concern still uppermost, I see her. She is a short way down one of the corridors held tight in the French lad's arms. They are kissing with great concentration. Then, as I watch, she breaks away and leans up to peck his cheek and immediately after leaves him and makes her way towards where Tela and I are standing. She doesn't see us at first, but then does, and hurries towards us.

"That was fun," she says. Her eyes are shining. She looks as though she could last until dawn. "I'm glad you waited for me, though. Christophe was getting a bit too keen."

Tela is right, of course. I have no need to worry about my daughter.

While we were in Wales we had gone again to Castell-y-Bere just the two of us, Gus and I, on the morning of our last day in the valley, leaving Tela to do the last little bit of packing ready for our departure. We hadn't talked much afterwards. Indeed, we had been strangely quiet, each of us, as we trailed back to the cottage. Now, back in New Zealand, we talk of our feelings then.

"That last visit to Castell-y-Bere," I say. "Did you have the same sort of reaction then as you did the first time?"

"Myeh, sort of," Gus says. "But not quite. I still felt a bit of what I'd felt before. But I also felt a bit as though the place was telling me: 'It's been nice to meet you, and yes, we mean something to each other; but you can bugger off now. I know your heart is elsewhere.'"

181

I'd felt something similar, a sort of release, a sigh of resignation, but I couldn't have put it so well.

"And Tan-y-Bwlch? Did you get any of the same sort of feeling when you saw the old house?"

"Yeeaaaah. Nah. Not really. I didn't feel much there. I didn't mind not going inside. I mean, it would've been interesting, but I didn't feel any great pull. I suppose in part because I don't much like Tomas Gerold, or whatever his name was. My Great-Great Grandfather. From your description, and from what I read in the Journal, he sounds a bit dodgy. So I wasn't much interested in seeing his family house."

"Fair enough. I know what you mean."

"In Wales, it was more the landscape that interested me and that I felt some closeness to. Even at the old castle ruin. It was more the setting than the actual walls and things. In Wales, for me it wasn't specific people we met or thinking of my ancestors, it was the land itself. I loved the feeling it gave me, even though it was a little sad, too, I suppose. That valley. Wow! There was a connection there. Something was going on."

"Yes. It's spooky, almost. I'm happy you felt it, too. It means I didn't imagine it."

"Yet I wonder why it was just there, especially in that valley. And only in Wales. If it's ancestral memory or something, you'd think I'd feel it in Fiji, too."

"You didn't feel any connection in Fiji?"

"Well… yes I did. But it wasn't the landscape or anything like that. It was the people."

"Your Mum's family."

"Yes, but more than that. More than just the fact that they are Mum's family. Aunt Margie, for instance. She's so warm and welcoming as a person. I would like her even if she wasn't related to me. And Grandfather Ollie. I got on really well with him."

"People."

"Yeah, that's when I feel Fijian. When I'm with my Fijians. And with PEs, of course. I feel like one of them. And Fijian men. Fwooah! That's why I like watching Sevens rugby. What could be more 'Fwooah!' than a Fijian man reaching high for the ball, plucking it out of the air, then racing away like a… I don't know. Something fast and uncatchable. That's another time I feel Fijian – and wish that I was built like a Fijian."

"Yet you seem to fancy white boys, mostly."

"Yeah. Not really. I mean, I haven't had much chance to get up close with Fijian boys. I've tried flirting a bit with one or two when I've had the chance, the ones here in Palmy. But those ones have been more interested in some of the girls I've been with. You know… white girls."

"Oh dear. Tragedy."

"Yeah. No, actually you're right. I do seem to be more attracted to white boys, hormonally. Funny, that. They're mostly not nearly as good looking. Mostly."

"But what do you mean when you say it's not so much your Mum being Fijian, or part Fijian, that makes you feel affinity to Fiji, that it's more the rellies?"

"Oh, no. It's Mum, too. But I suppose it's because of her personality. You know. She's all very Fijian when she's with other Fijians -- full of hugs and things – but she's never really been like that with me. Not much, anyway. I mean, I sort of understand it, but it's all part of her being a bit of a crap Mum."

"There's no right and wrong way to be a Mum. Everyone's different"

"Exactly. And she's been a Mum in her own way. And that means at times she's been a pretty crap Mum. I understand why. I'm not complaining. I used to think it was her fault, but it's not really."

"I'm not sure I can agree. Not about the crap Mum bit."

"Not always, Dad – but just think back. My very earliest understanding of what a Mum was didn't even include the word 'Mum', or my actual Mum. I can still sort of remember that in my early years, when we were in Fiji, the word that meant 'Mum' to me, as most people would understand it, was ''Nisi'. 'Nisi meant Mum, to me. 'Mum' meant something different. Mum meant that other person, who expected me to behave the way she told me to and who gave me presents occasionally, and who sometimes took me with her in the car, but who mostly seemed to be much more interested in other things than in dealing with my wants and needs. 'Nisi did that. 'Nisi was my word for Mum."

She's right about that, I have to admit. Our house-girl, Akanisi did most of the seeing to her needs. "But not after we left, Fiji. She's been your Mum in all those ways in New Zealand. You must admit that."

She laughs. "No Dad. Not really. Every now and then, maybe, but mostly it's you that's been my Mum. And my Dad."

From the Journal of Adelaide Gilbard

October 1880:   These are quite hard times. Some say it is because the country is in debt due to the policies of Vogel, but it seems rather unfair to blame one who has not even been a member of parliament, let alone its leader, for so many years. What is clear, though, is that the great hopes that pervaded during his time in office, hopes generated mainly by the prosperity of the South Island with its wool and its gold, have mostly vanished. Some have despaired that those years of relatively easy wealth have gone forever. Some settlers, quite large numbers in fact, have left these shores and sought their fortune elsewhere.

It is a number of years now since provincial government was abolished. When the question was being considered, there was much debate in the newspapers concerning the likely results. I was one of those who feared that Taranaki might lose some of its particular character if it were to be denied the right to make decisions for itself, yet what right did I, a mere woman, have for entertaining an opinion on the issue? These were matters that could only be decided by the men who sat in parliament and those who had the ear of such men – mostly the bigger farmers and town businessmen, and certainly not their wives, nor even those who worked for them.

When I was little more than a girl in England, soon after I finished my schooling, I spent a few months assisting the local vicar in his pastoral work. What I saw then were examples of poverty that repelled me. Yet my reaction was not to question the reasons for such poverty, but simply to try to overcome my fastidious nature and to fulfil my charitable duties while ignoring the wretchedness of the conditions under which the poorest people in the village lived. I accepted without question the privileged position I myself occupied within our small rural society and looked upon the poor as being irritatingly needy by their very nature. That, I believed unthinkingly, was simply the way things were.

But my experience here, in this country, has shown me that that is not the way things have to be. Many of the settlers who have arrived here have come from impoverished backgrounds, but they have come with the hope that this country will give them and their children the chance to live secure and rewarding lives. To be, in other words, equal to those who in England might have been seen as their inevitable and deserving betters. And there is encouraging evidence here that these worthy aims are indeed achievable and are being achieved. To take one apparently trite example – the

185

community picnics and sporting events that take place here are characterised by a lack of class awareness and by an easy comradeship that is heartening. Though there are exceptions, unfortunately. There is still a small section of our little community who seem to believe that they have some God-given right to a higher place in society and to be accepted as naturally superior and worthier to rule.

It is in our nature as human beings to put 'me and mine' before all else, yes, but surely it our duty as Christians, or simply as human beings, to also want the best for 'thee and thine', and to create a society where no one at all is impoverished or powerless?

I cannot talk of such matters as these with Tom. Our ideas are too far apart. Even Clement and I cannot talk freely on the topic. On the few occasions when I have tried to talk of the way I feel, he has listened to me but his responses have been condescending. Or so they have seemed to me. But Hannah and I do share our views, and on this as in so many other things, those views are close. What is more, she has taught me new ways of looking at the issues. Maori ways, I suppose. And I believe I have similarly made her see that at heart our notions of what an ideal society should be are not very different at all.

Of late, Hannah has been going more and more frequently to visit with her whanau, her wider family, and to remake connections in her home village that circumstances had weakened. She tells me that there seems to be a new spirit growing amongst the people of her tribe, a spirit of optimism and determination that has rather miraculously arisen out of the miseries caused by the loss of lands to the settlers backed by the government, and by the resulting conflicts and defeats. She has lately re-visited the large village to the west of this

186

town, which she calls Repanga but is mostly known today as Parihaka, where numbers of her people and others affected by the troubles have come together under the leadership of men who preach peace and co-operation, and who believe that Maori and settler can and should mutually respect each other's ways. These leaders are also strongly of the belief that there must be no further loss of their lands, and that some of the lands reputedly confiscated after the earlier troubles were taken without proper authority.

Last year, several men from this community went out to plough and fence some of those lands and thus to demonstrate their view that the sales or confiscation had been unjust and illegal. Some were arrested and jailed, but since then it has been agreed to establish a commission to discover whether or not the land confiscations were justified. This development is evidently the reason for the new spirit of optimism at Parihaka; and indeed, it is surely in the interests of all that a solution is found that is acceptable to settler and Maori alike. But just weeks ago, some men and boys from Parihaka were sent out to repair fences that had been pulled out by soldiers who had been told to build a road through those disputed ancestral lands, and as a result, some hundred or more of them were arrested and jailed. Despite this, the spirit of optimism, Hannah tells me, is still strong. The people seem to believe that Te Whiti's methods will eventually bring success.

Hannah shares in the spirit of optimism regarding these matters. Alas, while I fervently hope that she is right, I cannot but fear there will be harder times still ahead for Taranaki, and that those hard times will be borne mostly by Hannah's people –although it deeply saddens me to think it.

Jamie

We have this propensity to apply an adjective to decades as though each and every ten years that passes has its own special character. It's not true, of course. A decade is an artificial construct, and time itself is seamless. But by the time the nineties come around, it seems the eighties, for example, are to be remembered as the decade of Thatcherism, or, in this country, Rogernomics, after Roger Douglas, who, as Minister of Finance, engineered the ideologically-driven changes that have fundamentally altered the direction our country is taking.

When I look at the politics of our country and I see what seems to me to be an outright betrayal of the notion held by many early settlers, such as my own great-grandmother, a notion that is also at the heart of much (though not all, it must be admitted) of the culture of the Maori -- the vision of an inclusive society, a co-operating and compassionate society, a society and a partnership of equals – I become angry and depressed. The fact that I have chosen not to have many contacts with the world outside my family really just adds to this. I have no one to debate the issues with. I listen to the radio, watch television, read the papers and become increasingly frustrated by what I see and hear.

I know that Tela has many of the same values as I, but she doesn't seem to be afflicted by quite the same emotions. She is a pragmatist, I suppose. That weasel word. Where I rant and rave over the injustices reflected in the system that now operates in this country – user pays, the privatisation of the precious communal assets that have been bequeathed to us by those who dreamed of better things for us collectively, the exploitation of the resources of the land for private or corporate profit, the threatened handover of even our education system to those who would see it as a means of increasing the wealth of already rich investors – she simply adjusts to the prevailing conditions, making what she deems to be the best of the situation that now prevails.

At least, though, she does not allow herself to become a victim of the pressure to buy, buy, buy. We are modest in our material requirements, both of us. She allows me to indulge Gus a little, but we do not indulge ourselves unduly. And Gus is herself well aware that many of those things that her peers or the telly advertisers tell her are necessary for her happiness are not that at all -- that they are, rather, shackles designed to enslave us and to ensure that we carry out our true function (as the masters of the universe conceive it) to consume, consume, consume, and to borrow the money so that we can continue to do so and thus to fill the pockets of the bankers and their client capitalists.

And so I rant, rant, rant -- in my head if there's no one around to hear me.   And there usually isn't.

It is late winter of 1990, Gus's last year at Mapledene. I have driven up to Auckland to see the School's First XI Hockey team play in a secondary schools tournament, my dislike of Auckland traffic being overcome by my strong desire to see Gus lead the Mapledene team.

And a great little tournament it is, with Mapledene winning their division and Gus playing like a demon, all concentration and authoritative commands.

Afterwards, in my room at the motel into which the team has been booked, and we parent hangers-on too, Gus and I settle into one of our frank conversations that cover just about everything from the meaning of life to the inadequacies (still) of the Mapledene cuisine.

"So," I say. "A few more months and a you're a schoolgirl no longer. How does that feel?"

She shrugs. She's in mufti, wearing a tattered but favourite natural wool jersey that her Aunt Jenny knitted for her years ago. Judging by this and the holey jeans and sloppy tops that I've seen other girls in the team wearing, it seems shabby and well-worn must be the current fashion.

"Yeah, well. It was always going to happen."

"And it's been worth it, you think? Better than being at home and going to Girls' High or somewhere? Better teachers? More fun?"

"Most of the teachers are really good, but the teachers in the schools back home probably are, too. It's something else, a lot of other things. You know. I wanted to go to boarding school. And I suppose I'm glad I did."

"And you've made good friends."

"Yeah. Though probably none as good as Nora."

Nora Watene, her friend from Primary and Intermediate. She'd gone to boarding school, too – but to Turakina. At first, Gus had said that that was where she wanted to go, too, but she had been persuaded to go to her mother's old school easily enough. She and Nora still get together over the holidays, though. On those occasions, they don't greet each other with the sort of hysterical excitement that seems to be the usual habit of other teenage girls when they meet up with friends again after months, or even in some cases just a few hours, of being apart. Nora and Gus simply resume where they had left off. They are more like members of the same family.

"Livvie?"

"Yeah, she's cool. And Rosie. Quite a few of them, really. Blaise is another one."

"Blaise?" I can't recall that name being mentioned before.

"Yeah. You've seen her. The really pale girl with wispy blonde hair. She's so pale that if she stood up against a white wall, she'd just about disappear."

A good description. I now know who she is talking about. "So that's her name. Blaise. She's not here though, is she? She's not in the team?"

"God, no! She doesn't play hockey. Poor old Blaise. She

190

wouldn't last five minutes on the hockey field."

"Bit of a wimp, then."

"Yup. But nice. She only started at Mapledene at the beginning of last year, and she was a Day Girl at first. But this year she's been a boarder. Her room's next to mine, so I've got to know her quite well."

"That's good."

"Yeah, she's cool, too. But you know what? Once I got to know her a bit, she told me that her mother made a point of telling her that girls like me shouldn't be allowed at Mapledene. We had a laugh about that."

"Girls like you?"

"Brown girls."

"Oh." I bristle with protective anger. "But not Blaise herself?"

"No. Hell no, not her. She and I even devised a fiendish plot to teach her mother a lesson. The next time her mother came to see Blaise at school – she does that whenever she can just to keep an eye on her, Blaise reckons – we pretended we were the greatest buddies ever. Blaise told her mother that she was sorry, that she knew she didn't think she should be friends with someone like me, but that she couldn't be without me. That we were true bosom friends. We even held hands, and gave each other air kisses. All very OTT."

"And?"

"At first you could see that her mother was really pissed off. But then she saw the joke. I think she felt ashamed of herself. She's actually quite nice. We get on well now. She even invited me to lunch with them one weekend."

"Gus the Piss-taker, eh? Good on you."

"Well… you know. I just like to… be myself. I'm happy enough with the way I am, and I can't do anything about it even if I wasn't. That's why I try to understand why people behave stupidly instead of just sounding off at them when they do. Blaise is gay, by the way."

"Oh?"

"Yeah. She's known she's gay for ages. She's even told her Mum. We talk about what it's like, being gay, and I sort of agree with her that our bodies – girls' bodies – are more interesting and aesthetically pleasing."

"I can't disagree there."

"But in case you're thinking... For me, even a glance at a fit boy's buttocks is enough to send waves of lust through me."

"Really?"

"Well... bit of an exaggeration. But you can be reasonably confident that I'll push out a grandchild or two for you in due course, conceived in the usual way. And that I'll get considerable pleasure from the start of the procedure. At least, I'm assuming I will. I hope I will."

"But you don't... know?"

"No, Dad. I'm just assuming for now. And you can be sure that I won't be telling you when it becomes more than an assumption."

Our daughter. In control of her life. A seventeen-year-old Sybil.

Later in the day, I get permission from the Deputy Head, who has accompanied the girls to the Tournament, to take Gus back in the car with me so that she can spend the weekend at home. It is another chance for conversation, and I'm grateful for it. It occurs to me that we probably wouldn't have pursued our talks in such depth and with such honesty had she stayed at home and gone to Girls' High. The fact that there would have been ample and ongoing opportunity to do so would probably have meant that we hardly did it at all.

"You know, Dad," she begins, as we settle to our journey, "one other thing that Mapledene has done for me is give me a better appreciation of Mum."

"Oh? That's good. But how?"

"Well, for the last five years, I've sat down in the Dining Hall and seen Mum's name on the Honours Board. And I've thought about it, and you know what I think?"

"Tell me."

"I think it was Mapledene that made her into a New Zealander. Mostly that, anyway. There she is, up on the Honours Board in what even I must admit is one of the best schools in the country. It would have given her a real connection, her experience there. With this country I mean. And thinking about it made me see that although she's sometimes been a fairly crap Mum, she's a strong woman who knew what she wanted and went out and got it. Even as a girl in a foreign country. And a brown girl at that."

I can't let her introductory comment pass, but I try to moderate my touch of pique. "You've called her that before, but I wish you wouldn't. She was and is everything else you said, but I think you're being unfair calling her a crap Mum, as you put it."

"Well… I don't mean it in a super critical sense. It hasn't done me any harm. In fact, it's probably done me good." She grins across at me. "God knows what I might have become if I'd had two doting parents! But open your eyes, Dad. Mum being the way she is was one of the main reasons why I was willing, in fact wanted to go to boarding school. I used to resent her virtually ignoring me, but I don't any more. People are what they are, and I know she has lots of other qualities. I can see them now where I didn't really before. I am grateful to her for giving birth to me and I admire her for what she's done in her life. But she was at times and still is… a bit remote. As a Mum, I mean."

I am still more than a little shocked at her assessment. Even though I've heard her go on about this before, I am certainly jolted to hear her bring it up again. It seems it must be something she has dwelt on a lot and not just a passing fancy. I almost feel as though she is wanting me to take sides on the matter but it is not something I can do. I want to preserve my image of them both.

"Well… of course she wasn't always there, but that's because her job meant she couldn't be. That's hardly her fault. Anyway, whatever she did or didn't do," I say, "you can't doubt that she thought it was in your best interest, even if you didn't. I'm sure you also love her."

She is silent for a while, then: "Yes. That too. Of course."

21

Tela

The Nineties have begun, and I'm thinking of Gus, and whether or not I have been a good mother to her. It is not, I admit, a question that I have ever given very much thought to; but on balance I think I have done sufficiently well by her. I am pleased, at least, that she shows every sign of becoming the strong, independent woman I hoped and I think always knew she would be. How much of this happy outcome is down to me? Probably very little. It's mostly down to herself. But though it has not been in my nature to be a constantly adoring mother, I have given her love and she knows it. Other than that I have expended most of my time and energy in my other world, the world that is mine alone. For me, it really could have been no other way.

What is my world? Or maybe I should start with an even more difficult question. I remember this question being put to me years and years ago by one of the girls at school, at Mapledene – one I had offended, I imagine because of my skin colour. I must have done something to trigger the latent offence she took at having to share her space with me. 'Who do you think you are?' she asked. Indignant. I had heard the colloquialism before, of course, but it had never before had such a direct effect on me as it did on that occasion. Who, indeed, did I think I was? I didn't answer the girl, of course. I turned away with my nose in the air – my normal response to insult.

Later I did think about it, but not in the way she had intended. Who am I? Now that is a question! But it is not one I can easily answer – no more, I suppose, than anyone can know themselves. I do know, though, that who I am determines how I view the world. And I know, therefore, that there are at least two 'I's. One 'I' is truly independent and single minded. It is the 'I' that has brought me to where I am in my career. It is the 'I' that finds fulfilment and satisfaction in books and the worlds inside their covers. It can easily shut out the rest of the world, this 'I', but it can also happily point out to others the joys of this alternative world it inhabits. It is the 'I' that has extended its range to find a commitment to and an excitement in teaching.

But the other part of me, the other 'I', participates in, I suppose, the 'real' world – and from that world it sometimes gets another sort of satisfaction altogether. Jamie and Gus and Fi inhabit that world. It is a world I have some control over but one that can also be unpredictable and capricious. It is the world of my physically based senses and emotions. I do not altogether trust it. In that world it is as though I have to be, I am, another person. But I am not, of course. That other person is just as much 'me' as the one whose mind moves freely, safely, confidently (for most of my life it has been confidently) in the realms of literature, and who is its enthusiastic ambassador.

For a long time I used to think that those who did not share my passion for literature, especially for the literature of the nineteenth century, were somehow deficient in intellect. I knew, I still know, that those who shun the opportunity that is there for all of us to pick up a novel by Charlotte Bronte, or Gustave Flaubert, or Anthony Trollope, or by any one of a large number of other novelists who created whole worlds into which we can enter and roam are missing one of the surest ways of enriching their lives. I do now have a greater understanding of the myriad reasons why so many people are unable or choose not to do so, and I understand that it is not always, indeed it is not really at all a matter of intellect. For many it is largely a matter of having little time to do so – their lives are taken up with the business of survival for themselves and their families, and when they do have time they find it simpler to let visual images and spoken words entertain them.

These are a poor substitute though, or so I believe. Not enough is left to the imagination, for the stimulation of those creative impulses that are surely the true mark of our uniqueness as a species. I am fortunate indeed that I have been able to indulge my passion, and make my living by doing so.

And I know that many who do read choose to read only modern literature. Fantasy, romance, crime, or science fiction, perhaps. Sometimes I pick up such a book myself just to keep in touch with what is being written and hoping, perhaps, to find some sign that there are in the world of today writers of a genius comparable to the great novelists of the nineteenth century. And there are writers of talent in the world of today, I grant. But there are no great novels. Not a single one that I have discovered. Not novels of the classic sort. I am with those critics who claim that the last great novels, novels that carry on the tradition established by Jane Austen and William Thackeray and Henry James, novels that re-create the worlds they knew or imagined, worlds that in most essentials are exactly like our own and that are populated by people just like you or me and that take us into the minds of those characters, allowing us to become them, to be enriched by them, to learn from them, to suffer with them, to experience everything with them (or almost everything – I admit that the 'respectable' Victorian writers were not permitted to describe certain life events) were written no later than early in the twentieth century, and that nothing published since bears comparison.

But… who do I think I am, to make such a claim? I am a woman of over fifty years whose own world is passing, a woman whose mother was a Fijian villager and whose father was a part-European Foreman at a Sugar Mill; a woman who, as a girl, knew little beyond the dusty compound where she lived and who played like an urchin with a group of tearaway boys. But… but I was also a little girl who very early discovered the magic created by words on paper and who quickly harboured a desire to read everything she could lay

197

her hands on. A little girl who developed a passionate, unquenchable love for the novelists who had lived a hundred years or more before she was born.

So... who am I to make such a claim? Well, I suppose the answer to that is that I am better qualified than most to do so. Yes, I am. I am. If I am not, then my life has meant nothing. Nothing at all, except... except for the living evidence I existed. Except for Gus.

It is Gus's final year at secondary school, at Mapledene. She has come back with her father after a Hockey Tournament up north to spend a weekend at home. On Sunday afternoon, when Jamie must take her back to school, I decide to go with them.

I have only infrequently been able to find the time to go up to Mapledene while Gus has been there. It's not that I don't want to. I enjoy seeing the old school again. Outwardly, at least, it has changed little since my days there. Even the uniform the girls wear is pretty much the same. It is not so much nostalgia I feel when I do visit, though, as a kind of relief. Seeing Mapledene is somehow reassuring to me. I suppose it is to me much as the sight of the white cliffs of Dover must be to a returning Englishwoman, or the Statue of Liberty to an American. The welcoming gates to the land of promise, or something like that.

We drop Gus off. Hearing her brief goodbyes and watching her walk away and disappear through the door of the familiar building renews a feeling of deep satisfaction. My daughter, following in my very footsteps.

As we drive away I tell Jamie: "I always enjoy these chances to see Mapledene again. It's a bit like what you felt on that trip we made to Taranaki, I think. Seeing Te Mata Peak and the Giant's Bite again is almost like a homecoming for me. It brings back to me my feelings when we'd drive back from the Finlay farm to start a new term. It was always exciting." I sigh, and it's not altogether theatrical. "There won't be the excuse or the opportunity to come back here for much longer."

He glances across at me, giving me a look I can't quite interpret. "You must regret not often being able to come along, to pick her up or drop her off. Go to her hockey matches and all that," he says.

I laugh. "No. I'm glad I've been able to leave most of that to you. But the occasional visit – that's been enjoyable."

He doesn't answer, and we travel through the town and out onto the main road, past all the apple orchards with their sales stalls closed up and deserted until the late summer harvest begins.

"Do you miss her while she's away from us? When you're away?" he asks, out of the blue. What's brought this on I wonder.

"Well… yes, of course I do. But sometimes it's also been something of a relief. Not having to worry about her. Her moods. Anyway, I know it's the best thing for her, not having me around all the time. She doesn't need me. She never has, really, except maybe at the very start. When she was suckling."

Those few words get me thinking about the three of us. Just thinking, so we travel on in silence again.

We are very, very different, Jamie and I. He needs emotional connections. If he is not making those connections directly, then he is certainly doing so in his head. I know this. He is, in a sense, goal-less otherwise. He is happy to drift along in the currents of his emotional soup. Or maybe I should call it an ocean considering how much he used to like Swinburne. Maybe he still does. He loves me, I know that. I have always known that, even before he did. And of course he loves Gus, every bit as much, though differently. We are his life. Nothing much else matters to him.

And I need him; but it is not so much an emotional need as a reasoned one. A logical one. The real world, the world outside my head, is something I have to deal with though I'd much rather not. In that world, this world, Jamie is my reference point. My constant. He is the one certainty I can always locate when I need to deal with the real world. It is not that I leave all the worldly decisions to him – far from it – but I know that he will be faithful to the decisions made whoever makes them. He'll deal with the nitty-gritty.

Why does Jamie love me? I think about this question, too, occasionally. The only answer I can come up with is that it's because he needs to love me. Only that, it seems to me, could explain his constancy despite the fact that I am so often unable or unwilling to give him more than my often preoccupied presence in return.

Gus, on the other hand... I know she doesn't need to love me. And that is a good thing, I think. On the other hand it gives me a warm glow to know that she does love me. In her own, Augustan way. And that means, in the normal run of things, not needing to display it. Which is rather like me, really.

"You okay?" I ask, a bit perturbed by his silence.

"Me? Yeah, yeah. Just thinking about Gus. Missing her already."

I smile to myself. Perhaps there is a little wryness in it, a little twinge of something else. But really, the world is as it should be.

22

Jamie

The old oriental plane trees along the Avenue have been removed by Council workmen. The debate over whether or not they should go was long and hard-fought. The practical reasons for getting rid of them were that they were not in good health, that their roots were destroying the pavement around them, and, most stridently, that there was a need to improve traffic flow by making the roadway wider, won out over sentiment and history. There were protests, though, right to the end. I have a photograph of Gus who was one of those who took temporary residence up in the trees to try to save them. She is looking down at the camera with a stubborn but resigned smile. It made the front page of the local newspaper. Gus the Warrior.

During the later nineties and the early years of the twenty-first century, after she has finished her undergraduate degree and begins to take on the world, we see Gus only periodically. Our lives, Tela's and mine, settle to new routines. I take on extra work as a proof-reader and editor for a local publisher. It is not particularly rewarding work in any way but it makes me feel that I am contributing a little more substantially to the family pot, and thanks to the internet it enables me to continue working entirely or almost entirely from my study.

Tela seems ever more absorbed in her teaching and her research, and she has certainly seemed rather more at ease with the situation at home since we have been by ourselves. She has never much liked distractions and although she clearly misses Gus – it is her achievements and adventures that are by far the most frequent topics of our conversation when we are alone together -- it is equally clear that she is in a sense relieved not to be exposed to the occasional and apparently inevitable disagreements between the two of them. Inevitable, because they are two strong and opinionated women whose opinions do matter to each other, though they would probably both dismiss that notion out of hand.

There's a fish and chip shop just up the road that caters to our needs at least once or twice a week. It's quite fun, opening the steaming packet on the living-room coffee table and sharing its contents while watching the six o'clock news. Licking our fingers and reaching for the tissue box. Our revised domesticity.

It is September, 2001.

"Even after seeing it over and over again, there's still something unreal about it, isn't there?" I say, wiping the grease and salt from my fingers. The noiseless images. The silvery fuselage of the plane seemingly swallowed by the building. Then later, the sudden but eerie collapse and the onrushing clouds of turbulent dust seeking passage through the canyon-like streets. The images are offered over and over again, inviting a vicarious sharing of the terror from the safety of a cosy couch remote from it all.

Tela doesn't comment. She has ceased watching and has picked up her book.

"I'm glad she's out of it," I try. Gus has been in the States but is now in Europe.

"She wouldn't have been in any danger, anyway," Tela says. "Not on the west coast. Nor if she'd been just about anywhere else in the country for that matter."

A perfectly reasonable observation; but I'm still relieved that our daughter is now on a different continent. Then the ever-present concern returns. "I think the whole world will change now. Become more dangerous. I won't be happy till she's back here."

Another page is flicked over, and she glances across at me before turning her attention to the revealed words. "The world is always changing," she says. "And always remaining pretty much the same. It'll always be bloody awful for some people, somewhere. Gus will look after herself."

Yes, yes. Of course she will.

Of course she did. She returns safe and sound and full of ideas. There are many days and nights of sharing the comfortable reassurance of her presence, of questions asked and sometimes answered. Many of her experiences she has already related to us in letters and emails, others she seems reluctant to say much about. There was a young man called Simon from San Francisco, who took her to Las Vegas in his T-Bird. "It was fun, sort of," she says. "But depressing, too. Simon wanted to stay another night, but I was very happy he'd run out of money." And another young man called Cristoforo (and I remember another Christophe in the hotel near Heathrow when she was seventeen) who took her to Arezzo to see Piero della Francesco's frescoes in the chapel there. "They are breath-taking," she tells us. "Out of this world. And Cristo…" she sighs, shaking her head at the memory. "He is gorgeous."

Safe and sound. She is safe and sound. That's all that matters.

She is now almost thirty, I realise. But she looks like a teenager still. She comes home laughing one mid-week afternoon, telling us that she and Nora had arranged to meet in the Esplanade Café for an ice-cream and a catch up, and while they'd been strolling around the gardens afterwards a Truancy Officer had approached them and asked what school they were from and whether their absence was legitimate.

I laugh with her. I am not surprised.

She stays at home with us for a few months, then finds a place in a flat with some other young adults of around her age, a household with a fluctuating ratio of both men and women. It's not so very far away from us, just the other side of the

Square. It is almost like having her at home still while allowing her to continue her own life.

The biggest news of the year 2005, for a few days in April at least, is not related to politics or terrorism or even the Prince of Wales being greeted by protesting bare-breasted women on his tour of New Zealand, but to my old friend Cossy.

'Police Conduct Raid on Major Drug Operation in the Coromandel', the Dominion headline reads; and that night, the same item leads on TV One's Six O'Clock News. At first no names are revealed, but the description of one of the properties raided as 'fronting as an export orchid business' immediately brings Cossy to mind. Later, the name of the principal behind the operations is indeed revealed as 'Gideon Job Cosswill'.

Gideon Job? My first thought on reading this information is not so much surprise at Cossy being named as the principal – I had already come to terms with that probability – as the inappropriateness of his given names. They sound Jewish and ancient and supremely dignified. They seem wholly unsuited to the man I know. Then I think of Fagin. Yes, I suppose Cossy as a sort of Fagin is not so far-fetched.

There's a photo of him, too. 'Cosswill, the sixty-eight year old superannuitant and alleged master-mind, whose name suppression has been lifted', the caption says. And it's Cossy, alright. Lean of face, his expression unreadable. Or perhaps there is just a hint of quizzical surprise in his look, eyebrows raised.

Much later in the year, Cossy comes to trial. It is covered enthusiastically by all the media. The full extent of his activities is revealed. It is mainly cannabis, but evidence is presented that demonstrates his involvement in other drugs as well, including cocaine and heroin. Overwhelming evidence, it seems. The police had been conducting clandestine operations for many months prior to his arrest and the case against him is solid.

The verdict is guilty. It is a surprise to no one. All his property is confiscated, and he is sentenced to fifteen years. He doesn't appeal. Cossy, brought low. It seems to me that the world is out of joint. Cossy the Untouchable. Cossy the All-Knowing.

Cossy, my friend, has been put away.

Through it all, I wonder what I should do. Clearly there was nothing I could do while the trial was on, but now that it is over... Should I write to him? At least let him know that I... that I what? I suppose, that I am thinking of him. But he would probably laugh at that. What good is it to him that I am thinking of him. Besides, he has been revealed as a criminal, involved in a particularly harmful activity, vicious and uncaring.

But he is still Cossy. I suppose, looking back, I must have been aware that he was capable of such things. At the very least I knew him as secretive in his habits. Mysterious, even. But he was Cossy, my friend. I liked him. He knew that. He not only accepted that, he took me in as a sort of protégé. He certainly never wished me any harm. He even encouraged me away from stupid or illegal activity when, as a first-year student, I'd hinted I'd like to place a bet on the horses with him when I learned he was putting himself through University by running an illicit book-making operation. Save your money, he said, it's a mug's game.

I decide to share my quandary with Tela. We have talked of him occasionally, especially since the shock of his arrest and his trial. She has never met him, though.

"What do you think I should do about Cossy?" I ask

"What do you mean? There's nothing you can do for him, is there? He's been tried, convicted and sentenced."

"Well, yes. But do you think I should write to him? It might cheer him up or something. Just to let him know that I still think of him as a friend."

She shrugs. "Do you still think of him as a friend?" She sounds unbelieving.

"Yes. Yes, I do. I don't like what he did, but... I'm somehow not surprised. It's sort of... Cossy. Taken to extremes."

"Then... If you think you should write to him, just do it."

Not much help there, then. But I do write, on an arty post-card I pick up at my favourite bookseller's in George Street. It features a reproduction of an Albert Durer self-portrait. I've often thought Cossy looks a bit like Durer. Except for the long hair, of course. Cossy and long hair don't go together at all.

I agonise over what I should put on the card. Agonise, and grin a bit to myself at some of the possibilities that occur to me. 'Enjoy your stay.' 'Backed the wrong horse, eh Cossy?' 'Still getting someone else to cook your meals, then?'

But I just put down a few cautious and probably cowardly words, the sort of thing that won't even raise a grin for Cossy but that won't let whoever else might read them think that I'm somehow complicit in his misdeeds and so add my name to the suspicious character list. If there is such a thing. 'Let me know if there's anything I can do for you, Cossy,' I write. But I add: 'Within the bounds of the law, of course.' And I think of a few more words, something along the lines of: 'I'll be remembering the help you gave me, and your usually sound advice. I'm sad at the thought that you are where you are. I'm your friend, always.' But I hesitate, then decide not to put them down. They are too corny by far. Cossy would dismiss them, probably with a sneer.

I send the card off but I don't hear back from him – but I never really expected to. That wouldn't have been Cossy's style.

Then two years later Cossy is in the news again, but not front page this time. Still, it is a reasonably long column in the papers and it did make it onto the first bulletin of TV News.

His body was discovered in his cell one morning. A heart attack was the presumed cause of death, but an autopsy is to be held. Readers and viewers are reminded briefly of the reasons for his incarceration. With a certain inevitability the most salacious of the popular bloggers posts the news as: 'Notorious Drug Lord meets his end. Was it revenge?'

Later, a few words report that the cause of death was indeed a heart attack with no evidence of inducement. Veil drawn. Episode over. Exit Cossy from my life.

But not quite. A few weeks later still, I receive a parcel by courier. The sender's name and address is scrawled and illegible, except for the city. It has been sent from Auckland. I open the package to find inside, carefully wrapped in sheets of polystyrene foam and bubble wrap, the still-framed drawing by Turner that had made my heart skip a few beats when I had first seen it hanging on the wall in Cossy's luxurious bach in the Coromandel.

I stare at it unbelievingly. After the initial shock I study it, holding it with great reverence. There is no doubt about it. It is indeed the exact drawing, precisely as I remember it. J.M.W. Turner. By his hand.

My own hands are now shaking with the knowledge of what I am holding. I put it down on the kitchen bench and look again at the packaging it had been wrapped in. I see then that there is a postcard amongst the discarded material – a postcard depicting exquisite orchids. I turn it over to find no signature but just ten words written in violet ink: 'What are you going to do with this, young James?'

The last laugh. I can almost see him as he was in the old days, back there in Christchurch, raising his head from his book in amusement at my latest bit of angst. 'Go and read some Dorothy Parker. Either that or put the kettle on. Make yourself useful,' he'd say.

What a bloody question! Damn you, Cossy. I need you to tell me what I should do with this. Except, of course, I know what your answer would be. And I'm not 'young James' any more. I'm sixty-seven years old, and I'm holding an original art work by J.M.W Turner that has possibly been stolen, and that has certainly been obtained through unofficial channels.

What am I going to do with it?

I pick the drawing up again and hold it at arm's length. It is a masterpiece, as was everything that Turner ever did. A minor masterpiece, true, but a masterpiece nonetheless. Utterly, totally, perfect of its kind. The rarest of treasures.

What am I going to do with it?

23

Tela

At the age of thirty-five, Gus at last seems to have established a long-term relationship. Not that either Jamie or I have been putting any pressure on her. Even Jamie accepts that that part of her life is entirely her own. But I must admit that I had been occasionally thinking how nice it would be to have a grandchild. Now, a year or so after this partnership began, that occasional yearning on my part has become rather stronger.

My desire is indicative of something of a shift in the way I have been viewing the world lately. I know I have the legacy of my work, of my books and articles, but this no longer seems to be quite the justification for my life that I once imagined it would always be. Besides, literary criticism appears these days to be going down paths I have no wish to follow. It is altogether too clever, in the worst sense of that word. Smart and superficial. That's how much of it seems to me, anyway.

This year, 2007, I went on what I fancy will be my last overseas conference. It was in England once again, this time at a redbrick university in the Midlands. There were very few of my contemporaries there. Instead, the conference was dominated by a new and awfully young crop of academics and I felt somewhat out of place. I felt as though the treatment I received from the organisers was warm enough but unmistakably condescending, as though my name was known and that perhaps even some of my work was still being read but that I was a relic from a time that had passed. I suppose you could say that I felt my age.

So when I returned home I turned my thoughts with even greater hope to Gus, and the possibility of a legacy of what would surely be of a rather more enduring sort. And these days my hopes have taken on this rather firmer shape as it appears that at last she has established a proper connection (to use the term that Jane Austen might have used) with an apparently worthy man.

Gus's partner Max – his full name is Maximiliano – is Chilean and Irish by birth and nine or ten years older than Gus. He is quite tall but very thin. Almost skeletal, I thought when Gus first brought him home, but closer acquaintance leads me to think of him rather as sinewy. His physical attributes could be partly down to what Gus tells me is his passion for mountain-climbing. He wears his slightly greying reddish hair long, in one of those surprisingly alluring pony-tails. They've been together now for over a year. Better still, Max has recently bought a Victorian-era weatherboard house from a legacy left by his mother and Gus has moved out of the flat where she has been living and into the nest that Max seems to want to give her. To give them. A nest. And nests require filling.

So the signs are good, though when I tentatively suggest the possibility of a child to Gus the 'mind your own business' glance she gives me is unmistakable. "Plenty of time for that, if we decide that's what we want," she says; curt and dismissive. But is there? She is about to start the second half of her thirties. I don't remind her of that, though. I don't want my head bitten off.

Max is a freelance photographer and cameraman. They met up at the Polytech where Gus occasionally helps out, and through their mutual interest in film-making they began to meet quite frequently. So that is how it began. He seems steady enough though rather serious and intense. He speaks Spanish, of course, but he and his mother evidently came to this country when he was around ten years old so he speaks fluent English with just a trace of his mother's Irish accent but mostly with only the inevitable New Zealand one.

Ah yes! A grandchild or two or three would be nice. I occasionally wish they would marry but I dare not even mention that wish to Gus. Anyway, I do have considerable sympathy with the modern attitude to the institution.

There's no getting away from it; I am beginning to feel some of the effects of my advancing age. Mentally, that is. Physically, I suppose I have long begun to feel them. But I am… sixty-seven? Yes, sixty-seven, I think. Not really such a big age, yet I am having to put in much greater effort, mentally, to achieve the things that once came very easily. Martialling thoughts. Remembering quotes. Thinking things through to the appropriate end. Devising elegant turns of phrase. My teaching still comes easily but my research is more difficult than it was.

Gus and Max come to see us quite frequently. I think Gus still has the habit of thinking of this as her true home. The conversation over dinner on this particular occasion, a special dinner cooked by Jamie and featuring a lamb roast with one of his domestically famous sauces, is becoming a little awkward. Gus appears to be angry about something. Exactly what, it is hard to tell. Max seems to be trying to humour her but she is not responding to his efforts with anything other than quick glances loaded with censure.

"Is everything okay with you two?" I ask Gus; and Jamie immediately gives me a 'back off' look. But I ignore him. I want to know.

"Yes, Mum."

"Oh, good. I just thought…"

"Gus is not all that happy with me at the moment," Max says. "Right?" His head is lowered and he's looking uncertainly at Gus as he speaks.

"You could say that," Gus, says. There follows a rather heavy silence, but after a few seconds she puts down her fork and sighs, seemingly resigned to making some sort of explanation. "It's nothing really. Just me being selfish."

"No it's…" Max begins.

"Yes it is," she snaps; then she turns to me. "Max is planning a trip next year. An expedition. To Peru."

"Oh?"

"There's this mountain he wants to climb. Someone called it the most beautiful mountain in the world, so of course he wants to... climb all over it. Get on top. What's it called again?"

"Alpamayo. Or Shuyturaju. It's got the two quechua names," Max replies. He can't quite disguise his enthusiasm though I sense that he wishes he could. "It's in the Cordillera Blanca," he adds, rather lamely.

"Peru? Have you done any climbing there before?" I ask.

"I did a bit in the Chilean Andes a few years back with the same friend I'll be doing the climbing with this time. He's Canadian. But no, I haven't climbed in Peru before."

"Is it... particularly dangerous, then? Is that's what's worrying you, Gus?"

"No. Well, a bit, maybe. But he'll have to be away for six weeks or so. Setting things up. "

"So? You don't want to be alone in the house that long?"

She snorts her derision. "I don't care about that. It's just..." She looks at him, faintly accusing, but also, now, with an element of forgiveness or at least resignation. "We... usually do things together. We were going to do some kayaking around Golden Bay. I suppose we still can. But this trip is going to cost a lot of money. We'll have to put other things off. And it's... well, mountains. It's something we can't sort of... share. I like to look at them but I've never been at all interested in climbing the bloody things. I don't really understand it."

"That's a bit lame. Besides. I suppose a trip over there will give Max time to catch up with some of his family in Chile on the way." I say. "Will it, Max?."

212

He shakes his head. "I don't have any family left there, except for some distant cousins I've never known. No, I'd just be going over for the mountain."

"Another friend from Christchurch was going to go with them," Gus adds. "He and Max have done a lot of the Southern Alps together. But now he's pulled out. Right?"

"Yes. We'd been planning to do this for... for a long time. But he's... decided it'd be too hard to take the time off. Too many... other commitments."

"Yeah. Like a wife and two young kids," Gus says. She looks at Max. "Sorry. I'm just being selfish." She takes a sip of her water, then announces to the table generally: "I find it hard to understand how anyone can get so obsessed about climbing mountains. But that's me."

"Didn't someone famously say it's because they're there?" Jamie says. He wants to lighten the mood, I know. "Was that Ed Hillary?"

Max looks a little uncomfortable, but answers: "Actually, it was George Mallory. An Englishman. But he was talking about Everest, so... near enough."

"Yeah, and look what happened to him," Gus mutters.

Max is still looking uncomfortable, as though he wishes the topic had never been raised. He clears his throat; then: "This'll probably be the last serious bit of climbing I'll do. In fact, I promise it will be. Anything overseas, anyway. After this, I'll give all my attention to... things closer to home." And he gives her an apologetic look and a half grin that speaks more effectively than any further words could.

And I know exactly what he means. At least, I hope I do. But Gus and her expectations will be a bigger challenge for him than any mountain. I have no doubt of that.

24

Jamie

It is a Saturday in July of 2008, cold and windy, and Gus has come around to see us. She is pregnant with our grandchild. A granddaughter, we're told. The very sight of her lifts my spirits.

"Any news from Max?" I ask.

"I had a text. He's in a place called Huarez. It's the closest town to the bloody mountain, evidently. They'll be another six or seven days before they even start on it."

Not a happy Gus, then. "Everything else going well, though?" Everything else. We both know what that is. She is just starting the third trimester.

"Yes. I suppose."

I look at her again. She is concentrating on something, totally oblivious to my attention. It gives me a chance to examine her face. There is a tension in her features, an anxiety of a sort I have never before noticed. But that is understandable, surely. She is temporarily on her own at her place. Alone and pregnant and still busy with work.

"You could move back here, till he gets back," I say, hopefully.

She looks up at me then but seems to take a while to process my offer. Finally she says: "Oh God, no. Sorry. Thanks, but no. That would not be a good idea. It's only another three or four weeks till he's back, and there'd have to be too much rearranging of timetables and things if I left and then went back again. I've got all my stuff there, and people know where I am if they need me."

"Well, the offer's there."

"Thanks, Dad."

I am not happy that Max has gone off on his mountain-climbing expedition and left Gus, especially at this time, but

I'm also very conscious that I must tread carefully and not tell Gus of my concern. I have decided that I like Max, but it has taken me some time to come to that conclusion, and there are some things about him that worry me a little.

For one thing, he is nine years older than Gus. This is not so important in itself, I suppose – but it is what happened to him in those extra nine years of life that does ring some alarm bells with me. Those were his first nine years, of course, the years he lived in Chile as a child. By cautious questioning of Gus and of Max himself I have learnt that his mother and father were both very active supporters of President Allende -- left-wingers, and therefore marked as enemies of the Pinochet regime that with the connivance of the CIA overthrew Chile's democratically elected government in 1973. Max's father was one of hundreds, maybe thousands shot dead by army units in the days after the coup, and Max and his mother went into a terrified hiding before managing to escape to Ireland.

Both his mother and father were medical doctors, it seems, who had first met at the Dublin School of Medicine when both were studying there. It is not so strange that his father had travelled to Ireland to receive his medical training, as his family, too, was partly Irish in origin. Then not long after escaping to Ireland Max's mother decided to emigrate to New Zealand. Here she had first been a GP on the West Coast of the South Island then later made a move to Hamilton when Max had finished his secondary schooling. Max's early years, then, had been marked by disruption and loss.

But he does seem steady enough. I probably have no need to worry, particularly because he is clearly very patient with Gus; as well as being supportive and very much in love with her, of course. As he should be.

It is just one week later, and I am sitting in my office peering at the screen, proofreading a dense and exceedingly boring academic text on international trade when I hear the front door slam. I raise my head, listening, but there is no other sound. I am just a little concerned as Tela is at work and no one else, apart from Gus, is likely to have made such an entry. I leave what I am doing and go down the stairs.

Gus is there just inside the door, standing stock still. Soundless. I stay by the stairs, watching. A huge dread floods me, but at first I have no sense of why. She looks up and sees me.

"He is dead," she says. Each word is enunciated clearly, the faintest of pauses between each one. Then she is suddenly in motion, running past me to the door of her old bedroom, then through it, closing it firmly behind her. I am wordless. It has all been said. Those three words. From behind the door I hear a series of muffled groans, of whimpering. There could be no clearer sign to me. Keep out. Keep out. Wait. Wait.

So I wait. I go to the living room and wait. I listen, fine-tuned, and I wait. There is only one person it could be, the one person who has put himself in danger. Max.

I wait. I wait.

She comes into the room and walks up to the mantelpiece over the fireplace. She doesn't look at me.

"Max?" I ask, quietly. Of course I know the answer.

She keeps her back to me and takes in a wrenching gulp of air. "Yes." Choking.

She turns to me then and I take a step towards her, but she gestures with both hands, stopping me, rejecting me, shaking her head. I stop.

We both stand there, separated by no more than a pace. "I want him, not you," she says.

"I know. I know."

Then at last she surrenders, moves into me, and I hold her shivering body. "I want him, Dad," she says, barely coherent. "But he's gone. He's gone." Then her voice strengthens with anger. "Stupid bastard. Stupid, stupid fucking bastard. I hate him. I hate him."

Then she pushes me away and turns back to the mantelpiece, holding the edges of it, her knuckles white and her body sagging.

There is nothing more I can do but wait. Wait.

25

Tela

It is three years since Gus's Max was killed. We have a granddaughter, Jamie and I. Her name is Myfanwy, but she is always referred to as Vanu. She was born here in our house, Gus having moved back home soon after news of Max's accident had been confirmed and the terrible details related – the breaking away of a massive block of ice above them and the resulting fall of hundreds of metres and burial deep under the resulting avalanche. They had no chance.

So we are a family unit again, expanded by one.

The house is almost constantly noisy. Not just with Vanu's several voices – demanding or breathlessly excited or grizzling and every conceivable variation in between – but with the hum and thump of the washing machine and the roar of the clothes drier and the constant ringing of the telephone. Gus's friends or colleagues, mostly.

Mornings are the time when Gus and I manage, usually, to share our lives a little, just the two of us. We stand around in the kitchen together, me eating my toast, sipping my tea and crunching on my apple slices, Gus taking mouthfuls of her whole-grain natural muesli between dashes to the bedroom to put out Vanu's clothes for the day and supervise her toilet activity.

"Mum," Gus says. "I know I'm a nuisance, that we're a nuisance, and I don't clean up after myself often enough, but please don't just take my papers and things off the dining-room table and put them in random places. I can never find anything."

"I didn't…"

"Well someone did, and it's not likely to be anyone else."

"Why would I do that? That's ridiculous."

"I'm just saying, Mum. I'm not criticising. I know you don't like clutter. But things like that, if you could just ask me first. Tell me to move my backside and tidy up if you like. Just… please don't do it yourself. Not with my stuff."

I'm about to snap back at her self-righteousness, to make another denial, but then I recall all those many odd little problems I have been having lately. Problems with time and space. Well, not so much problems as gaps in my memory or ripples in my senses that upset my equilibrium for a moment or two. Nothing too serious, I thought at first. Nothing that influenced my daily activities to any great extent, or that prevented me functioning effectively. At first. But it has been getting worse, I can't deny that even to myself. Mostly, those absences, those gaps in my memory, fill in again. Given time. So… perhaps I did take things from the table, even though I now have no immediate memory of having done so.

And I have recognised a tendency in myself of late to react more strongly than usual to anything that smacks of unwarranted criticism. To take umbrage, and get worked up. I need to do what I have always done before – to step back and let things go. Not dwell on things.

I have read up on these symptoms. I believe I know what is happening to me, but having discovered the possibility, I have dismissed it from my mind. I do not want to think further about it.

"I wish you'd taught me Fijian," Gus now tells me, changing the subject. "All I know are a few of your swear words, and I can't use those when I go there."

She must be planning another trip. Maybe she thinks it's time to introduce Vanu to our Fiji family. She's occasionally been on about learning Fijian ever since she took a trip there on her own before she became pregnant. On that occasion she spent some of her time in the west of the island with her Fijian cousins, as well as in Suva with Margie and Ant. With Talei, too. Talei, who is long married with two children but evidently still very much a fun-seeker as she was when Gus and I made our visit together all those years ago. The last time I was ever in Fiji.

"You never asked me when you were younger," I say. "Anyway, there would've been little point being able to speak Fijian here."

"But it would've given me a better chance to get to know that side of me. I suppose you're right, though. I wouldn't have had much chance to use it here. It's just that… when I was there in the village I felt awkward that they were all making a big effort to talk to me in English when I know they would've been more comfortable if I'd been able to speak Fijian. I'm definitely going to learn."

"Good on you," I say. "I'll help you if I can. I'm not sure how much use I'd be. I haven't used my Fijian in years."

"But you were brought up bi-lingual. You can't have forgotten much. Not really."

"Well, it's probably there still. Somewhere."

Yes it is probably there, somewhere. It's not that I have never used the language here. I have involved myself with the small Fijian community in this city at times. Perhaps not as much as I should or could have; but I have often enough in the early days of our residence here gone along to their occasional gatherings, and I have shared news, shared jokes, mostly using Fijian to communicate. It has been with an increasing sense of alienation, though; from both the language and the culture. And I think that sense has been detected, too, by the Fijians here. I no longer receive notice of any gatherings and haven't done for years. I don't believe that is because they are no longer held; I think it is because I am no longer thought of as being one of them. I don't mind. I have brought that on myself, and it may well be that it is what I wanted.

But despite all that I am pleased that Gus is interested. Yes, she has probably learned those few swear words from me. When I am frustrated I still occasionally spit them out, unthinkingly. Not nice. And yes, I've heard Gus use some of those words, to my shame. But I'm glad that she is not content with just that. She speaks and reads French and she speaks and reads Maori, neither of which is part of her natural heritage. It is understandable that she should also wish to know Fijian, particularly because she seems determined to maintain contact with her Fijian cousins. I understand that, and I am glad she hasn't shut herself off from Fiji, from her cousins.

We are different in so many ways, Gus and I.

There is a shriek of impatience from down the hallway. It seems Vanu is having trouble getting dressed, calling for her mother. "Oh shit!" Gus says, spooning the last of her muesli into her mouth before rattling her bowl into the sink and racing off down the hallway to Vanu's bedroom.

26

Jamie

It is wonderful having Gus with us – Gus, and Myfanwy, my bees-kneesy granddaughter. She was born in the first week of November of 2008, and her birth had the salutary effect of helping Gus get over Max's death, and, for me, her new presence almost obliterated the resentment I felt at the National Party victory in the November election that year and at the country consequently having a Prime Minister whose sole qualification appears to be his success as a currency trader and thus making piles of money for himself and the American Bank in whose interest he did his gambling.

As the years go by our new domestic arrangements focus on the needs of a new baby, those needs all too quickly changing as she grows.

Now the first decade of this new century is over and we're well into the second. 2012. Twenty Twelve. We seem as yet undecided how to refer to the years of the current era. Some say Two Thousand and Twelve. Some say Twenty Twelve. Whichever way it is announced it is the year the Christchurch Recovery Plan is released, two years after the first of the two devastating and deadly earthquakes there. It is also the year we become truly aware that Tela's world has begun to fall apart.

Unlike the earthquakes, Tela's troubles creep up on her, in silent, incremental steps that at first no one even notices, least of all Tela herself, apparently. Or me. The falling apart of Tela is in the slowest of slow motions, allowing her, and allowing us to make adjustments in our minds so that the changes don't seem like changes at all. For we who are living the process, that is. For Tela, and for me. It is one who is removed from it just a little and who sees and wonders and becomes concerned. It is Gus who first brings it to my notice.

Yes, it is Gus, who is working furiously in her new job at the Polytech as well as directing a new play and being a mother to Vanu. Gus, who you would think thus had little time to pay attention to anything else outside her personal interests and obligations. She is the one who has observed. She has obviously been giving what she has seen and experienced some careful thought. She has drawn conclusions she wants to share with me.

"You need to persuade her to make an appointment with the doctor," she says. "It could be serious. It might be Alzheimers."

"Oh, come on Gus. She's always been a bit forgetful, particularly of things she doesn't place much importance on. It's really more like she ignores them."

"This is more than forgetful, Dad. She gets confused. I don't think she should even be driving."

Gus's concern is real, and I know from experience that when Gus shows concern, there is usually good reason. I start to think back to incidents that had puzzled me a little at the time, then passed out of my consciousness.

I remember, now, a recent incident when Tela and I were going shopping together. She was driving. I am normally quite happy to let her drive me around town even though she has never learned how to get into top gear. Around town, it doesn't matter so much. But on this occasion she was driving up Victoria Avenue heading for the Supermarket when she slowed down, pulled over to the side, and sat there with her hands on the wheel, the motor running.

"What's up?" I asked.

"Nothing," she said. "It's silly of me, I know… but… where are we going?"

"Supermarket," I said.

"Yes of course," she said. "Silly me."

But she continued to sit there for a while before she looked at me again, a frown on her brow. "How... how do we get there again?" she asked.

I chuckled. I still didn't see it as an incident of any significance. "Right at the second roundabout, then left at the next." I said.

"Of course," she said. And she put the car into gear and moved on.

I thought nothing more of it at the time. We all have those moments of forgetfulness, of confusion, don't we? But... yes, there have been a trickle of little episodes like that over the last few weeks. Or months.

"Just take her, Dad," Gus says. No doubt she can see the uncertainty in my features as I recall these things. "Even your GP should be able to give her some sort of a test to see if she needs specialist help. I think she does. In fact I'm sure of it."

Gus has no time for our GP who once, years ago, when he was still GP for the whole family and she went to discuss with him some issue to do with contraception asked her questions she thought he had no right to ask. You trample on Gus's sensitivities at your peril.

Later that day I suggest to Tela that it might be time for her to have a check-up.

"What for?" she says.

"Well... just a check up. You've been a bit forgetful lately. It's probably lack of sleep, but it's better to be sure. Don't you think?"

She looks at me. I imagine I can see a kind of resignation in her features, and perhaps a little fear as well. I get the sense that she herself must have become aware that she has been having difficulties.

"Yes. I haven't been getting as much sleep as I should, have I? That's probably it."

At least she is admitting to a problem. "So... will you make an appointment, or shall I make it for you?" Though she often professes to have little faith in the medical profession she will normally not hesitate to make a doctor's appointment for any minor problem she feels she has.

"I could just pick something up from the chemist," she says.

"They might be able to give you some advice, but they won't be able to give you anything really useful, you know that. Not without a prescription."

She is silent for a while, her eyes watching me closely. There is clear reluctance in them; but the resignation, the logic, wins out. "Alright," she says. "You phone. But make it for Thursday. I can't go today, or tomorrow."

Things move quickly after that, or so it seems to me. The doctor first gives her some simple tests then arranges a visit to the hospital, to a specialist. He doesn't say a great deal but there is that look of impersonal concern on his face when he ushers us out of the surgery.

We receive a letter informing of us of the time of the appointment at the hospital. We go there together, of course.

It is mainly a kind of interview, the specialist, a woman, taking notes and offering at first very little comment. After a time she appears to reach some sort of conclusion and I can tell by the way she glances at me that it is not one that I'm likely to want to hear.

She addresses both of us, and at the same time hands us explanatory brochures.

"We call it Mild Cognitive Impairment," she says. "MCI. At least in the early stages. But you'll see in the pamphlet it's also called dementia."

Dementia. The word hangs there like the sword of Damocles.

Tela appears to take the news calmly, but the word fills me with dread. The fact that it was dropped into the conversation so matter-of-factly makes it seem even worse. "What... what can be done," I ask.

The woman doesn't answer my question directly. "It will probably develop only slowly, though every case is different," she says, turning her attention to Tela. "There are many things you can do that might slow its progress. Or that will at least help you to... come to terms with it. There's quite a bit of information in those pamphlets. Routines that should be established. Like getting plenty of exercise. That sort of thing. Mental exercise, too. Some people find that crossword puzzles are helpful. And I can prescribe some medication that will help you deal with any anxiety you might feel. Some things are likely to become increasingly... difficult, you see. "

Tela nods, but it is as though she isn't really taking anything in. As though she is thinking the words might be true enough but that they don't have any reference to her.

Later, as Tela walks ahead of me along the corridor to the exit, the specialist has a quick word with me.

"You'll see that in the material I've given her the medical term dementia is used," she reminds me. As if I needed reminding. "But it's easier to think of it as Mild Cognitive Impairment. Easier when you have tell others, I mean."

"Dementia," I say. I want to vocalise the term, to put it out there while I face her alone, this specialist. There is a truth behind it that I don't want to accept but I need to know. "Is it... is it like Alzheimer's then?"

"There are many kinds of dementia. We can't put a name on your wife's form of it. Not yet. But it will get worse. You need to prepare for it. One thing you should do straight away – and I can't urge you too strongly when I say immediately – is arrange for Enduring Power of Attorney. If you leave it too long, you'll find the difficulties will have crept up on you and it will be too late."

"Too late?" I ask.

"Meaning that she won't be able to make necessary decisions herself – about her own well-being, her finances, all that sort of thing. I know that will be hard for you to accept, but I'm afraid it is so. She needs to agree now to give someone the power to make those decisions for her when the time comes. Someone she trusts."

She looks at me. I would really much rather not to have to even think about it. I don't even want to believe it.

"Right," I say, because she is clearly expecting some response.

"Your lawyer could arrange it. Or you could go to the Public Trust. Meantime I'll arrange for her to attend special programmes put on by a local charity. They're supported by the government and the local Council, so they won't cost anything. I'll need to see her again to talk about these things. She'll get a letter telling her of the time for her next appointment."

"Right."

"Has she been having any problems at work, do you know?"

"Not that I know of. She's been offered retirement."

"Yes. And?"

"She is going to take it. She'd decided on that already."

"That will be for the best, I think. And one other thing. She must not drive a car. That's definitely a no-no."

"Right." Our GP has already told her that. He has insisted on it. She has accepted that.

It won't go away. I now know it won't go away. But for the moment I must be positive. I must take her home and talk to her on the way as though nothing has changed. Tell her that nothing has changed.

And I do. I try to reassure her, tell her that we'll work around things. Make adjustments. It is easier than I thought it would be because she doesn't respond beyond just nodding her head. She clearly doesn't want to talk about where we've been and what has been said. It is as though she has forgotten all about it.

She retires from her University post, and the Department puts on a pleasant little do for her. People are very kind and positive. The speechmakers talk of her international reputation, her outstanding skill as a teacher, how much she will be missed and how she will always be welcomed and have a desk made available to her whenever she wishes to visit. Whether or not there is common knowledge of her condition is not clear to me but I sense that it might be when I detect a degree of extra sympathy in the manner of some of those who approach me.

It remains for me to decide how I should tell friends, hers in particular, or indeed whether I should tell them at all. In the end, I take the coward's way out. I decide not to broach the topic with anyone but to let them find out for themselves. I think perhaps I am still hoping it has all been a mistake. After all, age brings changes, everyone knows that. People of our age have our problems, all of us. Tela is just having problems. On the surface that is how I deal with it. I suppose I expect everyone else to do the same. Make adjustments. Explain if I have to but mostly just expect people to understand, to accept. Especially friends, our friends. Her friends.

In some ways Tela herself is taking it very well indeed. In her typical matter-of-fact way she has taken the retirement in her stride and adjusted to spending her days either at home or on her special programmes where she shares experiences and activities with others with the same problem. I notice, though, that she no longer makes any effort to contact many of her wider circle of friends. It is as though she would rather they did not see her as she is but only remember her as she was.

Tela's closest friend is Fiona Cameron, but we don't see her very often as she lives on a farm to the north of the city.

She does call in a few times a year, though, and when Gus was younger all three of us would sometimes go north to visit them on the farm. That was a habit we have largely dropped in recent years though Tela would occasionally make the trip by herself. Not any more now, of course.

Fiona. Fiona Finlay was her maiden name. That is how I, too, first knew her. Then she became Fiona Cameron, married to the man she had first met at a High School Ball. Or a Collegiate Ball, I should say, because Fiona and her husband are both from the ranks of the landed, the ranks of those who still send their children to boarding schools and retain other traditions that date back to an earlier, class-ridden vision of what New Zealand should be. Not that we are free of such inequalities today. Far from it in fact.

But Fiona herself is no snob. For years when I was myself a student I was a slave to the image of her that I had created in my mind. Perhaps I even vaguely wished that I, too, was from a landed family so that my wishful thinking had some chance of becoming a reality. I worshipped what I saw – a popular girl with honey-blonde hair and an easy, playful manner – but even more I worshipped the image of her in my mind that bore no relation to any reality. Fiona Finlay: a young woman in large part manufactured in my head and made all the more desirable because I considered her far beyond my reach.

Time has kept the same pace for all of us. She, too, is now in her seventies. But age hasn't changed the relationship between Fiona and Tela. I know that their friendship is significant to them both even though they are not often in each other's company these days, but despite this knowledge I cannot bring myself to phone Fiona and discuss Tela's affliction with her. I tell myself it will be best if Tela tells her herself. I know they still exchange phone calls and emails occasionally.

So I decide to let such matters take their course.

Many weeks later, Tela has become used to her day-long programmes of organised companionship and mental and physical stimulation. She goes twice a week. At first she had regarded the advice to do so with deep suspicion. Now, though, it seems she rather looks forward to the occasions or at least accepts them as some sort of necessity.

It is late in the morning after I have dropped Tela off at one of these sessions when Fiona knocks at the door. I am at home by myself, Vanu being at Day Care and Gus at work.

"Fi! Lovely to see you. Come in. Tela's at her programme, but come in and have a cup of coffee."

"I will, Jamie, thanks. What's this about Tela? What programme? Has she gone back to work? I thought she'd taken retirement?"

"No, no. It's to do with this…" I stop. Clearly Tela has told her nothing.

"What?" She eases herself into an armchair. Her figure has become quite matronly over the years. I also notice that she walks with a lurch, favouring one leg over the other.

"What have you done to your leg?" I ask, happy, for the moment, to avoid the other issue.

"Oh, just an accident. My fault. Something spooked Raggy and he slammed me up against the railings. Bruised my hip. I shouldn't've been riding. The doctor's told me that often enough since I broke my ankle."

Fi and her horses. It's hard to imagine her giving up riding. "How's Alistair?" Her husband was diagnosed a year or two ago with ALS. It had begun with a sudden inability to change gears on their ute. Now he spends most of his day in a wheelchair.

"Still frustrated and bad-tempered and weepy. I think mostly it's because he can't express himself properly; and he hates forcing down all the medication I have to give him. For me, it's worst when he has those bouts of crying"

"Tough on you." But she has her youngest son and his partner living with them, looking after the farm, I remember. Her gay son. The only one of her three children who has maintained any interest in rural life.

"Well, you know. One old crock looking after another. But what's this about Tela?" she asks again.

It has to be said, now. Fi is Tela's oldest and best friend. I decide to broach it obliquely. "Have you... the last couple of times you've seen her or spoken to her have you noticed anything about her?"

"How do you mean?"

"Has she seemed... confused, not remembering things?"

She is silent for a while, watching me. "Yes," she says, finally. "I even asked her about it the last time I saw her, but she said it was... well, she laughed about it. Said she was just getting a bit silly in her old age. I did wonder, though. Is it..."

I nod. "Mild Cognitive Impairment they call it. But it's dementia. Yes." It's out. It's the first time I've said it to anyone other than Gus.

She struggles to her feet again and envelops me in a hug. No words. When she lets me go she reaches for a tissue and wipes the corners of her eyes.

After I've made the coffee and brought it in we exchange news of children and grandchildren. I let her do most of the talking as she has the greater number of each.

We shared a kiss, once, a long time ago, Fiona and I. An hour or two before that sharing I would have thought that it would have transported me to my personal heaven, that kiss. But in the interval it had been revealed to me that the girl of my head and the girl I had sat with at the movies were two entirely different creatures. One was unreal, purely imaginary, the other corporeal; and the one had refused to occupy the space of the other. One I was obsessed with, the other I merely liked. I sat down at the movies with the one I was obsessed with but I shared that kiss with the one I liked. And I still like

231

her, fifty years on. She is no longer the girl of my silly adolescent fantasies, of course – but then she never was. Fiona, Tela's oldest and closest friend.

We seem to instinctively know that we, neither of us, want to talk of what has happened, what is happening, to Tela. The fact has been absorbed, accepted. Nothing else has changed.

And after Fiona has gone I go up to my study to the journals of that other woman, the one who is now the most constant and most accessible of the women in my life. These days more often than not I leave her journals on my desk, and there they are. I pick one up and heft its solidity. I turn it over. I open it and begin to read:

December 1882: Clement and I were today talking inconsequentially, deliciously, about this and that. It was a light-hearted conversation. Less a conversation, in truth, than a sharing of whimsies. We had been considering the notion of reincarnation, and I asked Clement what he would wish to be should he be able to choose his next life. "Something ephemeral," he replied, after a moment's thought. "A dragonfly, perhaps, or a mayfly. So that I would live a short and joyous and carefree life, the sun teasing sparkles of colour from my wings as I flit over the chuckling waters to discover love and to consummate that love before dying a happy death. And of course I should then like to start all over again." I laughed. It was an attractive thought. When he asked me for my choice, I said I would like to be a glossy kereru, so that I could keep an eye on my garden while filling myself with delicious drupes from the puriri tree.

But in fact I did not tell him what I would really like. It would have introduced into our talk a melancholy that I wished to avoid. Clement does not know that I am dying. I suppose it must be further evidence of my selfishness – but what I would really like to be in another life is... myself. And I

232

would like this next life of mine to be lived out here, in this country, and under this mountain. It would be a life of fresh opportunities. Some things from this life I would keep. I would choose that my new life be given to me once again by my father, and my mother. My children would be there, too, duly appearing in the natural course of things. For the rest – well, in my wildest fantasies I would like a young Clement to be my partner and to grow up with me, the two of us side by side; and I would like Hannah to be with us, to grow up with us as my lifetime friend; and I would like this country to have become what I hope it will become, a land that has kept its most glorious dreams alive. By glory, I do not mean the sort of glory won by force of arms, but the kind of glory that comes with peace and understanding. The sort of glory that I once, in my innocence, might have thought of as the mark of the Kingdom of God.

Yes, I should like my next incarnation to be as myself. I, I should like to live again, in a future not so very distant; but with choices that were never given to me in this life. Adelaide Augusta Gilbard redux. Has there ever been a more selfish wish than that?

These thoughts are all part of an exercise I have been undertaking, prompted by the knowledge that there is little time left. I have been assembling in my mind a catalogue of people – of those whose presence in my life has been of significance in shaping me into this being I still am. It is naturally self-centred of me to think of those significant people mainly in relation to myself, but the knowledge of the fragility of life, the foreknowledge of my imminent ceasing to exist, will, I hope, justify this selfishness.

Firstly, there is my father. My memories of him are childhood memories. I only knew him from the perspective of a

233

child. But I adored him. For the first eleven years of my life he was very nearly everything of importance to me. True, he was often away from home – but during those periods of his absence my mind was filled with the delicious anticipation of his return. My life went on in those periods of absence, of course, but only as a kind of marking time. And I know why I felt that way about my father – it is because he adored me. It was, and is, an instinctive awareness. When we were in each other's company, our worlds were complete. It may seem excessive, but it is without doubt true – when we were together my father and I were each other's entire world.

Then death took him away from me forever. I was eleven years old, and the world I had created from the influences around me collapsed. The hero had been written out, and the heroine, it seemed to me, had no further part to play. Only very gradually did I discover, or perhaps rediscover, other reasons to exist. Reasons like my mother, and my brother, and my little sister.

Looking back, I think I can see that the main problem that existed between me and my mother was that we each believed ourselves to be the love of my father's life. It was not jealousy, of course. It was rather that such a mutually exclusive belief meant that we could never, mother and I, fully understand each other. We were, each of us, unthinkingly critical, the one of the other. Judgemental. That, I think, never changed, though we did come to accept that there was a strong mother and daughter bond between us – my mother long before I did. She was much the wiser. I understand that now, as I, too, have become wiser with age. It is just as well, is it not, that there is one thing, at least, that improves with the passing of the years!

I always knew, instinctively, that I was my father's favourite child. It was also clear to me that it was my quick

234

mind and my infinite curiosity that gave him the greatest pleasure. Our conversations were joyful. When we talked together our happiness was a palpable thing, a musical arpeggio and chocolate eclairs and multi-coloured butterflies. My mother's company, or that of either or both my brother or my little sister, could not compare.

I pause in my reading as the thought occurs to me that Adelaide's father's attachment to her when she was a child was probably akin to my own closeness to Gus; and I like that idea. But then I take the thought a little further and ask myself if that closeness could have had any effect on the relationship between Gus and Tela, as Adelaide hints that it might have had between her and her mother. But no… the idea seems silly. My feelings for Gus have never in any way diminished the intensity of my feelings for Tela – the contrary, in fact -- and surely Tela would always have known that. And Gus, too, equally surely.

And I remind myself that although Gus when she was younger occasionally made grumpy and, yes, I suppose judgemental observations to me concerning Tela's mothering skills, they surely had and have a loving if sometimes a little less than totally cordial relationship. A normal mother-daughter relationship, if there is such a thing. Still, the slight unease I have at the thought is difficult to dismiss completely from my mind, even as I return to my reading of Adelaide's Journal:

My brother Oliver. Slowly, after my father's death I developed a genuine fondness for my brother, but it was a regard that was ever accompanied by an awareness of his weaknesses. When we were young, I never for a moment saw him as one who challenged for my father's affections. The thought would never have even occurred to me, such was my confidence in my place in father's heart. To me, Oliver was, before my

235

father's death, an occasional and easily manipulated source of temporary amusement. Though he was my elder, and had the advantage of his sex, I took the fondness he had for me (and still has, I presume, if he thinks of me at all) very lightly. After I had absorbed the pain of father's death, I became closer to him, while at the same time often becoming annoyed with him for his thoughtlessness and his excesses, particularly his wastefulness with opportunity, and with money -- and his intemperance. I suppose I must also have harboured some resentment of him for his favoured position in our mother's heart. But really, that would have meant little to me.

Then there is, there was, Meg. My younger sister I remember now with guilt. I paid little attention to her. I excuse myself by remembering that for much of her childhood years I was away at school. I see her now as an almost wraith-like creature, taller than me even by the time she was thirteen. And dead a year later. A quiet and secretive girl. A girl I never made sufficient effort to know, and to understand.

My pageant of people whose memory I now cherish must also include my Uncle Philip and my Aunt Mary. Their admiration for me helped restore my belief in myself. I care little whether or not I elicit admiration in the breasts of most of the people I meet – indeed, I know that in very many cases the sight of me elicits feelings very far removed from admiration , but that bothers me little -- but the knowledge that my Aunt, and my Uncle, admired me is a comfort to me now.

27

Jamie

The diagnosis is made and the symptoms become ever more evident, but my Tela is still there behind the sometimes irritating but bearable façade of forgetfulness and increasing confusion. Even the irritation of having to repeat things, remind her of things, eventually fades until it is merely part of our new modus. There are incremental shifts in my means of dealing with her affliction, of keeping her happy – or at least to shelter her as much as I can from unhappiness. These shifts or increases in my attentiveness are almost unnoticeable to me, which in turn means that I am hardly aware of the deterioration in her condition that has necessitated them so that when people ask me how she is getting on I tell them that she's fine. And that is how it seems to me. She is still there, although the things that she is comfortable doing for herself are shrinking.

But how very glad I am that Gus is with us. Gus; and Vanu. While meaningful exchanges between Tela and me are becoming less and less frequent, replaced by a mostly mute togetherness, delight in my daughter and my granddaughter increases to fill up the spaces that are left.

"Nora's thinking of moving back here, or possibly I might move down to Wellington. We're getting really serious about our film-making," Gus tells me one evening in the spring of 2014.

I prefer not to even notice the second of the possibilities she mentions. "Nora? That's good. But I don't know where you're going to get the energy from. All these projects."

"No, energy's not the problem, Dad. Making time, that's the problem."

"Not possible, making time."

"Well, finding it, then."

"Tell me your outline again. The one you've been working on."

"We start off in a marae. Could be in the past, could be the present, or future. Then this changes to other scenes as we go along. Woolshed, church, state house – you know, all the iconic places."

"Interesting. Difficult."

"Not as difficult as it sounds, using a backdrop and projected images. That sort of thing. We want to set much of it in Parihaka, for the symbolism, and use a mixture of Maori and English dialogue. And cast, of course. We start off with Maori speaking Maori, but by the time we get to the end it's random. Using the two languages seamlessly, with understanding on both sides. But we've got to make sure the message isn't too obvious."

"I doubt it would be. Most of the pakeha in your audience probably won't be able to follow it, anyway. Not all of it."

"Oh, they'll be able to follow it, alright. Even if they don't understand Maori they'll get the gist. If they don't we've failed."

"What about you, then? Is your Maori good enough by now?" I know she's been doing an immersion course, and her Maori has always been quite good. It's being aware of her progress that spurred me on to try again with the language myself.

"Yeah. It's pretty good."

That means it's very good.

The following day I casually announce that I'm going to the Mall to get a new key cut. I suppose I announce it because it is a somewhat irregular thing for me to go to the Mall. I don't like it, the temple to consumerism. I avoid going there if I can. But needs must.

"I'll come with you if that's okay Dad," Gus says. "I need to use that gift card you gave me for my birthday before it

238

expires."

Oh yes. The gift card. My unimaginative means of dealing with significant anniversaries. I leave it to Gus herself to decide. But it works out better that way, I know. She gets what she wants, and she is quite fussy about her clothing. The choice of colours and styles, that is, not the brands. She is not a brand person nor does she often buy anything new. In fact, she gets most of her clothes from Op-Shops.

I wait outside when she goes into the store to use the card. The shop is one of the swankier chains that I have had some success with on previous birthdays. I expect to wait some time; and I do, taking a place on one of the benches and surreptitiously watching the passing human parade as they gaze about them, mesmerised by the displays of glamorous goods, and thereby getting myself into a mood of inward despair. Eventually she emerges. She doesn't look happy, but she's carrying a large bag,

"Found something?"

"Yes. Thanks, Dad. I'll show you when we get home."

"You don't seem very happy about it."

"Hah. It's not the skirt and top. I like them. It's what happened in there. I'll tell you. Let's get something to drink and sit down."

We buy a couple of fruit juices in the food hall and sit at one of the tables to drink them.

"Well?" I say.

She sighs. "It's not that it hasn't happened before," she says. "In fact, it's happened a lot. But it always pisses me off."

"What?"

"Everywhere I went in that shop, I'd look up to see one of the sales girls watching me. It was always the same one. Following me around. I was on the point of walking out, but I thought, bugger you, bitch. So I just kept looking till I found something I liked."

"Why would she do that? Follow you around?"

239

She shakes her head at me as if in wonder. "Well, why do you think? She was assuming I'd probably try to steal something. Stuff it under my jacket. She'd probably been warned to keep an eye on me."

"Really? That's never happened to me, as far as I know."

"Yeah. But you've never been brown, have you."

I'm shocked. Probably more than I should be. "And... This has happened to you before?"

"Often enough."

I'm angry, now. Angry that she should have been treated in this way. Angry, and bewildered. Had she imagined it? No, not Gus. She isn't given to fantasy. But... in New Zealand? Today? "You're quite sure?"

"I don't know why you're so surprised, Dad. Well... yes I do. You just drift around in your own little bubble. Everything's rosy. If it doesn't touch you, you don't notice."

"I'm noticing now. And it's making me very angry."

"Hmm. It works both ways, you know. I could walk up to a group of brown skinned strangers in a bar or somewhere, and they'd just glance at me and carry on talking. Maybe even make a place for me. You couldn't. If you went up to them, they'd stop talking and look at you sideways. Probably tell you to piss off."

She's right, I realise. I recall an incident that occurred when I was on a trip north to see my sister. It was around lunchtime, and I'd stopped at a dairy on the outskirts of Tokoroa to get a pie. A group of four or five High School girls was just coming out of the shop. They were exchanging quips, laughing, and I, too, smiled to myself, affected by their good humour. I must have let my glance linger too long because one of the girls glared at me with considerable hostility and said 'What are you staring at, Honky?' I'd felt acute embarrassment. It was only then that I realised that all of the girls were brown-skinned, probably Maori. Had they thought I was ogling them? I'd bought my pie and hurried back to the car trying to put the incident out of my mind. But clearly it had lain there all these years.

"It's… sad."

"It's just the way things are, Dad. It's getting better, I think. Though… with what just happened, I'm not so sure."

"So, what did you do when you got to the counter? Did you say anything?"

"I looked at the girl who'd been following me around and said 'Churr. Lotta sweet stuff in here, eh? Best I come back when you's're not watching me.'"

I grin, but I'm not taken in. "Really?"

"No. Not really. I'd've liked to. But I just smiled sweetly and kept looking at her until she blushed. She was a bit ashamed of herself, I think. I felt sorry for her. I suppose she was only doing what she was told to do."

From the journal of Adelaide Gilbard

January 1883: I have just been rereading one of my entries in this Journal from about two years ago, and with the knowledge of the disgraceful events that took place at Parihaka little more than a year ago, how depressing it has been to reread the hopes Hannah and I held at that time!

I have been thinking deeply about where my sympathies lie. I know I am not alone amongst the British and other settlers in believing that the actions of those who responded to the peaceful and welcoming gestures of the Parihaka villagers with such outrageous villainy are deserving of nothing but contempt and horror, but my feelings are possibly deeper than most who are not Maori. I know more than most of what it must have been like, for Hannah has told me of the accounts of it she has received from many of those who were there.

241

I do not feel guilt. I am not culpable. I feel anger. I feel sorrow. I feel Hannah's anger and her sorrow, even though I know that I cannot feel it with same depth as she does herself. Dwellings were burnt to the ground, the whole village virtually destroyed. Property was plundered, crops were destroyed. Objects of great family importance were stolen. Worse still, many of the village men were deliberately clubbed or otherwise beaten, even though they offered no resistance, and women, some of them little more than children, were violated.

What have such perpetrators to do with me? I cannot, I will not, feel any affinity with them, none at all. None, none, none! Their shame is not mine, though I hope they feel it. But deep anger? Yes, I feel deep anger. Deep sorrow? Yes, I have deep sorrow. I am the wife of a military man, one who came here with her husband because that is what a woman must do. Because he chose to enlist in support of the government's aims, then he, I suppose, must feel some culpability, some shame. I think he does, but that is little comfort to me, or to Hannah.

Am I culpable? I was in danger of feeling so, then Hannah had the grace to come to me, to take me into her arms, when I suggested that perhaps I had a share in the shame simply because I am what I am. I wept with relief at the total understanding Hannah displayed. 'You are my sister,' she told me. 'You are as much a stranger to them as I am.' I felt redeemed, absolved. And she is right. I am not them. I cannot even begin to excuse what they did. They are strangers to me.

Yet he came here, my husband, at the request of the settler government, and his purpose was clear – to take part in the putting down of what that government deemed was rebellion. And in those first few years of our time here, that is what he

242

did. I was not happy about it, especially after Hannah and I had become friends and she was able to share with me her intimate knowledge of the often brutal treatment of the local Taranaki people as they attempted to resist what they clearly (and, I now believe, fairly) judged to be the improper dealings in their lands. I would talk with Tom about such things, and if he was sober, he would listen. Over time, I believe he came to have ever greater sympathy with the grievances of the Taranaki people, though he had little choice but to carry out his duty as a Captain in the Volunteers.

Then came an incident when he shamed himself and his fellow officers by his preposterously excessive drunkenness, and though he was permitted to keep his rank, he was taken off any duties directly concerned with the use of arms, and given tasks relating solely to the surveying of roads. I think, or I want to believe, that he was relieved to no longer be directly involved in fighting for a cause that he had come to question. Perhaps I had a slight influence in his change of attitude. If so, I am glad.

And then, in more recent times, the nature of that resistance by the Taranaki and other local tribes to government decisions regarding land has changed. The chiefs Te Whiti and Tohu and, yes, even the once feared warrior Titokowaru became the leaders of a movement that encouraged stubborn but peaceful resistance to injustice. And how was that very Christian decision finally met? With vicious injustice. How could I not feel Hannah's outrage and sorrow and hurt? We are sisters. We are.

But... to write of more cheerful matters: this year there have also been some signs that hope for a more prosperous future for everyone may soon be renewed. The successful shipment of a cargo of frozen meat to England has people dreaming of

243

New Zealand becoming Britain's farmyard, supplying it with not just meat, but butter and cheese as well. A large Dairy Factory has been built in the South Island, this development adding to those hopes for a renewed prosperity. And it is not only the South Island that looks forward to better times. Here in Taranaki there is also a sense of new possibilities, particularly amongst the farmers. And when the farmers prosper, so, too, do the townsfolk.

Yet how hollow even these hopes seem while the sad results of Parihaka are still fresh in our memories!

March 1883: Tom has become more consistently thoughtful and considerate of late. It is due in part to his acceptance (long overdue) that his vague dreams of wealth and influence are never going to be realised. It is also a reflection of his renewed resolution to stop his immoderate drinking. Most of all, perhaps, it is because of my illness, and his probable knowledge of its origin. Guilt, it seems, can be a powerful promoter of change.

Poor Tom! There have been many disappointments for him over the years. No doubt some of those disappointments are to do with us, his family.

Have I disappointed him? He is no longer the central concern in my life, I can admit that now. But I can think of none other of the vows we made that I have broken. Certainly not in the flesh, at least. And I have given him children. A son, and two daughters.

George, our son, has disappointed him. That, too, must be admitted. George, with his deliberate, methodical, inward-looking habits could never be the kind of son to please Tom. George is quite clever with his hands, but he shows little interest in knowing people. By himself, he appears to achieve a kind of contentment. With others, especially girls and women, he is awkward and shy. When he's with his father these habits have always been especially pronounced. Tom used to work himself into a fury trying to get George to respond to his questions, his exhortations, but these days, blessedly, he tends simply to ignore him.

When Inez, our elder daughter, was younger she, too, was another disappointment to Tom, as I think he took her partial deafness as somehow a reflection of imperfection in him as her sire. In time, though, Inez's proud nature and her shrewd intelligence, and what appears to be a natural affinity between the two of them, have meant that Inez is his favourite child, and perhaps the only one of our children who has given him any true joy. When Tom is back from his office in town, they spend much time in each other's company. It is a comforting sight, Tom reading his newspaper, pointing out passages to Inez and passing it to her to read. She will then comment to him in her thick-tongued voice, and he will nod his head. Sometimes he will attempt to answer her, raising his voice, but more commonly he will simply nod his approval of her comments, and they will continue with their comfortable companionship. I am pleased for them both, but when I see them together I can't help reflecting that they seem somehow like stuffy relics from a past that has little lasting relevance to our life here. My husband and my elder daughter. I have grown away from them both. We have grown away from each other.

I am surprised that Tom has not made Ellen, our younger daughter, another favourite, as she is a sweet-natured girl who likes to please. What is more, as the youngest child, Ellen has only known her father as the relatively subdued man he now is, and never as the restless, unpredictable, and very often

245

drunken man he once was. But no... He notices her occasionally and offers her a tender gesture, but otherwise her essentially happy nature doesn't seem to suit his prevailing mood of resigned disappointment and... yes, it is not too strong a word... his resentment of his failures.

28

Tela

Sometimes memories are simply there, having emerged out of the primal soup. Or like an iceberg looming out of the sea mist, or a creature humping up from the depths. They are just there, unsummoned. There without apparent reason.

I remember a book I read once. It might have been recently, or it might have been years ago. It doesn't matter. The title of the book I don't remember, but that doesn't matter either. The author's name I do remember. It was Ishiguro. It follows the thoughts and experiences of one who has a strong sense of purpose. Something he must do. Exactly what is not clearly defined, though it has something to do with words he must speak, with persuading others to do something. He moves in a space-time that conflates and confuses the logical mind. Moving from one area of a building to another results in impossible distances being covered and activities that must in the 'real' world have taken hours are undertaken in moments. It is the sort of defiance of logic that sometimes happens in dreams. Inconsistency that annoys and confuses the reader momentarily but doesn't seem to influence the protagonist in any way at all. He is not aware of, or simply accepts, the anomalies. But his sense of purpose is there at all times. It keeps him going. And the reader goes along with him. Accepting. Eventually not even questioning.

It is like that with me. I no longer have the means to summon memories at will, and at times the sequences of the memories I still can access have become jumbled. But none of that seems to matter much. Pieces have been taken out of the jigsaw puzzle of my past life, but the gaps are not detectable. The gaps have vanished with all that was once in them, both the time gaps and the space gaps, and the remaining pieces of the puzzle have locked together seamlessly. Conflated.

The sense of purpose in me, though, remains strong. The sense. But exactly what that purpose is… well, for me it is like that of the protagonist in Ishiguro's book. It is unclear to me as it is to the book's reader, and increasingly elusive, but always strong. It is frustration at my inability to define purpose that at times used to lead me to episodes of anger. It threatens at times to do so still, but those feelings are dulled by the medication that Jamie ensures I take. So my modus now is to ignore the question; and mostly, thanks to chemistry, that is reasonably easy to do.

But my world is shrinking, I know that, though the sense of purpose remains. Reasons for being. Things that I know should be done if only I could discover what they are.

How much longer will I be able to remember even disconnected moments, like a memory of Gus in her teenage years, of the three of us together? Not much longer I suspect. When I do remember incidents they often seem confusing. Certain arguments with Gus, for instance, when the memory of them seems to include feelings I didn't even know I had had. Yet I must have, I suppose, or why else would I now recall them, those feelings? But how could I have been so successful in suppressing them that it is only now that I can feel them again? Jamie trying to reason with me. Jamie taking her side. Resentment. Jealousy. My resentment. My jealousy. But… no, no. That can't be right. I am not like that. I am confused. Surely I am confused.

I fear my memories are like the bus that brought me to Mapledene when I was fifteen years old; the bus that dropped me at the terminal in Napier and then disappeared into the night, driven off to be locked away in some unknown and inaccessible place. Or perhaps one day soon some clever chemist will discover a formula that will reopen all those blocked synapses and I can travel with those memories once again.

Oh yes, I would like to believe in fairy tales and the supernatural and the perfectibility of humankind. In God, too, I suppose. I would like to, but I cannot. I have read widely of the sort of fairy tales beloved by the Victorians but only in an attempt to better understand their world and the nature of the intricately realised human beings who inhabit their novels. I have studied myth and I understand its importance in the history of humankind's attempts to explain itself and other natural phenomena. All of this I know that I must once have understood, but my mind even then would shut down any inclination I might have had to actually experience the relief, or the excitement, of belief in such things.

As I grew ever older I began to regret my inability to roam freely and imaginatively in these realms. I see it now as it truly is – a weakness in me. My thinking is too logical. I leave insufficient room for magic and marvel. I am not a believer. I do regret, especially now that the world of logic and certainty in which I have lived all my life is closing down on me. Collapsing. Removing itself. The world of here and now, I mean. How I would welcome the chance to lose myself in the realms of the marvellous and the illogical where anything is possible! What a fine substitute that would be for this world of now, of an hour ago, of yesterday, that I am losing! But I cannot. It is too late.

I have lost my way in this world, the physical world. That concerns me rather less than the fact that I am also losing my way in the worlds created by the great novelists. I pick up a book and just by looking at the cover and riffling through some of the pages I get that feeling of warmth and secret excitement that I have always had. But if I begin to read, the words on the page seem unfamiliar. I have to puzzle over them, dredging around in an attempt to rediscover their meaning. It takes me an age to read a paragraph, to make sense of it, and when I do the meaning is gone without properly registering itself and I have to begin again. Except that I mostly don't bother any more. Instead I hold the book, riffle its pages, and content myself with the feeling, the certainty, that I know it well. That I knew it well. The effect in my mind when I do this is something like holding a kaleidoscope up to the light from a window and slowly turning it. I am gifted with shifting images, flashes of recollection that are gone almost before they arrive. A passing awareness of beauty and delight.

And that is all. That is all. The rest has been stolen from me.

29

Jamie

Tela is beginning to become confused even about people of some significance in our lives. Well, not so much of significance in her own life, perhaps, as some of those of significance in the lives of the rest of us.

Yesterday Gus was in the downstairs sitting room talking with an old friend of hers about the staging of this year's Summer Shakespeare, which is to be Midsummer Night's Dream. He is directing the production this year, and as Gus is a Shakespeare aficionado he is consulting with her on ways to cut the script.

Anyway, the friend is familiar to us all, including Tela, though he hasn't been around to the house in some time. When Tela saw them sitting there she came back out and whispered to me: "Who is that man in there?" I told her, but I fancy the name didn't mean anything to her. Nevertheless she went in to the room, exchanged affectionate words, and even sat down with him for a while.

Today he was here again and she asked me the same question, and the exact scene was replayed. It seems that once forgotten, always forgotten – that a renewed sighting, even the exchange of friendly words, doesn't mean that the memory is refreshed.

Vanu is Gus's chosen diminutive for Myfanwy, and it suits the girl perfectly, the name. She is eight years old now and tall, slender and lithe. She is the most enchanting little creature in the known universe and possibly even beyond. She fills whatever space she occupies with actual or potential delight. When she is at school, and her mother is at work, this house is as silent as a (very untidy) tomb.

Vanu has the blue eyes of her father, though no doubt some of Gus's genes also played their part in deciding this. She is light-skinned, dreamy, rarely excited, often uncommunicative, and very, though silently, wilful. At unpredictable times, though, her tongue will run on and on letting the world know what is going on inside her head, the complex stories and adventures of her extraordinary imagination. At such times she constantly chatters – to herself if there happens to be no one within earshot. Although stubborn and self-possessed she is also essentially good-natured and compassionate. Despite her fair skin, she is unmistakeably her mother's daughter, and her grandmother's granddaughter.

My first duty in the mornings is to my granddaughter. While Gus showers I get Vanu her breakfast. At the moment, she doesn't like cereal, she doesn't like porridge, she doesn't like yoghurt, she doesn't like scrambled eggs – she doesn't like much at all except toast and butter. Lots of butter, right to the edges – she is fussy about that, which is a little odd as she doesn't eat the crusts. It is a matter of honour not to do so it seems. I take my offerings in to her.

"I thought I'd make boast and tutter, instead of toast and butter, just for a change," I say.

She looks up from whatever it is on the telly that has been holding her attention.

"What?" asks Vanu.

"Boast and tutter. I hope you like it."

She looks at me in a faintly irritated way. She is interested but apparently against her will. Will she respond? It's touch and go. Then she says, almost reluctantly admitting to a very uncool curiosity: "What's that?"

"Well, it's exactly like toast and butter, except it puffs its chest out a bit and makes disapproving noises."

She makes no comment but turns her face back to the telly, which is much more interesting, it seems. Another failure, I fear. I put the plate down on the side table near her seat.

She glances at me, with the hint of a knowing smile. "Thanks for the boast and tutter, Pompa," she says. It's her own word for me, 'Pompa'. She devised it when she first began to talk, and it has stuck.

At this moment, I'm happy with my world.

My granddaughter. Evidence of the continuation of a dynasty of remarkable females. I discount myself. I even discount the late and truly lamented father of my granddaughter. We are, were, no more than the regrettably necessary catalysts. Or so it seems to me. We, Max and I, were or are, relatively speaking, insignificant.

Things are changing in various and mainly unpredictable ways. The world, of course, but also our tiny part of it. For me this is the more significant. I doubt I am alone in this, as surely for most people it is the changes in their personal environment that are the most immediately affecting. Vanu continues to grow and to change. There is something new about her every passing week. Gus continues to grow, too – though mentally rather than physically. And in the middle of all this is Tela, who is also changing. But in her case, it is a diminishing.

Though it was at first scarcely noticeable, those incremental steps in her deterioration have added up to a huge difference between then, when it first began, and now, when it would be obvious to anyone. I am too used to our routines to notice or to have registered in my consciousness the daily shifts towards a total disappearance but if I mentally step back and remember how it was compared to how it is, the dreadful and inexorable effects are there. I don't want to see what is in front of my eyes. I spend most of my day blocking it out; but it is a little like a slow motion replay of what used to happen when the old-style television sets were turned off. It is an inescapable fact that Tela's awareness, that which makes her Tela, is shrinking, shrinking, shrinking; and in time, we are

253

told, it will become little more than that dot in the middle of the screen. Then that, too, will disappear.

I come slowly down the stairs, attracted by the sound of voices from the sitting room. One voice is raised, angry.

"And what am I fucking told? That they're as much in the fucking dark as I am!"

"Yeah? Useless arseholes. Typical."

The first voice is Gus's. Angry Gus. The second, quieter, sympathetic, I recognise as her old friend Nora's.

I know Gus must be talking about something to do with her place of work. Only work frustrations could cause her to swear so emphatically. I still flinch when I hear her use certain swear words though I don't judge as I once would have. Girls, women, shouldn't use the more extreme words, those relating to body parts or body functions, I once thought. Now that judgement seems ridiculous. Another example of sexism. It's a different world in so very many ways and I have trained myself to hardly notice any more.

I continue down the stairs and look in. There is a pile of papers on the coffee table and the two armchairs Gus and Nora are occupying are drawn up on either side of it.

Gus looks up. "Sorry Dad. I was just sounding off at the ridiculous inefficiency of the Admin people at work."

"Understood," I say. "How are you Nora?"

"Yeah, good thanks."

It's some months since I last saw Nora. I'm a little surprised to see that she has cropped her hair, and has allowed a natural greying to show. She is still lithe and youthful looking though. She and Gus could almost be taken for students, still, rather than women in their forties. Mothers, both of them, and women who are creative in a copious number of ways. Old friends.

Nora is based in Wellington these days; but I know that she and Gus are working on some sort of new film project together.

"Is this your script?" I ask, with a nod towards the papers on the table.

"No. It's just some notes on a few new ideas I've had that I brought up for Gus to have a look at. We've not really got going on the script yet. We keep finding reasons not to."

"True, so we must talk about these new ideas that you've got here," Gus says. "That's what we should be doing now. My fault. Bitching about work. We've got to make the most of it before you have to head back."

"How long are you here for?" I ask.

"I'm just up for the day and I'll have to be back before six. Both of the kids've got kapa haka practice and Alek's got to go out tonight."

Alek is Nora's partner. He's a musician, and originally from Latvia. I was a bit surprised when Gus told me they were together. Nora had always seemed to me to be the sort of girl who'd not even think of getting with a man who wasn't Maori. But Alek's very much into things Maori, I'm told, and he dotes on Nora's two children from a previous relationship, or relationships. The last time Nora came to see Gus, Alek was with her and I met him -- an earnest young man a few years younger than Nora.

Both Gus and Nora are now looking at me. Their wish is evident.

"Right. I'll leave you to it, then," I say.

"Oh, by the way, Dad," Gus says, just as I turn to go. "Nora's going to look around for a house for us. In Wellington and somewhere close to her. I've had that offer of a job tutoring drama and I think I'll take it. And I've got all the money from the sale of... of Max's place, our place, sitting there, so I should be able to get something reasonably comfortable, even at Wellington prices. With any luck we could be out of your hair before the year's out."

I'm stunned into silence, and I advance to the door with my head spinning. Leaving? Gus and Vanu? Of course it was always just a temporary arrangement, though one that has lasted nearly nine years now. But... Leaving us? Leaving me?

"Right," I say. With any luck, they'll be leaving she says. Just like that, she tells me.

But that's Gus.

Is our daughter like her mother? In some ways the link is obvious enough. They are both very practical. They are both very clever. But is that all? Is that where the similarity ends?

Gus experiments with just about anything that takes her fancy (other than drugs or alcohol – she is her mother's daughter once again on that issue). In the course of the forty plus years she has now spent in the world she has been, amongst other things, a Science student majoring in Chemistry (Chemistry having been her least favourite subject at school, she of course chose to do a first degree in that field, which tells much about her stubborn nature), a campaigner for animal rights, a very successful stage actor and later Director, a Masters student in Economics whose thesis has been published here and overseas receiving widespread condemnation from neo-Liberals and enthusiastic support from just about everyone else, a designer of functional and beautiful household furniture, a Small Business Advisor, a teacher of English in French Polynesia and in France, a knitter of jerseys and other woollen garments that she has given away to friends and their children, and a player to a high level in a number of sports. At present she is a resource person at the local Polytech, devising and teaching courses for new migrants, but she is now decided, it seems, on a return to the dramatic arts, that will no doubt include script-writing on the side. After that... who knows? Whatever she chooses to turn to next the certainty is that she will get things done. She is a problem solver. A project deviser. She is also a superb and caring mother. She is the perfect woman. Of course, I say that as one who is totally objective and unbiased in any way.

I think of her mother, of Tela as she was before the affliction became apparent. Tela when she was Tela. That Tela, the real Tela, was single-minded. She had little apparent interest in most things outside the area of her passion. In what we might call the real world, the world away from her books or her teaching, she was intensely practical, dealing with whatever came along impatiently but efficiently. In her field, she was brilliant; she was a world leader, but the field is a very narrow one.

Is our daughter like her mother? She is very different in both the nature and the extent of her interests, yet she is also, in other ways, very like -- though both mother and daughter would reject that notion out of hand.

Now, of course, that Tela-who-was has mostly gone. Those things that defined her are disappearing. But she will always be one of the twin centres of my life, and the one who now needs me most. Really, she is the only one who needs me at all. The other half of what has been for the past forty years or more of my life my binary star has, for the moment, dismissed me from her presence, and has casually announced that she plans to take herself to another city. She has her life to get on with. I understand that. She, and my granddaughter, the enchanting Vanu. Soon, she announces, they will be out of my hair.

What's left of it.

Changes. They are happening all the time. It is simply a matter of adjusting to them. Some of them are for the better, others are not.

There have been deaths.

Dougal was the first to go. The first of my siblings that I actually knew, that is. Now Jenny, too. Well into her nineties, she was. I went to her funeral earlier this year. I went by myself. It was a big funeral, a town and country funeral, with nieces and nephews and great-nieces and great-nephews and even great-great-nephews and -nieces in attendance. Most I had never seen before. Those who noted my presence looked at me with either mild curiosity or indifference.

That funeral was the last time I travelled east through the gorge. It is just as well that there is not much reason any more for me to travel to the other side as the road through the gorge has been closed to all traffic, permanently it seems. There are too many unpredictable and dangerous rock slides and apparently no way to prevent them. The alternative routes are longer and more frustrating to drive. But there are plans to build another road, one that will be easier and shorter.

Some changes I welcome. The departure of the man who has led the country for eight long years, for example – the tuft-hunting ex-currency trader, bland and vapid, who for some inconceivable reason was (as A. R. D. Fairburn put it of financiers generally) 'triumphant and much looked up to.' The government he headed, though, still remains.

It is mid-morning and we, Tela and I, are sitting together in the living room as the late autumn sun angles through the windows. It is a scene of domestic harmony. We are simply together – in each other's company.

"I was just thinking," Tela says, "I haven't seen Cynthia since… How long has it been?"

"Cynthia died, my love. Over twenty years ago now."

"Cynthia's dead?' She pauses, evidently giving the information some thought. "Oh. Would you like a cup of tea?"

"I can make it."

"No, no. My turn."

And she gets up from her chair, slowly and deliberately, as with all her actions these days, and disappears into the kitchen.

I hear her rattling about there. It is something she can still do. Though she takes a long time over it and often makes mistakes she gets there in the end. It is something she enjoys doing, I think. That sense of accomplishment I suppose. Of being useful. Or is it really just a desperate grasping at what is slipping away?

I pick up the book I am reading. It's a heavy tome, a biography of Samuel Marsden. I knew little about Marsden before I started. Now I see him emerging from the welter of detail as a significant figure in our history. A man with a rare gift for making friends amongst the Maori as he set about helping to establish the early missions in the Bay of Islands and further south. A man subject to all the arrogance and prejudice of the age yet with the sort of compassion that enabled him to relate at a human level to the 'poor benighted savages', awarding them a dignity and an equality of intelligence that many others of his kind refused to acknowledge or even to recognise.

I am enjoying the book. It is minutely researched, the prose elegant. I have not been reading many such scholarly history books of late and it is pleasant to do so again now. It is something like putting on a familiar garment and being reminded of how comfortable it is, and was.

Tela returns and puts her head through the door.

"Do you take milk," she says, a little embarrassed, as though she knows it is a silly question. "And sugar?"

"No milk, no sugar, thanks."

I have never taken milk or sugar in my tea or coffee. Never, in all our life together.

I resume reading.

Eventually she comes back into the room, places my cup of tea on the table in front of me and takes her own seat, opposite mine.

"Thank you, my love."

"That's alright." she says. And then, as she settles: "I was just thinking how long it is since I've seen Cynthia. Do you think we could go and see her?"

"Cynthia died a few years ago, my love. She'd lived long and well."

"Oh. Poor Cynthia."

She takes a sip of her tea and looks over at my cup. "Silly me," she says. "I forgot to put milk in your tea." She begins to get to her feet but I wave my hand in restraint.

"No, no. I don't take milk."

"Oh. Right. Of course. And sugar?"

"No. I don't take sugar, either."

30

Tela

I am here in the sitting room, and I am shocked almost to anger by its untidiness. The whole house seems to be very untidy. We used to have someone, someone who… But not any more. We don't have her any more. As soon as the weather warms a little I must scrub the floors and the carpets. Now that we don't have someone.

And I can never find anything. I put things down but they are not there when I want them. Do others borrow my things? The little one, perhaps. She is always taking things, the little one who lives here with us, in this house.

Just as I am thinking about her, she appears in the doorway. Vanu. I remember her name. My granddaughter. She doesn't say anything at first, but comes in and looks around the room.

"Have you seen my fidget spinner, Bubu?" she asks.

She calls me Bubu. She always has. I like to hear her calling me that. It is Fijian for grandmother. "Have I seen your what?"

"My fidget spinner," she says; or something like that. That's what they sound like, the words she uses, but who has ever heard of such a thing? Fidget, fidget. She is fidgeting in the doorway. Is that what she means? I shake my head and she leaves the room.

I stand there for a while after she has gone. I think there is something I should be doing. Perhaps it is a book I should be reading. I go down the passage to my study, but when I look in there I find that the girl, my granddaughter whose name is Vanu, is now seated on my chair in front of the computer. She doesn't say anything, so I sit in my armchair and wait. From here I can see the tallest of the bookshelves, the rows and rows of books. My books. They are all my books. Books I have read.

"Vanu! Get off the computer! No more screen time today, you hear. You know the rules. You can save what you've got there, but off you get. Bubu's probably come in here to do some work."

It is Gus, my daughter. Vanu's mother.

"But I've nearly finished this..." the girl complains.

"No, I said. Minecraft can wait. Clear the screen. Off now!"

"Bubu doesn't do work any more. She can't," the girl mumbles; but she gets off the chair and stomps out of the room, past my daughter. Her mother.

I stay in the armchair for a while then I get up and sit down on the chair in front of the computer, the chair on which the girl was sitting, and look at the screen. It shows a picture of a little girl, a baby girl. For a moment I wonder who she is, then I remember. Of course! She is my granddaughter! Just a baby, but such a pretty baby. Her name is Vanu. Yes, Vanu. How pretty she is! I look at the screen and it makes me feel happy and warm to see her. Vanu, my baby granddaughter. Then, suddenly, the screen goes blank, and she is gone.

I sit for a while longer, then my daughter comes to the door again.

"Has Vanu been in here again, Mum?"

"Yes. No. She was here, I think." Wasn't she here? I remember seeing her, the baby. I'm sure I do. Or maybe not.

Gus goes to the window and peers out. "Oh there she is, out on the trampoline. Little beggar. I told her to empty her lunch box and hang her bag up. Might as well talk to a brick wall."

I feel she must be wrong, as surely Vanu is too young to be outside by herself. "How come?" I ask. "Did you leave her out there? Where has she been?"

"At school, of course. We've just come back."

"At school?" It doesn't seem right. Babies don't go to school. Vanu is just a baby.

"Yes, Mum. She's just come back from school."

"Oh."

She leaves, and I still sit there, but I am back in my armchair. I am facing the big bookshelf. It is tall, ceiling high. It has rows and rows of books. Isn't there something I'm supposed to be doing? I hold my hand out in front of me. My hand. It seems to be more wrinkled than it should. I must be old. Eighty, at least. Or ninety. How old am I? I need to know.

I go down the passage to the kitchen and he is there. He is getting a pot out of a cupboard and putting it on the sink bench.

"Hello, my love," he says. "So there you are." He is taking potatoes from a bag and putting them in the sink.

He. Jamie. My husband. He will tell me. "I'm old. I'm ninety," I say.

"No, no my love. You're seventy-six. I, on the other hand, am seventy-seven. *Whitu tekau ma whitu*. Which makes you younger than me by a few months. You'll always be younger than me."

"I don't want to be younger than you." He has told me his age in something that sounds like Fijian. But it is not proper Fijian. I don't know why he is speaking to me in bad Fijian. Anyway, I'm not Fijian. I am *kailoma*.

"I'm afraid there's absolutely nothing that can be done about it."

It doesn't seem right that he is older. If he is older, he might… I need him, my husband. What will happen to me if he is not there? I have always needed him. I will always need him. And why has he spoken to me in bad Fijian? He is not Fijian. And I am not Fijian. I am a New Zealander. And I am *kailoma*. Part European. In the middle. And a New Zealander.

31

Jamie

And here we are. Another year more than half gone. A year that at last brings some hope, at least for the country. The elections are over, the results in. After all the doubts and negotiations we at last have another Labour-led government, this one headed by a talented young woman. Let's hope they keep more firmly to their supposedly socialist aspirations than either of the last two.

These days, much of my time is spent reading. I have always read. It has been necessary for me to do so. All my life. For many years, I mostly read documents essential to the histories that I was contracted to write – histories of voluntary organisations or commercial enterprises or local bodies. These were not uniformly interesting. Indeed, many of them were very dull indeed. I would much rather have been reading material of purely my own choice. Now that is what I am able to do, and I take constant and joyous advantage of that fact.

I try to spend a little time on most days learning Māori (and in my eagerness to do things in what it has now been decided is the correct fashion, I envisage the words replete with macrons where required). My renewed interest probably has something to do with Adelaide's Journals, especially the friendship she describes between herself and Hannah. I am unlikely to get very far with Māori, I know. I am not good with languages. My first two years of secondary school I had to take by correspondence, and I opted to do Māori, but I made little progress. Now, I'm trying again. I suppose you could say that I have wanted to be able to speak Māori all my life. A forlorn hope, but it gives me some satisfaction to pretend to keep that hope alive.

I have also just finished reading a treatise on Patrick White, the magnum opus of my old friend Anders Malmo. I haven't seen Anders for years – it was in England, in Cambridge, where I last saw him, a devilishly handsome and carefree young man he was then, and one who behaved as though he saw his major purpose in life was not so much to finish his doctorate as to offer the gift of his joyous manhood to as many young women as could be persuaded to accept it. Most, it seemed, took little persuasion.

Anders published his book, based loosely on his thesis, about ten years after receiving his doctorate but I did not read it at the time. It has become something of a classic of its kind. I sought the book out only recently, after hearing from him – a rare but welcome letter, not an email, in which he told me that he had retired from Canterbury University where he had spent most of his career and intended taking a leisurely tour of the North Island. He said he might call in to see us. He had known Tela, too, as they had been doctoral candidates at Cambridge at exactly the same time. In fact Tela has seen him much more recently than I, having crossed paths with him occasionally at Conferences. Not that she would now remember.

Still, I reflect – I hope he does call in on us. Seeing old friends again is a strong attraction to me these days. I shall write and tell him of Tela's affliction so that he is prepared.

We, Tela and I, are told that exercise can be beneficial for her. Exercise on a regular basis, the specialist tells us; but she is addressing her words to me even though she includes Tela in her glances.

So we walk, four days a week. For a half hour or an hour. Sometimes we walk to the Esplanade, which is quite close, and there we wander through the bush near the river.
Usually we talk very little on these walks.

On this day, when we take one of the river paths, it is to find that the Manawatu is high and brown and broad. We stop and look out over the reach of the waters flowing silently but rapidly past. Tela gives a gasp of surprise.

"It must have rained in the ranges overnight," I say.

"I... I hope she's alright," Tela says. I glance at her to see that she is agitated, wide-eyed.

"Who?"

"Maggie. She and Tom... they went..." She gasps again, clearly distressed. I follow her gaze and I see a section of a dead tree lifted from somewhere upstream drift past its branches raised like the arms of a drowning man or woman.

"Maggie?" I say. I can think of no one we know called Maggie.

"Maggie," she reiterates. There is confusion in her features now as well as the distress. "You know. Maggie, the one with the dark hair. The little brown girl and her brother. Like me, she's like me. But... I'm not Maggie. Maggie and... and Tom. Yes, Tom." She looks at me, pleadingly.

I can't help her. I don't know where her mind is. Maggie? Tom?

Then her features relax. The confusion is still there, but the distress vanishes.

"I thought... Silly me. I thought Maggie... She drowned, didn't she? She and Tom. But she is not... Is she? She is not..."

I understand now. Maggie Tulliver. She must have passed through the portal into her other world, then stepped back again.

"No, she's not real," I say. "But yes, she died. She was drowned. She and Tom died in each other's arms."

She smiles at me, grateful. "Yes, yes. They drowned. Of course. In the book."

She turns in the direction of the path, grasping my arm, and we continue walking. "What was that book again? I've forgotten."

"The Mill on the Floss," I say. "I remember you telling me once that when you were little you thought it must be the best book ever written." As I say it I have an O God moment myself. This is my life from here on in. Having to deal with more and more incidents like this. My new ever-diminishing world matching hers. But no, that's not right. I now have this other world I am discovering in the sort of books that were once her world, the books in her study that I am now constantly raiding. They are tendrils of another life that was once hers and that are now enriching mine. They bring me closer to who she is, my Tela. Who she was.

We move on and I shorten my steps to match hers. She clutches my arm harder, leaning into me. "You're a good man," she says.

Once we are home again she says she is tired out, and she goes upstairs to our bedroom. I make sure she is comfortable there then I go next door, to my study, my office. There I do what I nearly always do these days when I first enter the room: I go to my desk and pick up one of Adelaide's journals and begin reading at random.

November 1871: We frequently share our frustration, Hannah and I, at the lack of progress in our plans for increasing understanding between Maori and settler women. And not simply understanding, but appreciation also, for there is very much we can learn from each other. It is deeply disappointing to admit, but our initial fires of enthusiasm have been doused a little by our lack of success. We talked, and we talked and we talked together, Hannah and I. Then I braved the streets of our little town and broached the topic with any women I could find who showed the least interest in conversing; and Hannah did the same. Some responded, Maori and settler, and we arranged little gatherings to talk further about ways and means. Occasionally, we even shared in demonstrations of our different crafts. But overall, it seems we have achieved little of real value.

"Too much talk", Hannah tells me. "We have a saying," she says. *"'Hohonu kaki, papaku uaua.'" (Hannah spells Maori words out to me whenever she uses them, so I believe I have written this correctly). She tells me the literal meaning is 'deep (or strong) in the throat, shallow (or weak) in the sinew'. Metaphorically, of course, it means 'much talk, little action.'*

I put the volume down and pick up the other, the later one, and open that, too, at random:

November 1883: I have been looking back at some of my earlier entries in this Journal, and have been reminded of many of the little triumphs and failures that have marked the years. Now that my illness has become such a heavy influence on the way I must now play out my life, I need to remind myself of what I had hoped for in those former days. Though I still do have days when I can momentarily ignore my afflictions and get out into the world, mostly I am simply too tired, or in too much pain, to do more than sit or lie down, and read. Or talk, of course. With Hannah, mostly, but also with Clement when he calls in from next door, and with my happy, sunny-natured little girl, Ellen. She is still at school, where she does quite well without being exceptional. If I am resting, she will always come to my room to see me when school is over for the day. Or if I am feeling well enough, I like to be there, in the kitchen, when she returns. I pour us both a glass of lemonade and we sit and talk. She tells me about her friends, and what she has learned.

My other two are much less sociable. George spends most of his days tinkering with things he is making in his little workshop at the back of the stables. He is good with his hands, but prefers his own company. Inez, now a young woman, uses her deafness as an excuse to spend much of her time in her room doing embroidery and sewing or altering the rather severe gowns she likes to wear; or perhaps with her church group, doing similar things for charity in company with those who are familiar with her affliction.

Hannah is not always here with me. She still maintains close, though irregular, contact with her family, her whanau. I have never had any difficulty with this, though others who have employed Maori in any capacity often complain at how often 'they' disappear, ignoring their duties in order to attend a funeral or other family gathering. Sometimes Hannah is away for days at a time. I miss her when she is away, of course, but I do not grudge her absences. I know that she needs these reassuring meetings with her kin. When she returns (and she always seems happy to return, I am relieved to say) she is full of stories of the goings on. I teased her once about the chance such meetings must give her to meet another man, and thus to forget the bitter disappointment of her husband's abandonment of her. She looked at me with the semi-serious sideways stare she sometimes adopts and said: "No. No more men. My stew pot doesn't need any more onions." I was shocked for an instant, but I couldn't restrain a bark of laughter. Then I said: "Nor mine!" Yet I felt my cheeks flush with my naughtiness.

It is true, though. While for a time I used to wish, pointlessly, that Clement and I could consummate our love in the flesh, that silly notion passed soon enough. For him, too, I believe. Now our love for each other is something we have come to accept as purely a mental comfort. When we meet these days, we do not touch, even if the circumstances are such that we would be able to do so without fear of discovery. We exchange a smile, or a look, and that is enough to sustain us. And we talk of many things. We are comfortable in each other's company. We care for each other. We love each other.

269

Tomas. Where is Tomas now in my life? He comes home after work hours most of the time these days. He has established a small business in town, undertaking surveying, and drawing plans of an architectural or engineering nature. Clement tells me he is doing quite well. Tomas does not talk to me of these things. He has become almost meek in his relationship with me. It is guilt, I suppose – but I do not blame him for my affliction, and I have told him so. It is more than just that, though, I know. It is because he feels that he has disappointed me in other ways. He has not been able to provide me with a great house, or a ballroom, or a vast park. There is no array of grand carriages calling at our door.

But I do not want any of these things. I never have. O yes, he has indeed disappointed me at times, but not for the reasons he suspects. I was particularly humiliated a few years ago when one of his drunken episodes put him in gaol for a time. I was far less upset by the drunkenness than by the revelation that the episode also involved a young woman, little more than a girl. But after that, he, too, seemed so utterly shamed by his weaknesses that he has ever since moderated his behaviour. He has become 'respectable'. I believe at times he resents having to behave in a manner that he thinks of as being somehow not suited to one of his class. I am quite certain that if he were rich, he would have laughed off his humiliation and resumed his way of life, that being the way of life he considers, or considered, to be his by right of birth. But he is not rich. We are not rich. He has failed in his efforts to become rich. This much I know. I know it is circumstances rather than deep conviction that has forced him into 'respectability' – into behaving like one of the common kind rather than a member of the gentry. As he sees it, of course.

And I must record here that Tomas does show and has shown for years now deep feeling for Inez. He seems to see in

270

her the ideal daughter – one who admires him for what he is, or that she imagines him to be; that is, a man of the best blood, a man above ordinary mortals. In fact, Inez does far more than admire him. She adores him. He can do no wrong. He gives her something that no one else can give her, I suppose – a feeling of superiority, despite her affliction.

Do I have a favourite? I should not, of course. But I do. She is not particularly clever. She has no secrets that she will not share with me. She is Ellen. She is my hope. I admit to these pages that I have occasionally day-dreamed about the time when I am not here, and it is Ellen who features most in those dreams. I imagine her grown to be a young woman, I imagine her finding love, and being a mother to children as sweet natured as she. I imagine a worthy legacy.

32

Jamie

"Jamie. Jamie."

Tela's voice awakens me instantly, although it is little more than a whisper. I am used to the early morning interruption to my sleep. I know what it is, I know what she needs. I reach out and switch the light on.

She needs the bathroom. She cannot find the light switch on her side of the bed. She has no idea where it is.

"Okay now?"

She is standing by her side of the bed. I don't know how long she has been there. I turn over and glance at the clock. It is not quite four. There is a morning chill in the air.

She is still standing there. "Are you okay?"

"No. Where's the bathroom?"

With the light on, she has never before had to ask directions. I point. "The door is over there, in the corner."

"Over there? Where?"

I get out of bed and show her the way, then return. I leave the light on so she can find her way back. I can hear her make use of the toilet, flush, then turn the tap on at the sink. Seconds later I hear the bathroom door close gently, as if she doesn't wish to disturb me.

I am fully awake by now. I know it is no use trying to get back to sleep again, but I keep my eyes closed, waiting to feel the weight of her getting into bed again so that I know it is safe for me to turn the light off.

I wait. I wait. There is no sound, no movement; but now I am conscious of her presence close to me. I look up, and she is standing by my side of the bed.

"Where do I sleep?" she asks.

I pat the other side of the bed, her side. "Here."

"Oh. Thank you." She makes her way around the bed and takes a little time to lie down, pull the sheets and blanket about her. "Thank you," she says, once more.

I wait a few minutes until her regular breathing tells me that she has gone back to sleep, then I gently tip myself out of bed and place my feet into my slippers, thinking of my tasks ahead. There is nothing unusual on today's schedule, no worrying additions to the regular routines. With any luck, I may be able to catch up on sleep with an afternoon snooze, after I take Tela to her day of supervised activities.

She still spends hours in her study, the shelves lined with books and her computer screen blank as she sits in her favourite armchair there, reading, reading. At least, she will be holding a book she has selected from the innumerable ranks impeccably displayed. Perhaps she has chosen a Trollope, or a Gaskell, and she sits there, holding it in her lap. Turning it around. Opening it. Looking at the words. The words.

There are other, much less tidy piles of books on the floor elsewhere in the house, along with papers whose proper stowing she has long since abandoned. She has also secreted collections of pencils and ballpoint pens in various places, including the kitchen cupboards. Anything connected with words, with writing. Squirrelled away. Perhaps she thinks of them as caches of the sort of things that might be essential for a rebuilding of her imploded world.

But the bookshelves in her study are tidy. Sometimes I have looked in on her and found her standing in front of them just looking, looking, the expression on her face one I cannot quite describe. Awe, perhaps. Or desperation.

It is several weeks after Gus and Vanu have left to settle into their new house in Wellington. I am in the sitting room, and I push my favourite armchair towards my favourite spot near the heater. As I do so, I hear a rattling sound from somewhere in the chair's innards, and when I sit down I slip one hand down the side, beneath the cushion and to the side of the spring base. I can feel something there, oddly shaped and metallic.

It is quite a struggle to bring it up, as my hand barely fits between the sprung base and the wooden frame, but eventually I manage it. I hold it in my hand, turning it around in my fingers. It is a strange object, quite heavy, with a circular central portion outside which is a trefoil section that spins around at the slightest touch. I smile to myself as I remember what it is called. A Fidget Spinner. I remember Vanu being obsessed by the thing for a week or two, balancing it on her finger or on a tables top, before misplacing it or simply losing interest. I remember her once moodily accusing Tela, her Bubu, of hiding it from her, and stomping off in a dudgeon when her mother told her not to be silly.

These brief memories are accompanied by a sudden and extraordinarily deep awareness of absence, of loss. Both my daughter and granddaughter are gone from me, and my wife is no longer aware of the passing of time or anything much other than the moment she is living in. I wonder if the depth of my feeling of loss is because, like Knausgaard when he writes about the effect on him of the death of a parent, I no longer have anyone to witness my life. It is a feeling that I do not want to foster, so I slip the thing, the fidget spinner, into my pocket. It will go into the box of rediscovered items they will one day return to collect. For now, I choose to forget.

We could sell this house now and do what we once, years ago now, used to talk of doing, Tela and I. We could find something smaller and easier to maintain, something easier and less expensive to keep warm in winter. Something more suited to an old man and an old woman living by themselves. We could, but we won't. It would upset her now, I know. It would be taking away those things with which she is still familiar, with which she still has a kind of connection.

I reach out to the coffee table and pick up one of the books I am currently reading, one I have only recently purchased. It is a collection of interviews with Noam Chomsky, my favourite commentator on the major issues affecting the world. I also pick up a 5B pencil that I left with the book. I use it for marking passages with exclamation marks of approval. That's how I read Chomsky. I am like one of those enthusiastic people you sometimes see on television at evangelical church meetings, the ones who leap to their feet and shout out 'Amen!', 'Halleluja!' 'Right on, Jesus!' 'You're sayin' it!' and so on. Chomsky expresses my own views, or prejudices, in ways that truly excite me. Out with the pencil, on with the exclamation marks. Right on, Noam!

But my thoughts are banished by an awareness that I am not alone and I look up to see Tela in the doorway. She is animated, clearly wanting to tell me something.

"I was in my study," she says. "Just sitting, reading. And, and... it came in. Through the window. It came in, and right up to me. There it was. On my, my, my... my book. Then it flew away."

She is beyond animation now. Agitated. Confused.

"What did?" I ask.

"You know... A..." She cannot find the word. It, too, has flown from her mind. Yet another one of her constant companions, deserting her. They are the most precious things in her life, I have long come to accept that. The distress on her face is evident. Her hands are fluttering in frustration. She wants to tell me.

"A bird?" I suggest. "A butterfly?"

"Butterfly," she says; but the word issues from her throat flat and dead. Like a corpse. It was not her who found it, it did not come to her as it should have. It is not one of hers. It is the right word but it is not a native. "Yes. Butterfly."

All trace of excitement has gone from her voice, and only the distress remains. She turns and goes slowly upstairs, and I

275

am left to my book. But Chomsky's views on the global issues, even the issues themselves, no longer seem so significant, and I put it aside.

Soon she will be lying down, resting, I know. In my mind I can see her standing beside the bed, dimly aware. Now she puts a hand down, confirming the solidity of the bed clothes, the mattress. I see her cautiously lower her body, move her limbs, stretch out. Soon she will be asleep. She sleeps a lot, possibly because of the pills she has been prescribed and that I must ensure she takes every morning and night.

It is now very late afternoon and I head to the kitchen to prepare our evening meal. It is something simple but I know Tela will like it. 'Delicious' she will say. It is what she always tells me.

I am setting a pot of water to boil to cook the pasta when I hear her hesitant footsteps on the kitchen tiles.

"Ooo, yes! Lunch," she says. "I'm starving."

"Well... not lunch," I say. Should I explain? I can't suppress a sigh. I know it really doesn't matter, one way or the other, but: "We had our lunch hours ago. This will be our dinner."

She is at my side, still and silent now. Hardly even a presence. A ghost. Is that how she thinks of herself, I wonder. As something now mostly immaterial? Is she uncertain even of her own existence? Then: "I didn't eat lunch," she says. "I'm starving."

"Yes you did. I made sandwiches. With our own tomatoes. You said they were delicious."

She ignores the information, or doesn't process it. "What's that in there?" Pointing at the pan.

"Chicken and mushroom. Sauce for the fettucine."

"Yum, chicken. I'm starving."

"Won't be long."

"Can I do something?"

"No. It's all done. Thank you."

She moves away from my side, then turns to me again. As I watch I see the blank curtain of confusion and doubt lift for a moment, like a cloud passing from the sun. She doesn't smile but her eyes are alert. She is there, behind them, properly there. Her expression is one of sudden awareness, as though something hidden but of huge significance has been revealed to her. And what she says next takes me by surprise. It is something she has never before said to me.

Or is she saying it to me? It is as though she is repeating a deep secret to herself, only herself. But she is looking at me, with that expression of wonder and sudden conviction, when she says: "I love you."

But a moment later she is gone again. Standing there, gone; and I am alone.

After dinner we sit together for an hour or so, the television on, then I check that the doors are locked and the curtains drawn and return to the room and suggest it is time to go up. Tela obediently follows me as I mount the stairs, and I supervise her night-time preparations, see her comfortably into bed. But I am not yet tired myself. All day I have been aware that I must finally resolve another question, one I have been avoiding for years.

Tela is soon asleep, and I leave her and go next door to my study where I stand for a moment looking about me. I think of the hours I have spent here, in this house if not in this particular room, and wonder briefly just what percentage of my life those hours represent. In a natural progression my thoughts move from there to the more fraught question of what my life represents. Much of it, most of it, has been firmly centred on those two people who have shared this space with me. In this house. Really, without them my time on earth would have had the relevance of a passing shadow.

Two people. Tela, and Gus. My almost everything. Yet, with all the inevitability of life itself, they are both slipping away from me; one by perfectly reasonable choice, and the other by cruel chance. My almost everything. Without them, what do I have?

And this question reminds me of why I have come here, to my study. I deliberately try to focus my mind on what I know I must now do.

I lower my gaze, past my desktop and down to the locked drawer beneath. It is in there, the object whose fate I must now decide. I am the only one who knows it is there. It is ten years since I last saw it. The very thought that I am about to reveal it again excites me, but part of that excitement is an excruciating anxiety.

I resolutely cross to the bookshelf and reach up to where for some reason I still keep the key even though with the ever-inquisitive Vanu gone that precaution is no longer necessary. I open the drawer and look in. The framed picture fits snugly, barely allowing my fingers to take purchase either side as I lift it out and prop it on the desk.

It is exactly as I remember it, this fine drawing by Turner of an old and partly ruined town in Northern Italy. Cossy's gift to me. Or is it Cossy's curse? As was the case when it first arrived, I am filled with conflicting emotions and my heartbeat gears up a notch or two. Jealous pride at my possession of something of such exquisite beauty wrestles with the feeling that I should have passed it on to the police. Or to someone.

Yet I ask myself why I should feel guilty. I have no knowledge that it has been illicitly obtained, I only suspect that it has. Does that make me a receiver of stolen goods, if it has been stolen? Not knowing, but only suspecting?

Damn you Cossy. Were you really my friend? Is this a precious gift, or did you mean it as a curse?

It is nearly two hundred years old. It is tangible proof of mankind's astonishing creative possibilities, its all-too-rare genius. Yet it is also an affirmation, a celebration, of what it depicts -- of nature's dominance over whatever human beings can devise and make, of the ultimate triumph of the indifferent mountains and the tumultuous skies.

I pick the drawing up, cautiously, a hand to either side of the frame, and bring it closer. I let the light from the desk lamp fall on it, sharpening the detail. I imagine the decisive, immaculate strokes of the artist as the outlines first took shape.

My fingers tighten on the frame, gripping it. My knuckles are freckled and bloodless.

J.M.W. Turner, by his hand.

By the hand of a genius. A strange and perhaps, to most, an unlovable man; but a genius. A creator of the beautiful.

Art in whatever form it takes is surely the ultimate demonstration of humanity's intrinsic worth. It demonstrates our ability to intuit an understanding of things far, far greater than ourselves.

I turn my attention once again to what I am holding. Created by human hand, by human genius, and containing within it a precious fragment of the human soul. No artificial intelligence could ever equal it.

I feel a certain vindication. Yes, it is mine, I decide. Cossy's gift. Regardless of how it came into his hands, it is now mine. A gift, accepted in all innocence.

I am far from believing the essential truth of my own conclusion, but what does it matter now? I am old, and surely I can live a while with my self-deception. The Turner is something I should cherish and enjoy; a part recompense for what I have lost. For what I am continuing to lose. Given, perhaps – would Cossy be capable of such compassion? -- for that purpose.

I take a step or two across the room and remove a framed Degree certificate from the wall and replace it with the Turner drawing. I adjust it so that it hangs perfectly. Now I will be able to see it every time I come to my study. It will be a little something of precious beauty that I can appreciate each day. Yes. Yes. It is the right decision.

I step away from the wall. I try to dismiss my remaining doubts. I will not change my mind. No, I will not. Besides, I must keep it all in proportion. It is a relatively minor matter. There is asleep in the room next to this someone who needs me and whose need of me is of much greater significance than the question of whether or not I should keep my temporary possession of a work of art, no matter how beautiful or valuable it is.

So determined, but still troubled, I turn back towards my desk, and what I see there, the two old volumes of my great-grandmother's Journals, diverts my thoughts and triggers a surge of pure relief. My reaction to the sight of them is as strong or stronger than it has ever been, and the tainted pleasure that the Turner gave me is overwhelmed by a welling sense of redemption, by an awareness of my unqualified right to reclaim at will something of far, far deeper and more personal significance than the drawing. Someone else I can love. And really, there is nothing other than love that keeps me here.

I reach for one of the volumes and lift it from the desk. I imagine Adelaide's hands holding it. I picture her opening it to where she was to make her final entry and deciding what the very last words she would record there would be.

I turn the volume upside down. It is by now an automatic gesture for me, as the Journal entries begin at the back, and I flick through to those very last pages.

The writing here shows some evidence of unsteadiness, the occasional stroke of her pen clearly a little out of her control, but the hand is still neat and compact. I read:

29 May 1885. It is Thursday, and I have a strong feeling that it might well be the last Thursday of my life. Perhaps I will see another Friday, another Saturday. Even another Sunday, or

Monday. Those mostly unconsidered days of the week. Tiw's Day. Woden's Day. How strange it is to count them off like this! I don't remember ever feeling their significance so clearly, their names, their origins. But another Thursday? Something tells me... I will see no more of Thor's Days.

After I have completed this entry, I shall call for Hannah to take these volumes away with her, and, in due course, to give them to Inez. I have spoken to Inez about them. I have not told her that I have written in them anything other than the household accounts, but I have told her that I believe they are worth keeping. I have charged her with looking after them. She, of course, has taken the instruction to heart. Inez is nothing if not earnest in her determination to honour any commitments that she agrees to undertake. She puts me in mind of Ethel May in The Daisy Chain – she is censorious, self-righteous and a little awkward, but she is possessed of grave common sense; and, like Ethel, she will feel it her sacred duty to care for her father when the time comes. It is why I have chosen to leave the books, too, in her care. I have not instructed her that she is not to look at them. Had I done so, the result would probably be to ensure that she did look at them, and, if so, some of what she reads here would no doubt be troublesome for her. I do not want that. No, Inez will carry out my instructions because it is in her nature to do so, once she has given her word – but she will not be interested in the books. They are labelled 'Accounts', and she knows only that that is what they contain. Figures. She will accept that they are of some significance. She might open one of the volumes and glance at the figures, but that is all. She will not look further, but she will preserve them. They will not interest her, but they will be saved.

It is my hope that some day, someone will pick the books up and see past the figures. That someone will read these words.

A granddaughter, perhaps, or a grandson – or their children after them.

I now anticipate that my hope is not vain, and I greet you, reader. And I say goodbye. E noho ra.

I close the book and replace it on my desk. Haere rā, great-grandmother. Yet I'd rather respond to your greeting than your farewell, as for me you have not gone. As long as I live, so will you.

Therefore... Tēnā koe, Adelaide Augusta Gilbard. I greet you. You are part of me; but more to the point, given my own age now, you are part of my daughter, your great-great-granddaughter Augusta. Gus. She, too, has read your words, every one of them, and she carries two of your names.

As does Tela, I remind myself. Tela. Atelaite. Your brother's great-granddaughter. Yes, you're all together in this. Adelaide, Tela, Gus. And now, the little one as well. Myfanwy. Vanu.

And me, the hanger-on. The archivist. But also kindred.

Epilogue

From the Journal of Augusta (Gus) Ashcott-Gilbard.

Karori, 10 November 2018. Vanu has just turned ten years old. Double figures. I love to watch her becoming the beautiful young woman she so clearly will be, but I miss the baby, the toddler, the needy little girl she once was and at certain heart-breaking times still is. Some of my friends make comments like: 'It must be comforting to have her, to know that there is a little of Max with you still.' Of course it is comforting to have her. It is comforting to have her stretch my patience to breaking point with her wilfulness and her determination to be what she wants to be and not what I think she should be, because she seems to know that in the end I, too, want her to be what she wants to be. I love her totally for what she is; and true, part of that is her being Max's daughter. That's nice. That's special. I love remembering that. But mostly I love her because she is Vanu, and she came from me to be what she is. To be what she wants to be.

I am not bringing her up alone. When we first moved here she and I felt the same sort of absence, I know. We both missed the nearness of my mother and father, Vanu's Bubu and Pompa. We seemed to rattle around in a semi-vacuum, even though this house is much smaller than the one I grew up in and that saw Vanu through her first nine years. But since those early days of our arrival here we have created a way of living village style, with frequent shared gatherings at Nora's place with her two children, and our own house open to visitors at almost any time, night or day. Vanu has made new friends, and through her friendships I have gained new friends, too. Many live within walking distance, and we often share child-minding duties and help each other out with whatever projects we might have in hand.

Of course, we both still miss my parents, though we travel north to see them quite frequently. They have settled into routines without us, but they always welcome us joyfully, mother every bit as much as father. She seems still to recognise us, or at least to know that we are special features of her life. It is lovely to see; but I don't feel guilty about moving away. My father does not allow me such feelings, anyway. 'You and Vanu are as close to us now as you ever were,' he tells me. 'You are here, with us. Always.' I know exactly what he means. Exactly. And he is right.

I suppose most people wonder at times about how they came to be as they are. I know I do. These days it is less about myself than it is about Vanu – but in a sense when I wonder about Vanu I am also wondering about myself. She is her own self, yet she is also an extension of me. I am aware of her at all times, even when, maybe especially when, she is not here with me. And it is very much the same when I consider my own parents, both my mother and my father. I understand that I am not unconnected to those who preceded me in this human chain. I am an extension of them. And further back, and still further. Those who begat. We are temporally separated from most, yet we are linked by an indivisible chain.

In that chain there are some we get to know of whose presence means more than others – with whom the links are stronger, seemingly more direct. Mostly, of course, it will be those closest to us in time, the ones we actually shared and maybe continue to share experiences with. But I am lucky to feel a strong connection with another who is much more distant in time but who left evidence of her thoughts and her hopes and her loves and her humanity.

Adelaide Augusta Gilbard, I know you. I know you from the inside. I know you as a woman whose instincts are my

284

instincts. I read your words and I feel your frustrations as you encounter those stifling difficulties that a woman faced in your world, not all of which have even yet been overcome. I love your compassion. I admire your honesty and your courage, and I would like to emulate you. You are a major source of my wairua, that which gives spiritual meaning to my life. You have helped shape me more than anyone other than my parents, and I love you as I love myself. We are together in this. And Vanu is with us, because she will come to know you too. She will come to know you as well as I do. I promise.

www.ingramcontent.com/pod-product-compliance
Lightning Source LLC
Chambersburg PA
CBHW061549170626
46811CB00001B/139